Penguin Books
The Rotten Elements

Born in Romford, Essex, in 1903, Edward Upward was
educated at Repton and at Corpus Christi College, Cambridge,
where he was awarded the Chancellor's Medal for English
Verse. Christopher Isherwood's book *Lions and Shadows*
describes how Isherwood and he invented the village of
Mortmere when they were at Cambridge and gives the plots
of several Mortmere stories by them both. Edward Upward
took a degree in History and English, became a schoolmaster
and taught various subjects in various types of school. In the
1930s he published his first novel, *Journey to the Border*, and
he contributed to *New Country, New Writing* and the *Left
Review* and was on the editorial board of the *Ploughshare*,
organ of the Teachers' Anti-War Movement. He was for
sixteen years a member of the Communist Party of Great
Britain which he left in 1948 because he believed it was ceasing
to be a Marxist party and was becoming opportunist and reformist.
He published nothing between 1942 and 1961, mainly for political
reasons of a kind which he describes in this novel, which he wrote
in 1969 – the second volume, after *In the Thirties*, of his trilogy.
Also in 1969 was published his book *The Railway Accident and Other
Stories*. He taught for thirty years in a London grammar school,
where he was Head of the English Department and a housemaster.
He has now retired to the Isle of Wight to occupy himself mainly
with writing. He is married and has a son and a daughter.

'Upward is a rarity, a writer of perfect, uncomfortable seriousness. He is able to convey, as no other writer of his generation has done, certain intellectual realities of life before and after the war. The most extraordinary factual and imaginative document of our time' – Julian Symons, *Sunday Times*

'It has the same beautiful clarity and precision of observation in the writing that have been so satisfying all through his work. Mr Upward has an extraordinary gift for charging an external scene with philosophical significance' – John Lehmann, *Sunday Times*

'Upward is that rarest of writers; a serious Marxist, wholly dedicated to the misery of other people, sensitive to the fact that his own predicament as a failed poet is morbid and tiny compared with the sum of human suffering, intelligently suspicious of the "personal" basis of his political commitment, worried by everything, but hysterical about nothing ... These last pages of *The Rotten Elements* are some of the most moving I have encountered in contemporary fiction' – Robert Nye, *The Times*

Edward Upward

The Rotten Elements

Penguin Books

Penguin Books Ltd, Harmondsworth,
Middlesex, England
Penguin Books Australia Ltd, Ringwood,
Victoria, Australia

First published by William Heinemann Ltd 1969
Published in Penguin Books 1972

Copyright © Edward Upward, 1969

Made and printed in Great Britain by
C. Nicholls & Company Ltd
Set in Linotype Granjon

To Derek and Muriel Sutton

Author's Note

The Rotten Elements follows *In the Thirties* as the second volume of a trilogy about the life of an intellectual in the middle years of the twentieth century. It is subtitled A Novel of Fact because one of its aims is to give an historically accurate picture of policies and attitudes in the British Communist Party during the late 1940s – though the individual communists who appear in the novel are fictitious characters. 'Rotten elements' is a phrase that was commonly used in the party to refer to members who deviated seriously from the correct party line. The novel was originally to have been called *The Deviators*, but the author has since felt that this title might raise the wrong kind of expectations.

Alone in the back sitting-room Alan Sebrill was waiting to ask his wife Elsie what she had thought of the talk he had just given here to the Branch members. She was now seeing off the last of them at the front door. He stood in the middle of a dis-arranged ellipse of chairs, making no move yet to pick up the ash-trays that were on or under several of these, and he still held with both his hands the black school exercise book in which during the past few weeks he had written detailed and careful notes for all of the five talks he intended to give about Lenin's *State and Revolution*. He had aimed at presenting Lenin's ideas in such a way that they would be entirely intelligible even to a newly-joined member like Rose Barlow whose general educa-tional level was not high, as well as to comrades who had been a year or so in the Party but who seemed less well acquainted with basic theory than communists should be. Recently he and Elsie had become uneasy about the Party's post-war theoretical line, and they wanted the Branch members to discuss whether it was consistent with Lenin's views on the State, and, if it wasn't, whether this was because those views needed develop-ing to correspond with changes in the world since Lenin's day or perhaps because the new line might not be altogether a cor-rect one. The introductory talk he had given this evening had, he thought, been lucid enough, but he needed to get Elsie's opinion on how thoroughly his hearers had understood it. She seemed to be a long time at the front door. He moved to the bookcase and put back his exercise book on a shelf next to several spare paper-backed copies of *State and Revolution* which he had bought for the purpose of handing them out to comrades who might forget to bring their own. He could hear her voice in the hall-passage, and it did not sound as though she was saying good-bye but as though she was putting forward a political argument and might take more than a minute or two to finish. He went to the door of the room and opened it and looked out into the passage.

He saw that she was speaking to Les Gatten. All the other comrades had already left the huose. She was excitedly and cheerfully assertive, talking fast, not pausing for any comment from Gatten who stood facing the front door and – so far as Alan could see from behind – listening with interest though without indicating either agreement or disagreement. The hair at the back of his neck curved strangely sideways to the right and to the left, giving a soft whiskery effect – a pussycat effect, Alan fancied, but he quickly repressed the fancy as being rather uncomradely, and then was surprised that he should have found uncomradeliness in a comparison which if he had applied it to almost any other Branch member would have seemed harmlessly humorous. Elsie was watching Gatten as she talked, and gave no sign of having noticed Alan looking out of the room. Her lively face, topped by her uncontrollable curls, was bright with the summer evening sunlight that came through the glass-panelled upper half of the front door. The tints of a coloured-glass leaf-and-flower pattern were projected from one of the panels on to the skin of her cheeks and neck, and he remembered how in Keats's poem about St Agnes' Eve the moonlight through the emblazoned casement 'threw warm gules on Madeline's fair breast'. He saw that Elsie's face was tinged not with gules or rose bloom but with sulphur yellow and with a vivid green suggestive of the kind of seaweed which grows sometimes on sea-walls or on the iron supports of piers, though amethyst did appear in a rhomboidal lucency on the flesh near the point of the V-neck of her bosom-lifted brown gingham dress. She was desirable and he loved her, but her features had nothing of romantic delicacy about them, and she was a mother not a maiden. Les Gatten stood docilely listening to her while she told him, with a forthrightness that Alan himself might not have risked, her objections to some of the public statements that had come lately from the Party leadership. Alan was about to step out into the passage and to join the two of them at the front door, but he realized that if he did join them he might delay Gatten's departure yet further and have to wait longer before being able to talk with Elsie alone. He turned back into the room.

As he turned, a thought revived in him which had not even momentarily crossed his mind during the whole of this evening's meeting: it was that for the next three days he would be free from the school at which he earned his living as a teacher. Tomorrow would be the beginning of his half-term holiday. The thought made the room seem very pleasant to him. He liked the look of the plaster mouldings on the ceiling and of the little white-painted fluted wooden pillars under the mantelshelf. Usually these things, and the coloured glass in the front door and the sham Tudor beams beneath the gable outside, although they did not offend him – his experience of houselessness during the war having purged him of all his pre-war contempt for early twentieth-century suburban architecture – were uninteresting to him, as was the conservatory which was at the far end of the room and which he now found positively beautiful. Between the windows that it had in common with the sitting-room and the windows that separated it from the garden, the enclosed air luminously united the freedom of the garden with the secure homeliness of the house. There were no flowers in the conservatory, and he felt that it did not need them. The glass-door leading into it from the room and the glass-door leading out of it into the garden were both open still, as they had been throughout the meeting because of the warmth of the evening, and he moved across the room and through the inner doorway. He read once again on the pistachio green distemper of one of the side-walls in the conservatory the neatly black-painted words that had been left there by the barrage-balloon crew who had been billeted during the war in this house and whose balloon had been kept in the playing field beyond the end of the garden. Nails interconnected by wire had been driven into the plaster below the words, which were: 'Sandbag Lines', 'Bed Slips'. He would have re-distempered the side-walls at the time when he and Elsie had first gained possession of the house, but he had wanted to preserve the words as evidence in any dispute that might arise with the War Office about the payment of compensation. He had got used to them since that time, and at this moment he even found them decorative. But the door jambs and the window-frames would have to be repainted very soon if they were to be saved from rotting beyond repair, he thought, as he came to the outer doorway. Also the gaps between the jambs and the brickwork – which comrade Pete Naylor who was a quantity surveyor had called the 'reveals' – badly needed refilling with mortar. Alan stood in the doorway and looked out into the garden.

The sky was still very light, because today being a Sunday the meeting had begun and ended earlier than if the Branch members had arrived after a day's work. He liked the flowering weeds in the foreground under the evening shadow of the house. Elsie and he ought to have dug these up months ago, if only because the neighbours might object to them; but Elsie who before the war had been interested in gardening was too busy with the children now as well as with Party activities, and he had never been interested in it. He liked, without knowing their names, the enchanter's nightshade and the black horehound and the white dead nettle visible at the end of the garden beneath apple trees which the lengthened shadow of the house also covered. She would have preferred flowers of her own growing. The shadow came to a stop on the far side of the garden fence, and sunlight was still warmly bright over the playing-field beyond. This field suddenly had the appearance for him of a huge theatre stage illuminated by lamps which he could not see. A row of elms about three hundred yards distant from the fence formed the backdrop. The pleasure he had begun to feel already inside the house was intensified, became joy.

He knew that the intensification was caused not only by his having noticed the resemblance of the playing-field to a theatre but even more by something that the elms, or perhaps the chestnut paling to the left of the elms, made him remember from his middle-class childhood. Or had the remembrance come first and had it projected itself on to the elms and the chestnut paling, giving these an affinity to certain quite different objects he had observed thirty-five years before out of his nursery window? The nursery had been at the front of the house facing a road on the other side of which was a garden backed by a long brick wall, and to the right of the wall there was a fenced meadow – less broad but going much farther back than the garden – where two horses were often grazing. Sometimes he had seen them gallop round the meadow, the black horse following the brown as if in playful chase, and one afternoon when they had reached the most distant part of the fence and were moving along it they did not turn to come galloping towards him again but went straight on to disappear abruptly behind the brick wall into a hidden place that must have been of considerable extent (otherwise they would surely have begun to slow down as they approached it) and that until then he had not known of. His amazed delight, which had increased as he had speculated what the horses might find behind the wall – just visible top leaves of two trees hinted at an orchard, but a green-painted wooden spike rising between the trees might be attached to the roof of a big summerhouse – was resurrected in him now, with the difference however that though the emotion seemed hardly less keen than he remembered it to have been in childhood he was conscious that he was not so much experiencing it as observing it; but in the observing also there were amazement and delight.

The scene of the meadow with the disappearing horses was not the only one he was reminded of as he continued looking across the playing-field. He thought too of the honeysuckle-screened corrugated iron garage which when he was fourteen and in love for the first time he had been staring at from another window in his parents' house one evening just before he had begun to write his first poem. And he thought of the cliffs which he and his friend Richard had invented poetic images to describe during a morning walk along the seashore ten years later. The elm-trees that bounded the playing-field seemed to hold within the multi-shaped recesses and protuberances of their foliage the disguised outlines of many more past scenes which though superficially concealed could, like the concealed outlaws' faces in a Child's Annual puzzle-picture of Sherwood Forest, be discovered if he looked carefully enough. He was sure he had the power to discover them; and he was beginning to expect that all of them would be connected with occasions long ago when his imagination had been poetically active. He became aware that it was poetically active now. He believed he was going to be able to write poetry again – as he had not been able to do for the last seven years, in spite of constant wishing and trying.

The poem he would write to start with was already clear to him in much of its detail; and he was strangely confident that it would not come to nothing when he tried to put it down on paper, as other poems promising in conception always had during those years. It would be about his standing here in the doorway of the conservatory this evening and seeing the playing-field like a huge illuminated stage on which episodes from the days when his imagination had been creatively awake were about to be re-enacted; then it would go on to present the three episodes he had already remembered – and after those the others that every moment now were revealing themselves, not yet in fullest clarity but with sufficient definition for him to recognize their identity and the richness they promised. His mind was acceleratingly busy, and in his body there was a feeling of extreme well-being. And he was filled with the conviction, as he had often been in the past, that poetic creation was what his nature needed and ought not to be deprived of. 'At last I have come alive again,' he found himself thinking, 'after years of political activity.'

But immediately he took alarm. To have had such a thought indicated a serious deterioration in his attitude towards the Party. What sort of poetically creative mood was this that had brought him to the verge of revulsion against the necessary day-to-day work which as a Party member he ought to be always eager to do? It was a would-be deserter's mood, wholly impermissible, it was the mood of some renegade-in-the-making, capriciously weary of the door-to-door canvassing, the jumble sales, the small public meetings, all the unspectacular duties that must unceasingly be performed at this stage of the struggle for the future happiness of humanity. And yet, how much more gladly – how much more efficiently even – he would have done his

Party work during recent years if only he had been able in his spare time to write poetry. How much more gladly he would have been able to do it from now on if only the creative mood that had just come upon him had been of a kind he could have allowed himself to continue to indulge in.

The power of that mood was in him still as he stepped out from the doorway of the greenhouse into the garden. He had the sudden hope that his poetic excitement might when fully understood prove to be pro-Party after all. Perhaps it was not antagonistic to his everyday Party activities except in so far as these had tended to be zestless during the years when he had written no poetry. In fact, what it might be urgently telling him was that his political work needed the re-invigoration which only his return to poetry-writing could give. This idea, as soon as it occurred to him, seemed valid. His poetic excitement, no longer suspect, was released from the restraint that his Party conscience had put upon it. Filled to the full with it he went striding towards the end of the garden. There was no other happiness, he thought, to compare with this happiness of creation. Love could not equal it, either in intensity or in subtlety, nor would any drug ever be invented that could even temporarily produce anything like it. Mystics who felt themselves transported out of their bodies knew nothing of the physical ecstasy he was experiencing now. It was centred deep between the throat and the solar plexus, radiating its power to his muscles and nerves, giving him the sensation that he could if he had wished have jumped with the ease of a hurdler over the six foot fence on to the grass of the playing-field beyond. He seemed never to have been more exhilaratingly, more exaltedly awake in the body than now as he stood at the end of the shadowed garden under the evening apple trees.

Yet somewhere very minutely in him there was a doubt about the viability of this new happiness, a physical uneasiness which at first he could not define and which was perhaps hardly significant enough to be worth the effort of defining. After a while he thought it might have been generated in some way by the sight of the elm trees at the far side of the playing-field. Then he knew that it had to do with the actual poem he meant to write and that it was not insignificant at all but fundamental. He recognized that though the scenic details of the poem – the elm trees as a back-drop and the playing-field as a huge theatre stage for the re-enacting of episodes from his past – could be very good, the main theme would be fatally defective. He had only just become aware of what the poem would really be about: it would not merely present scenes from his poetically creative years before he joined the Party, but it would implicitly assert that those years had been better than his later politically active ones and that what he needed above all things was to get back to the kind of poetic life he had lived then. In essence the poem would be triumphantly saying 'Those were the days.' Even if writing it could give him a zest which would be helpful to his Party work – and with such a theme this seemed hardly likely – how could the poem be any good as a poem? The falsity of its theme would make it false aesthetically also, would taint it even as a work of art. The truth was that the poetic life of his pre-Party years had brought him to the verge of madness and suicide and that only by getting into contact with the Party had he been able to save himself. He would never write this poem. His mood of creative excitement, as so often before, had been fraudulent.

He turned away from the playing-field and faced the house. Then he thought: 'And yet why shouldn't I write a poem which would begin with the same setting and with the same hankering back after the poetic life, but which would go on to expose those years for the misery they really were and to show communism as the only way out?' He began to walk very slowly towards the house. But why should he write of his pre-Party experiences at all? They were essentially bourgeois and trivial. To denounce them in a poem wouldn't make them or the poem significant. Why shouldn't he write of the things that mattered, of the Party's post-war housing campaign for instance, or – if that theme did not seem large enough – of the world-wide struggle against hunger and racialism and against the imperialist preparers of a new war which would atomically destroy half the world's population? He looked at the blotchy sodden-seeming yellow-brown brickwork of the back of the house, and at the small wooden coal-shed to the left of the scullery doorway, and as he looked he knew he would not be able to write a poem on a political subject. Though he did not doubt that the present and future condition of humanity in general mattered to him far more than anything else, he had to recognize that no germ of a poem about it existed in him. And the poem which actually did exist in him, and which he could have started putting down on paper at once, was artistically as well as politically impermissible. He was back again to the sterility of the last seven years, without hope of creation.

He might never write another poem. His future might be wholly devoid of the kind of joy he had had this evening. There would be committee meetings, mass meetings, group meetings, Branch meetings, Borough meetings, District meetings, union meetings, jumble sales, ticket sales, leaflet distributions. Free weekends and even free evenings would become rarer. Revulsion rose in him, but he instantly fought back against it. He reminded himself that there could be no other life without disaster and dishonour for him than the life of the Party. 'What else am I here for?' he thought. 'I was not born to smell flowers or live like a cow in a field.' But this thought did not bring with it, as it had brought on several previous occasions when he had used it to extricate himself from despondency about his Party work, a pang of the inverted joy of renunciation. Instead, it was instantly followed by a revival of the mood he had been in while giving his talk to the Branch, of rebelliousness against the Party's post-war theoretical line, a mood which – as he suddenly recognized – had helped him to conceive the poem he had just rejected and which was all the stronger now in its rebelliousness because of the rejection.

Before he had got half-way back to the house from the end of the garden, Elsie came out towards him from the conservatory doorway. He had the extraordinary impression that the colours from the front door panes were still upon her, counterpointing the chequered pattern of her brown gingham dress. Her movement towards him appeared more like dancing than walking. She was still several yards away from him when she said:

'I believe you've begun to convince Les.'

Her eyes showed exuberance. Alan, looking at her and unable to bring his mind round immediately to Les, asked without thought:

'Of what?'

'He says your talk this evening made him realize that Lenin's theory of the State can't be reconciled with the Party's present line.'

'I'm not sure I'm convinced of that myself.'

She became for a moment slightly indignant with Alan:

'Of course you're sure. As you said at the beginning of your talk, Lenin thought the transition to socialism couldn't start without a violent revolution – except in a really free democratic bourgeois republic of a kind that's no longer possible under modern militaristic imperialism.'

In her wide bright face there was an excitement which all at once reminded him of Elsie in her early twenties when he had first heard her speak at a Party meeting, and which could not be explained by what she had so far told him of her conversation with Gatten. He asked:

'I suppose Les doesn't think that Lenin still holds good, and that the Party's present theoretical position is unsound?'

'Oh no, he agrees with the Party that the Labour government can be forced by mass pressure to carry out a genuinely socialist policy at home and abroad. He thinks that a fundamentally new situation has resulted from the Second World War and that Lenin's ideas need developing in order to remain applicable.'

'What did you say to that?' Alan was beginning to be able to divert his attention from her immediate presence and from the young sound of her voice and to focus in his imagination Elsie talking to Gatten.

'I mentioned Britain's post-war foreign policy and said it might suggest Lenin wasn't so far wrong in believing that no Labour government could or would do anything else than serve the interests of imperialism. But he asked whether I wasn't being a bit doctrinaire.'

'What,' Alan interjected quite hotly, 'even though the Labour government has been favouring the forces of reaction all over the world – in Greece and Malaya and Java and Indo-China – and has been steadily opposing the Soviet Union and the New Democracies?'

'I pointed that out to him, but he gave me the usual Party argument: it's all due to the right-wing Labour leaders in the Cabinet, and we must get them replaced. So I reminded him how at one time the Party had laid the blame for the government's anti-socialist policy on to the old-school-tie types in the Foreign Office, and afterwards on to Labour's Foreign Secretary Ernie Bevin, and I prophesied it would soon be blaming not just the right-wing leaders but the whole Cabinet and would be demanding a truly socialist Labour government, and in the end it might return to the Leninist view that before there could be a socialist foreign policy there would have to be a revolutionary smashing-up of the whole imperialist state machine – and I said a revolution was something no Labour government would ever bring about.'

'Oh, good,' Alan exulted. 'And how did he try to answer that?'

'He didn't. I think he was impressed by it. Though later he asked whether I thought that a government which was carrying out a progressive policy at home could really be so absolutely reactionary abroad as I maintained.'

'That was rather shrewd of him.'

'He mentioned the granting of independence to India, but he didn't disagree when I pointed out that the Indians could have made themselves independent by force and that the British government pretended to give way willingly in the hope of continuing to dominate India economically if not politically.'

'All the same, I think he'd got something when he doubted whether a government which is being more or less progressive at home can be wholly imperialist abroad.'

'I thought so too; but then, just after he'd gone out of the front door, I asked myself his question in reverse: Can a government which is reactionary abroad really have the kind of home policy that communists ought to support? And I realized that it can't, and that the Party's propaganda has been misleading.'

Alan was startled.

'What, do you mean there's nothing progressive about the new National Health Service, for instance?'

'The Party oughtn't to give the workers the impression that what they're getting now is in any way a *socialist* Health Service. We ought to emphasize that it's really no more than an extension of the doctors' Panel which was introduced by Lloyd George's bourgeois Liberal government thirty-five years ago. It's a capitalist reform, intended to increase the efficiency of capitalism. A genuinely socialist Health Service can't be established in Britain until the workers have won power here.'

'But you're not suggesting we should oppose the present Health Service, are you?'

'I'm suggesting that the Party ought to be urging the workers to struggle for something much better than the present one.'

'But what about nationalization of industry under a Labour government? Is our support of that unjustifiable too?'

'Lenin said state monopoly in a capitalist society is never anything else than a means of guaranteeing the income of millionaires who are on the point of going bankrupt in one branch of industry or another.'

'I wonder if that's still true.'

'I think it is; and it means the Party ought to stop talking as though the mines are now owned by the working-class, and ought to start pointing out that capitalism is still firmly in power and that the workers must get rid of it before they can expect the sort of public ownership which will be in their interests.'

'Do you think the demand for nationalization, for more and more nationalization, could be a weapon in the struggle to get rid of capitalism, provided of course the workers weren't given the illusion that nationalization was at this stage an instalment of socialism?'

'Yes, but I don't think the Party's present support for nationalization is a weapon.'

'Nor do I,' Alan had to agree.

'And then, worst of all,' she said vehemently, 'why is the Party in favour of conscription? They argue that a conscripted army is more democratic than a Regular one, as though that justified the compulsory sending out of young workers to shoot down the supporters of left-wing independence movements abroad. No doubt what really makes them adopt such a policy is their theory that Britain isn't imperialist any longer but has now become a great progressive country starting out along the British road to socialism.'

Her use of 'they' instead of 'we' for the Party was only momentarily a shock to him. He was becoming increasingly convinced by her.

'The truth is,' she went on, 'that the whole policy of the Party since the war has been wrong.'

This idea, he now knew, was the climax she had been leading up to ever since she had come out to him from the conservatory, and it was this that had made her walk seem like a dance. He felt the momentousness of the idea for them. She added:

'The policy has been wrong because the theory on which it's based is unLeninist.'

They stood side by side on the dry uneven ground among the tufts of grass and the patches of spurge and shepherd's purse, and they unseeingly faced the loose planks and plankless gaps of the wooden fence that divided their garden from their neighbours' to the north of them. An alarmed elation came to him, the stab of a sense of liberation, but the alarm soon grew and the elation diminished. He recognized that by criticizing the whole policy of the Party she was in effect – and he had agreed with her – saying that she no longer had confidence in the Party itself. If they both continued thinking as they were now the result would eventually be that the Party would have no confidence in them, and they would find themselves outside it. They were on the point of taking the road that would lead to this. He urgently tried to think of some flaw there might have been in their reasoning. All at once he believed he had found one.

'What about the Party's drive for increased production in the factories?' he asked. 'Is that wrong too?'

He looked at Elsie and knew that she was beginning to feel the same fear as he felt and the same need to find the Party's policy correct after all. But, reluctantly, she had to say:

'I don't see why the Party should urge the workers to work

harder if Britain is still an imperialist country and their work only helps to strengthen imperialism and increase the profits of the monopoly capitalists.'

Alan was able to remain doubtful:

'But think of all the shortages there are now – of food, clothes, houses, almost everything; the Party could hardly take an unconstructive line about the crisis we've been in since the war.'

'Why should the Party try to help solve capitalism's crisis?'

'You mean we ought to try to aggravate it rather than solve it?'

Now Elsie could begin to feel unsure.

'Perhaps not. We ought to aim at ending it – in the only way it can be permanently ended.'

'Ought we, for instance, instead of calling for increased coal production, to urge the miners to take advantage of capitalism's present difficulties and go slow at their work until they have won genuine working-class control over the mines? I must admit that I find the thought of our taking such a line at a time of electric power cuts and blackouts a bit frightening.'

'You're right,' she was relieved to be able to agree. 'And Lenin did say somewhere, didn't he, that it could never be the aim of the worker to cause a total breakdown of industry?'

'Yes, I think he did; though I can't remember where.'

Another reassuring idea came to Alan. He added:

'And as for nationalization – even though it couldn't be genuinely socialist under a Labour government, mightn't it be genuinely progressive? If so, the Party's support for it would be quite justified. After all it's something the miners themselves have been demanding for years, and I'm sure they find it an improvement on the old form of ownership.'

'If nationalization is progressive,' she said hopefully, 'then the Health Service is still more obviously so.'

'Perhaps even in foreign affairs the Government is not one hundred per cent reactionary; it does seem to be beginning to dismantle the British Empire.'

'Perhaps.'

'Perhaps there's nothing wrong with the Party's policy at all.'

They looked at each other, and each saw in the other a dwindling not only of unease but also of zest. Elsie said:

'If the policy is right the theory may be right too.'

'But what is the theory exactly?' Alan couldn't help asking.

'That's the point.' Elsie brightened. 'It's never been properly formulated. There's something almost hole-and-corner about it. You aren't even quite certain it does differ from Lenin's.'

'Oh I think there can't be much doubt it differs. And you said Les thought so too.'

'Then if it does why can't the Party leadership say it does, openly and clearly, and give their reasons for deciding that Lenin's theory is no longer applicable?'

'They may have perfectly sound reasons, and we're very willing to be convinced, but they don't seem to regard basic theory as worth bothering about now. That's what disturbs me.'

'They seem just to by-pass Lenin, as though he had become quite irrelevant.'

Elsie's voice had an exasperation which was exhilarating to Alan. He said:

'We must do something about it, quickly. These talks I'm giving at Branch level aren't enough. We must go and see someone at Headquarters.'

'I wish Dean Ayres were still there.'

'Yes. He was one of the best theoreticians the Party ever had. You remember those classes of his we used to attend before the war?'

'He's still writing articles occasionally for the Party press. I believe he's in the North somewhere. What about Digby Kelsall?'

'He would do almost as well.'

'Will you get in touch with him or shall I?'

'You'd better,' Alan said. 'You know him quite well, and I don't. And as secretary of the Branch you'll carry more weight with him than I would.'

'I'll try to ring him up this evening and arrange it.'

'He may not be as good as Dean Ayres but he ought to be

25

capable of explaining the Party's theoretical position convincingly to us.'

'Or if he can't convince us we might be able to convince him.'

This idea of Elsie's, which did not seem implausible to either of them, excited them both. Alan said:

'Quite possibly the leadership have been so busy during the war with various practical problems that they just haven't had the time to pay much attention to theory. By going to them with our difficulties we may help to start them thinking seriously about Leninism again.'

The prospect of discussing the Party's theoretical position with a member of the national Executive renewed in Alan a keenness for politics which, now that he was experiencing it once more, he knew he had not unreservedly had since his pre-war days in the Party. And, as he and Elsie began to move towards the house, there revived in him also a hope – which seemed to develop out of and to be powered by his restored political zest – that he would be able to write poetry again. His eagerness for her to go indoors and phone Digby Kelsall was accompanied by the same kind of alerting of the senses that had preceded his conception of the poem about the playing-field. He noticed now that a weed he just missed treading on had leaves like the saucers of a doll's tea set, and in the same instant he heard how the planks of the garden fence amplified the sound of a bird's claws scratching along the top of them. The poems he would write would have no resemblance to the poem he had conceived at the end of the garden, would not look back to a lost poetic life. They would be political – like those he had been able to write sixteen years before when he had first come into the Party. The fact that he could not yet think of a particular political poem he could write did not weaken his new confidence at all. He would work to find one. It might take time, but from now on he would make time for poetry, even if this meant cutting down his other Party activities a little.

Before he and Elsie reached the conservatory door their attention was caught by the movement of a curtain behind the bedroom window that was over the scullery. The curly dark-brown-haired head of their eight-year-old daughter Christina appeared just above the lowest part of the window frame, and quickly disappeared. Then, no doubt remembering that her parents had not seemed to look disapprovingly at her, she reappeared and remained grinningly in view. Her lovely face, strangely large still in relation to her square-shouldered body and reminding Alan of her babyhood when she had been so like a real doll that once she was mistaken for one by a guard collecting their tickets in a railway carriage, made them laugh; Elsie, however, who before having children of her own hadn't been a teacher for nothing, soon managed to put on an adequately severe look, and Christina removed herself from view again and perhaps went back to bed. But then at one of the windows above the roof of the conservatory their young son Stephen, who had evidently heard them laugh, brought his delightedly inquisitive face very close up against the glass and peered down at them. His hair, light-yellow and disordered, covered his forehead almost to his eyes which were as bright with vitality as though the time had come for breakfast instead of for sleep. When Elsie signalled to him to get back to bed he went even more readily than Christina, who was two years younger than he was. Alan and Elsie laughed again, but more quietly.

'These light summer evenings do make it difficult for them to settle down,' she said. 'They're both really very good, considering.'

'How glad I am that we've got children,' Alan said.

He put his arm round Elsie's waist, but had to unarm her as they stepped in through the conservatory doorway which was rather narrow.

2

They went up to town to meet Digby Kelsall during his lunch hour, a time proposed by him which was possible for Alan because he had a half-holiday and for Elsie because both of the children were at school all day now and had school meals. The route they took from the railway terminus was through a region of bombed sites, shored-up buildings, emptied static water tanks, where nothing seemed to have changed since Alan had last been here more than a year ago on the morning when he had come to fetch Stephen home from hospital after a minor operation. That day had been fine like today, anxiety about Stephen had been over, clock chimes had sounded from a tower, pigeons scattering suddenly up into the sunlight had cast their flickering shadows across the creosoted timber beams that buttressed an unsafe wall, and the sunlight had erected momentarily around him a new London of socialism and peace in a future Britain such as the Party expected the Labour government to begin to create. Now, as he and Elsie were passing a bombed church, he saw growing out from among its tumbled stones a profusion of the tall pink-flowered plants which he did not yet know to be rosebay willowherb – though ever since he had first seen them among war ruins he had been meaning to find out what they were called – and he strangely felt his former hopefulness return. Perhaps the Party leadership was right in thinking that the monopoly capitalists had learnt their lesson, and perhaps Digby Kelsall would be able to prove to him that what looked all too like a rebirth at present of militaristic imperialism was really no more than its dying spasms. Perhaps even, after the meeting with Kelsall, he might be able to write the optimistic political poem he had conceived on that morning a year and a half ago and had abandoned as being too abstract when he had returned home with Stephen from the hospital. 'But would I be able to think now of writing that poem,' he suddenly asked himself, 'if I hadn't arranged with Elsie at breakfast that she should be the one who would do most of the talking to Kelsall?' He wondered whether the bobbing vigour of her walk at his side might be a sign of agitation as well as of her customary vitality. He said:

'I should think he's a reasonable man to talk to, isn't he?'

'Digby Kelsall, do you mean?' She had never been willing to accept Alan's habit of assuming that certain of his thoughts were too obvious to require explicit statement.

'Of course.'

'He was reasonable and pleasant enough before the war. I was on bantering terms with him when he used to come out on those rambles organized by the Workers' Theatre Movement. I haven't met him to talk to more than once or twice since the war, but he's asked after the children each time.'

They had just turned into a street which appeared to Alan, as he glanced down it, to have had none of its buildings destroyed. The above-pavement iron railings of a below-pavement public lavatory rose out of the middle of a small open space at the corner. She said:

'This street reminds me of the moment eighteen years ago when I decided to join the Party.'

'Why?'

'Perhaps because the street I was walking along then was rather like this, with a lavatory at one end of it. I was on my way to be interviewed for my first teaching job, and the air was very hot and full of horse-dungy dust which helped to make me feel sick, and I thought of the cedared lawn in front of the teachers' training college I had just come from, and realized much more clearly than ever before the sort of conditions the working-class is forced to live in.'

'You motives for joining were more altruistic than mine. I wanted to save my own soul, I'm afraid.'

'I admit that I mightn't have decided to join if I hadn't had a cousin already in the Party.'

'Well, I hope today isn't going to be quite as momentous for us as that day eighteen years ago was for you,' Alan said only half humorously.

'What do you mean?'

Alan would not be explicit:

'I think we had better see ourselves as going merely to ask Kelsall's advice about certain theoretical difficulties we have got into. We don't want to start arguing with him.'

'I shan't. You needn't worry.'

The café where Kelsall had arranged to meet them was one that Party members often used, and Elsie did not have to look up for the name *Marco's* on the fascia in order to know it when she and Alan reached it. She opened the door and he followed her into the long and rather narrow eating room whose far end he could not at first fully see because of the very large cylindrical urn, nickeled and having many shining external pipes, that stood on the counter to the right of him, and also because of a frosted-glass screen jutting out from half-way along the wall on the other side of him. Behind the urn the dark-faced café proprietor, who might himself be a Party member and might even know that Kelsall was expecting them, seemed like the driver of an elaborate but clean continental locomotive as turning a tap handle he looked briefly towards them through steam. Kelsall was not at any table in front of the screen. But after they had walked past the urn Alan saw him in the right-hand corner at the end of the room. He was sitting with his elbows resting on a table whose surface was bare except for a sauce bottle and a cruet. His face, viewed against painted wall planks that had the colour of stale mustard, was as pale as his extremely fair hair and was bleaker and bonier than Alan remembered it. Alan's awareness of these physical details was almost instantly superseded by an awe, which he wanted to resist but could not, at finding himself in the presence of a member of the Party's Executive committee. Kelsall's smile when they came up to him seemed to have to break through resistance, and he did not greet them verbally. He pushed a chair out from the table for Elsie. She had to be the first to speak:

'Have you been waiting here long, comrade?'

'No. It can't be said you were ever one of our unpunctuals.'

Alan didn't know quite how they were meant to take the 'It can't be said', though there was nothing in the sound of it to imply that less favourable things could very well be said. Kelsall spoke with what seemed an intentional slow tonelessness, as if to avoid exciting himself any more than was necessary. Alan remembered having been told that he suffered from athlete's heart as a result of rowing at his university, where he had only just missed getting his blue. A similar remembrance may have come at the same moment to Elsie, who asked:

'How have you been keeping lately?'

'Much the same as usual.'

Kelsall wasn't going to be communicative about it, probably not because he intended to maintain his distance from them but because he wanted to avoid seeming to regard such things as important. Nevertheless he did not ask after their children. He sat looking in front of him, long-faced, until a waitress came up to their table, and then he ordered toast and a cup of hot marmite – in a way which made Alan guess that this was what he usually had here at this time of day. Kelsall showed no sign, when the waitress had gone, of wanting to hear in greater detail what the theoretical problem was that Elsie had told him over the phone she would like to discuss. He asked about her Party Branch, how many members it had and who they were and where they worked. Even after the waitress had brought food to the table and Elsie and Alan had begun eating he continued questioning her about them, until at length he gave Alan the impression not so much of showing comradely curiosity as of making an investigation. His face was ascetic-looking almost to sourness, but he had an unusually long forelock which – like Rupert Brooke's – was brushed back above his ear. One other vestigial indication of his middle-class origin was his green sportscoat, shabby now and with leather patches on the elbows but it had probably been expensive when bought and was the kind of thing worn by university aesthetes in the twenties. He fetched out from its side pockets an old suède leather tobacco pouch and an old and conspicuously large yellow calabash pipe. He filled the pipe very slowly. As soon as she had finished eating he asked, in a tone which seemed meant to sound slightly patronizing:

'Well, what exactly is this problem of yours that you want to talk about?'

Elsie was ready with the wording of her answer.

'Lately I've become a bit confused,' she used the apologetic phrase customary with Party members when they wanted to express inability to accept official policy completely – 'about the theoretical line that the Party seems to have adopted since the war.'

Kelsall asked almost snappishly.

'Why do you say "seems"?'

'I mean I'm not altogether clear about it. Apparently it's different in some ways from the line that Lenin laid down in *State and Revolution*.'

'In what ways?'

'I think it assumes we can begin to build up a socialist economy in Britain *now* even though the workers have not come to power and the monopoly-capitalist State machine is still intact.'

He waited for her to go on. She tried to remove the bad impression she could see she had made on him.

'Of course I don't for a moment believe that all of Lenin's teachings will remain true for ever. Obviously as objective circumstances develop there must be some development in our theory too. I know that Marxism must be creative not dogmatic. But on the other hand surely we ought not to depart from the teachings of the great Marxist thinkers without giving a detailed explanation of why we have to do so.'

There was very briefly something startlingly like contempt in his look as he said:

'What grounds have you for supposing that the Party has departed from Lenin at all?'

She wasn't prepared for this, Alan knew. She hadn't really doubted Kelsall would admit that the leadership had modified Lenin's theory, and she had expected him to defend the modification with reasons which would either convince her – and she was sure she was willing and even eager to be convinced – or which if she found them inadequate, as she suspected they might be, she could demolish and thereby set going in his mind a process that would end by his being persuaded, and in turn persuading the rest of the leadership, that the Party's present theoretical line was wrong. Before she could think how to answer him, he added:

'If you had taken the trouble to read Party publications over the last year you would be less likely to come out with such half-baked assertions. '

She was stung into saying:

'I think I've read them at least as carefully as most other comrades have. And I've taken careful note of what Party leaders have been saying in public speeches. As for instance comrade McNarney's remark, made on the day when the coal mines were nationalized, that "a great industry has now become the property of people".' In spite of Kelsall's minatory stare she continued with increasing assurance: 'Or comrade Baxter's remark, at the time of the Grimethorpe colliery strike, that the strikers were "enemy miners". Surely these leading comrades could not make such statements except on the assumption that Britain is already advancing to socialism under a genuinely socialist government.'

'Does it occur to you, as you sit nattering there, that you are criticizing comrades who are not only more experienced politically than most of us but who have international contacts?'

She was even less prepared for this than she had been for his implication previously that the Party's present theoretical line showed no divergence at all from Lenin's. Again she didn't immediately know how to answer him, and he paused as if to allow her time to recognize how much she had been at fault; then he sharply asked:

'Would you say that the revolution of 1905 in Russia was socialist?'

'No. It was bourgeois democratic.'

Alan thought Kelsall was a little put out that she knew this.

'What was the attitude of the Bolsheviks towards it?'

'They supported it.'

'Supported it?' His ironic tone seemed meant to persuade

her that she had made an understatement. However she was not to be caught out:

'It wasn't started by them – it was a more or less spontaneous outbreak among the peasants and workers against conditions under the Tsar – but the Bolsheviks tried to organize and lead it.'

She was holding her own; though Kelsall now had the initiative, Alan knew.

'Why should the Bolsheviks want to establish a bourgeois republic?'

'Because it's the freest form of government possible under capitalism and it enables the workers to organize openly and build up their strength until the point is reached when they can seize power from the bourgeoisie.'

He plainly did not like this: perhaps the 'seize power' grated on him, or perhaps he was irritated that she had not obviously laid herself open to refutation. Suddenly, as though up to now his questions had been no more than a feint, he struck home hard with:

'What did Lenin think of the line taken by Parvus and Trotsky about the 1905 revolution?'

He looked at Alan, extending the attack now to him also, sure evidently that he would not be able to answer the question either. If Alan had had more time to think he might have been able to show that he knew something though not much about Lenin's argument against Parvus and Trotsky in 1905; however, Elsie spoke first:

'I don't remember what line they took. I suppose it was leftist. Did they want the Social Democrats to aim at setting up a workers' government and not a bourgeois democratic one?'

'You don't remember,' Kelsall said, with a surprise that was quite crudely sarcastic, though he didn't say she was wrong. 'I advise you to go and read Lenin's two articles on the subject which were published in the thirteenth and fourteenth numbers of *Vperiod*.' Elsie's face was beginning to show a glumness recognizable to Alan as a sign that she had taken deep offence and would not soon get over it. Kelsall went on: 'I suggest too that you study what Lenin said and wrote in 1917 during the period between the overthrow of the Tsar and the start of the October revolution. I think this might help you to see there's no departure from Leninism in our Party's present policy.' He spoke the phrase 'departure from Leninism' in a tone of warning, as if to stress both the gravity of the accusation she had made and her irresponsibility in making it. She did not try to answer him. He added: 'And you may be interested to know that comrade McNarney himself is now preparing a book which will give a full analysis of the situation facing us in post-war Britain and will deal among other things with the kind of questions you have raised. It will be published early in the autumn. I recommend you to read it with very great care – and with humility.' Elsie signalled to the waitress and asked to pay for what she and Alan had eaten. Kelsall said with a slight though satisfied smile:

'Have you got to get back already?'

'Yes.'

Then, not as though dismissing their interview from his mind and returning to his normal friendliness for her but as though indicating that her political attitude hadn't yet made friendliness finally impossible, he said:

'How are the children?'

Alan answered for her:

'They're doing very well, thanks.'

She moved away from the table and Alan followed her towards the door of the restaurant. Outside in the street she seemed unable immediately to break from the sullenness caused by her sense of insult, but Alan freed her by saying:

'He wasn't very helpful.'

'Talking to him was worse than useless. His attitude was a disgrace.'

'It wasn't exactly "pleasant and reasonable".'

'He behaved like a teacher trying to score over a child who has asked a serious but awkward question – all the more awkward for being serious.'

'The sort of teacher who takes for granted that the question could only have been asked out of guile.'

'Or the sort who just doesn't know the answer.'

35

'I doubt that,' Alan said. 'After all, Kelsall's one of the best theoreticians the Party has. And as an undergraduate he got a First in the Moral Sciences tripos. He's an extremely able man.'

'Then the way he took my remarks about McNarney and Baxter was all the less excusable.'

'Perhaps it wasn't what you said so much as how you said it that upset him. I mean, he may have felt that your tone in criticizing the Party leaders was, well, a little too confident, too easy.'

'Are we expected to sound full of awe whenever we mention the leadership nowadays? Perhaps we are, because a respectful rank-and-file is less likely to think of being critical at all, and less likely still to make the kind of criticisms that can't be rebutted.'

'He may have an answer to us. We haven't yet read the *V period* articles.'

'I should be very surprised to find that Lenin had at any time written or spoken in favour of supporting a bourgeois government which had shown itself to be reactionary.'

'So should I,' Alan said. 'But when I ask myself if the Party ought to attack the Labour government instead of supporting it – even though as a result the Tories might win the next general election – I begin to suspect that the Party's present line may be more Leninist than we've supposed.'

'I don't,' Elsie said strongly. 'I think that unless we expose this government as not genuinely socialist its behaviour is bound to discredit socialism and help the Tories. Anyway, whether I'm right or a hundred per cent wrong, what sort of Party has ours become when the leadership can make major changes in policy without getting the rank-and-file to discuss them first?'

'It wasn't like that before the war,' Alan agreed.

'Now we're told we're "nattering" if we presume to express any doubts at all about the pronouncements of "experienced comrades with international contacts".'

During the journey by train and bus back to their home Elsie repeated to Alan at intervals with little verbal variation her opinion that Kelsall had resented not so much the particular criticisms she had made nor their tone but the fact of her having had the nerve to criticize the leadership at all. Alan became sure she was right, and he felt a deepening alarm, less for himself and her and their future in the Party than for the Party itself. 'If we'd behaved unconstitutionally,' he said, 'and had started coming out with our criticisms at Branch and Borough meetings, instead of taking them to a member of the Executive, his attitude might have been justified.' She also convinced Alan that Kelsall's sacrosanctifying of the leadership ought to be of even greater concern to them than whether or not the Party's policy was consistent with Lenin's theory of the State. Nevertheless after they got back to their house his first thought when they came into the hall passage was to go and read the two articles by Lenin which Kelsall had mentioned.

He went into the front room and picked out the right volume at once – paper-backed and with pages as thick almost as blotting-paper – from the bookcase there. He began in a hurry to read the opening paragraph of the first article, then he skipped through twenty or more pages without finding what he wanted, then he turned to the summary which the editor (whose involved style was fortunately of the type that did make sense if the reader took the trouble to unravel its involutions) had given of the two articles, and he read:

Contrary to Martynov and Martov, Lenin affirms the necessity of materializing the victory of the revolution, such materialization – bearing in mind the social importance of the petty-bourgeois elements – to be expressed in the revolutionary dictatorship of the proletariat and the peasants; contrary to Parvus and Trotsky he insists on the bourgeois character of the actual revolution and the distinction between the maximum and the minimum programmes.

Alan called out to Elsie, who had gone into the kitchen:
'I've found something.'
She came to have a look at it. He explained:
'It's only a summary. I haven't been able to spot anything much in the articles themselves yet. But the sentence here about Parvus and Trotsky perhaps gives a hint of what Kelsall may have been getting at.'
'I don't see what bearing it has on the present political situation,' Elsie said after reading it.

'Perhaps he meant us to compare the support the Bolsheviks were ready to give to what would in essence have been a bourgeois revolution with the support the Party is giving to the Labour government now.'

'But in England the bourgeois revolution took place long ago, as long ago as the time of Cromwell.'

'That's true.'

'Whereas in Russia when Lenin was writing those articles it had still to come.'

Alan couldn't disagree with this; nevertheless he wasn't willing to accept what her tone of scorn was confident in implying – that Kelsall if not deceitfully trying to fob them off with a show of knowledge was at best stupidly muddled.

'The *V period* articles aren't the only thing Kelsall referred us to,' Alan said. 'He also told us we ought to study what Lenin wrote in 1917 during the period between the Tsar's overthrow and the Bolshevik seizure of power – the period of the bourgeois revolution, in fact.'

'He was just trying to throw dust in our eyes.'

'I can't quite believe it. How I wish we had asked him at the time which passages in Lenin's 1917 writings he had in mind. Do you think one of us ought perhaps to go and see him again?'

'No I don't. He's not prepared to discuss anything with us. He's not even prepared to answer our questions. If you went to him again all he would do would be to ask you questions, and his only object in asking them would be to put you on the defensive and make you forget what you were trying to find out from him.'

'I'm afraid you're right,' Alan said. 'But what are we to do next? We can't just resign ourselves to going on as before. That would be unbearable now.'

There was a strong single knock on the front door.

'It's one of the children back from school,' Elsie said.

She went out of the room and Alan followed her. Through the lower part of the glass panel of the door he saw Christina's peering face and her amethyst-tinted grin and the flattened tips of her pressing fingers.

As soon as Elsie had opened the door to her she jumped in over the mat, saying:

'Why didn't you see me?'

'Why didn't we see you when, dear?' Elsie asked.

'Just now when you were opening our gate.'

'Where were you?' Alan asked.

'I was quite near you. I was with Sally Pendle. I was skipping on the pavement.'

'There were a lot of other children coming back from school who were on the pavement too,' he said self-defensively.

'And you didn't hear me either. I called to you four times.'

'We must have thought that some other Mum and Dad were being called by some other daughter,' Elsie suggested. 'We're sorry, darling.'

'I nearly believed you were quite deaf.'

However, Christina was not really indignant – even though Elsie, as Alan saw, was still thinking mainly of other things while answering her. Christina may have noticed this but without minding it, being so full of the news she now brought out:

'I did fifty bumps today. It's my record.'

Doing bumps meant swinging the skipping rope twice over the head and under the feet while the feet were still off the ground, and the bumps had to be done successively with no pauses between them. Elsie sounded convincingly impressed as she exclaimed:

'Fifty! That's wonderful.'

'I don't know how you manage it,' Alan said.

Christina took their praise with pride, her face shining warm from the skipping she had just done outside on the pavement, her body momentarily immobile in its mauve-and-pink-striped seersucker dress, her short thick plaits of brown hair red-ribboned near the ends and at rest on her shoulders. Suddenly she was wholly in movement again, and she had already begun to run towards the open door of the back room as she said:

'I'll show you now.'

Her skipping rope, which while she had been talking with them she had held dangling doubled in a long loop from her hand, was now – quite dangerously, so Alan as usual felt – trailing close to her ankle-socked feet and might in an instant have become entangled with her browned slender legs that leapingly took her out through the back room and through the conservatory and somehow safely into the garden. There, after glancing back at her parents to make sure they were watching, she began to skip – not facing them but sideways on to them – and then to do her bumps. Alan said to Elsie:

'It might be worth our while to go and see some other member of the Executive.'

'No. If Kelsall, their best theoretician, won't or can't answer us, who could?'

'But what else can we do now – without being unconstitutional?'

'We must try to bring as much pressure as possible to bear on them through the rank-and-file.'

After the fifteenth bump Christina's feet failed to clear the rope on its second downswing, and she paused in her skipping to glance again at her parents. Though their faces were turned towards her she detected that their attention was not. She called out to them:

'You've not been watching properly. Now you must count aloud how many bumps I do.'

She sounded commanding rather than offended.

'All right, we will,' Elsie answered her.

Alan could hear in Elsie's voice a compunction such as he himself had also begun to feel. When Christina started skipping again they did their best to concentrate entirely on her, and they helped themselves to do this by loudly counting out in unison the number of bumps as she made it. However Alan was soon concentrating without any deliberate effort, was entirely won by the movement of her limbs and her dress, by the contraction and expansion of her flared circular skirt as she jumped, by the linked whirling of her wrists and of the spherically-headed shiny wooden skipping-rope handles, by the energetic joy that emanated from her. He was held too, even more, by the sudden remembrance that this child so physically marvellous to watch was the same who had told them how at nights she had often stood in her dark bedroom near the window and had looked out at the moon and the stars, and who had once shown them a poem she had begun to write called *The Universe Verse*. Now, when she next came to a stop in her skipping and while she was getting set to start again, he said to Elsie:

'We really mustn't let our worries about the Party make us absent-minded with the children.'

'No we mustn't. For one thing, if we do we shall end by turning them against the Party.'

It was lucky they did not take longer to break out of their political preoccupation, because otherwise they might not have noticed, when Stephen arrived back from school, that something was disturbing him, and he might not have told them. After letting himself into the house – he had his own latchkey, unlike Christina who although she had been offered one had declined on the grounds that she might lose it – he hardly glanced at his parents as he came into the back room to put his satchel down on the sideboard, though he did answer their hullos.

'How did you get on at school today?' Alan lightly said.

Stephen's tenseness was not relieved as he came out with:

'Mr Fosket asked me if I went to church last Sunday.'

'Asked just you?' Alan was on the point of being indignant.

'No, he asked everyone in the class.'

As more than once before, a question evidently addressed by Mr Fosket to the class as a whole had been taken by Stephen to be intended for him in particular – a testimony not only to Stephen's sensitive alertness but also, Alan reflected, to Mr Fosket's effectiveness as a teacher.

'How many put their hands up?' Elsie was quite eager to know.

'Everyone did except me.'

Christina, who had stopped her skipping and come in from the garden to hear what they were talking about, said:

'Did Mary Pratt put her hand up?'

'Yes.'

'I know she never goes to church.'

'Nor does Norman Wilcox, nor does Peter Yalden,' Stephen said, 'and they both put theirs up.'

'Well, I think it was all the more to your credit that you didn't,' Elsie said, perhaps assuming from his look that he needed to be praised.

He stood strangely rigid in his unrestricting summer clothes, with his back to the sideboard, his yellow cellular shirt wide open at the neck and his striped snake-lock belt comfortably loose around the waist of his khaki shorts.

'Did Mr Fosket say anything to you after that?' Alan asked.

'No. He went on with the lesson.'

'Did any of the others say anything to you?'

'No. They soon forgot all about it. They don't care.'

Stephen's strained and serious look was unchanged. Elsie said:

'Mr Fosket may not go to church himself. Perhaps he's really an atheist and asked the question hoping there would be quite a few in the class who wouldn't put their hands up.'

'If he's a Christian he would have asked how many *didn't* go to church,' Alan too ingeniously suggested.

Stephen wouldn't have this.

'I'm sure he believes in the Bible.'

'What makes you sure?' Elsie asked.

'The way he tells the stories from the New Testament.'

'There was a teacher at my last school, Mrs Carson, who told them with very great reverence,' she said, 'though she didn't believe a word of them herself, but she said to me once in the staff-room that she enjoyed putting them across – she was an extremely competent teacher – and that she thought it was good for children to be made to believe in them.'

'What an attitude,' Alan said.

'Mr Fosket isn't like that,' Stephen said. 'He does really believe. He once said to us he does, and he said some people nowadays don't.'

'That sounds genuine,' Alan conceded.

'He is genuine,' Stephen insisted.

'If you feel he was putting pressure on you and the others to go to church' – Elsie, like Alan, was aware that they hadn't yet found out exactly what was troubling Stephen – 'we'll write to him about it, just as we wrote to Miss Parbury, you remember, who taught you during the war when you were at your first school.'

'Oh, she was quite different. She said we must all go to Sunday School. I don't want you to write to Mr Fosket. He wasn't trying to make us go to church.'

Then abruptly Stephen came out with:

'How can he believe?'

He was a little easier after saying this, as though he had at last achieved a formulation of what had been puzzling him. The unsettling thing for Stephen, Alan now felt, had been the recognition that such beliefs could be held by a teacher who was otherwise sensible and likeable. But before Alan or Elsie could answer Stephen's question, Christina said:

'Perhaps God is true after all.'

Though Alan and Elsie could hardly suspect her of not being deliberately provocative, they did feel a brief alarm. However, Christina soon added, with a wide smile of amusement at having succeeded in momentarily dismaying her parents:

'Of course I don't really think there is a God. I know there isn't, because I've tried.'

'How do you mean you've tried?' Stephen asked, very slightly jeering.

'I wasn't going to believe there's no God just because Mum and Dad said their isn't. So one night in bed I asked God to speak to me aloud to show they were wrong. And he didn't answer, so then I knew there was no God.'

'What more convincing proof could there be than that?' Alan said. 'If he won't even speak to a child – "one of these little ones" who must be "suffered to come unto" him – a child appealing to him to save her from the disbelief that her godless parents are bringing her up in, well, supposing he did exist he wouldn't be much good as a God.'

'I should like to hear how the theologians would try to explain why their God refused to answer Christina,' Elsie said.

'There are first-rate brains among them,' Alan said in a tone corrective of Elsie's contempt, 'and I've no doubt they'd produce explanations which we wouldn't find easy to refute. Perhaps they would argue it was sinful of Christina to try to force someone so all-important as God to speak just to her, and that's why he ignored her. Or they might say that God speaks only to very exceptionally holy children, such as young Samuel, his future High Priest.'

'What tripe it all is,' Elsie said.

'Some parents think,' Alan said to Christina, 'that they oughtn't to try to make their children either believe or not believe in God and that the children should decide for themselves, but we think this would be unfair because the children would hear about God only from believers or from people who pretend to believe.'

Noticing that Stephen still looked perturbed, Alan remembered they had not answered his question 'How can he believe?' and said now:

'Mr Fosket isn't to be blamed for being religious. I expect he was brought up like that, among people who all of them believe or think they believe, and the possibility that he might be wrong just hasn't occurred to him. We ought to respect the beliefs of sincere Christians.'

'I don't see why,' Elsie said. 'They don't respect ours.'

'By respecting theirs we show the superiority of ours. Besides, there are times when Christianity can be inconvenient to the fascists and reactionaries who plan new wars and new ways of keeping the coloured races down.'

'It doesn't seem to be inconvenient to the Dutch Reformed Church in South Africa. Nor to the fascist governments in Spain and Portugal. And plenty of Christians are in favour of the atom bomb which they say is the only defence of Christian civilization against communism.'

'Some Christians would argue that those Christians aren't real Christians,' Alan said.

'But other Christians would claim that the Christians who argue like this are disguised communists. So how are we to know which Christians are the real ones?'

'Not from the Bible. Both sorts of Christians could find plenty of support there. For instance "Blessed are the peacemakers" and "I came to bring not peace but a sword".'

Christina interrupted her parents with:

'Why do I have to go into Scripture lessons? I *hate* Scripture.'

The way she spoke the word 'hate', much more softly than the other words and half-closing her eyes as she spoke it, made them laugh.

'You don't have to go into them,' Elsie said. 'Parents are allowed by law to withdraw their children from them, and we could write to Miss Samson saying we would like you to do something else instead. But it might be better for you to stay in with the other children, because if you didn't you would learn nothing about the Bible, which can be a very interesting book. And there are a lot of things you wouldn't be able to understand in other books if you don't know the Bible.'

'All right,' Christina agreed, more easily than they'd expected.

'Another reason why it's worth doing Scripture,' Alan said, 'is that you'll learn how Christians think, which will help you to win them over when you're arguing with them about things that really matter.'

'But religion does really matter to our children,' Elsie corrected him. 'It's very much a part of their school life.'

'I know. What I'm trying to say is that they ought to aim first at persuading the others about such things as the need to be against the colour bar, for instance, and to be active for peace – rather than at attacking Christianity.'

'Religion is continually being put across to them. It's much more an immediate thing for them, and for all the others too, than war or colonialism. They've got to counter-attack it.'

'Mum is quite right,' Stephen said decisively. 'And Dad is wrong.'

'Yes, I am,' Alan agreed. 'I was thinking of school as though it were the same as the outside world.'

'I'm pretty sure religion in schools helps to make some children delinquents,' Elsie said. 'How can they want to behave well when they're taught they ought to imitate someone who died in Palestine two thousand years ago and who hadn't any idea what life today is like?'

'Being an atheist doesn't necessarily prevent a person from becoming a criminal,' Alan felt bound to say. 'Hitler, for instance.'

'He wasn't an atheist,' Elsie said. 'He was always bringing God into his speeches. As when he said that the burning of the Reichstag was a God-given signal for him to put an end to the Communist Party. The Reichstag was the German parliament,' she explained to the children, 'and it was really burnt down by the Nazis, so that they could put the blame on the communists.'

'All the same, atheists can be wicked people,' Alan said, 'though they are much less likely to be wicked than Christians are.'

'And yet Christians have the impudence to suggest that atheists who behave well are really being influenced by the Christian tradition.'

'The truth is that Christians who behave well are being influenced by modern humane ideas. The Christian tradition is a tradition of horrible wars and of the burning and torture of heretics.'

Christina, though she was still interested in what her parents were saying, now remembered something that – because it had been ousted from her thoughts for the last few minutes – became more interesting to her. She told Stephen:

'I did fifty bumps at school today.'

He seemed as though he would ignore her and as though he wanted his parents to continue talking about religion, but he changed his mind and said to her:

'Let's go into the garden.'

They didn't linger. As they turned to run out through the conservatory Alan knew from Stephen's grin that he no longer felt any uneasiness at all about Mr Fosket. Christina began her skipping once more and Stephen after very briefly watching her went to look at a hole which he had been digging the day before behind the nearest apple-tree and which he hoped to make into a pond for a toy submarine of his. Seeing him again as a child Alan admiringly thought how promising he was, how scrupulous, how brightly awake to everything and everyone.

Alan said to Elsie:

'Wouldn't it be dreadful if we became so absorbed in the Party that we didn't look after the children properly and one of them grew up to become a fundamentalist – or a Catholic convert, like George Fletcher's daughter.'

'That was a shocking thing. We thought of him as a model communist, tirelessly active; but when he was at home, which wasn't often, he was unpleasant to his wife – I daresay he despised her for not being a communist, though she wasn't religious – so it's not surprising the daughter reacted against everything he stood for.'

'And yet,' Alan had to say, 'there could be times when neglecting one's children for the Party would be necessary and right.'

'It would be horrible at any time, even for a Party whose theory and policy were perfectly correct and even in a period of extreme political crisis, but it would be worse than horrible for the sort of Party we seem to have at present.'

'We shall have to be careful,' Alan said, 'or we may find ourselves lapsing into the position of those well-intentioned bourgeois intellectuals who think personal relationships are more important than politics. We mustn't forget that if we devoted ourselves more to our children than to a Party which was genuinely struggling against imperialism we should be helping the reactionaries to start a new war and to destroy the children.'

'I know you're right,' Elsie couldn't help agreeing. 'Though we mustn't forget, either, that making no effort to stop the reactionaries wouldn't be quite the same thing as actively helping them.'

A very unpleasant thought came to Alan.

'Oughtn't we to be prepared to neglect the children now so that we can give all our spare time and energy not to supporting the Party as it is but to bringing it back to Leninism?'

'No.'

'Why not?'

She momentarily didn't seem quite sure, then said:

'Because, for one thing, we can work hard to bring it back *and* we can avoid neglecting the children. Why should we always assume that unless every Party activity we undertake involves us in sacrificing something we're not being good communists?'

'Yes, why should we? I think we've almost come to believe sacrifice is meritorious in itself, whether or not the situation requires it. That's an idea the Party must have bred in us. And it's a religious idea, not a Marxist one at all.'

In the garden Christina stopped skipping and they guiltily knew that once again they hadn't been concentrating on her. However, this time she had been skipping not for them but for Stephen – who wasn't watching properly either, as she now told him. Alan, relieved that Elsie and he hadn't been caught out, let his glance rise from Stephen to an apple-tree whose boughs together with those of a second tree farther off on the other side of the garden made an apparent arch beneath which was a circle-segment of brighter green indented by fringing apple leaves at the circumference. This circle-segment was the grass of the playing-field beyond the end fence of the garden. It reminded him of how a few evenings ago he had conceived a poem which would have compared the field to a huge theatre stage and which would have been in praise of the poetic life he had tried to live in his younger days before he had turned to the Party. His hope, soon after he had reluctantly rejected that poem, of being able to conceive a politically militant one in place of it hadn't yet been realized. But now, as he looked at the field, he seemed to come much nearer than before to knowing the kind of militant poem he wanted to write. It would not be about the housing shortage, or about racialism, or even about the atom bomb: it would be more general, would praise the Party's struggle against all these, would be in deliberate opposition to the poetic life poem he had rejected and would affirm that the life in and for the Party was the finest life. He wasn't able to begin to develop this conception in any detail, however, because Elsie said:

'We still haven't decided what we're going to do next.'

He had an instant of incomprehension before answering:

'I think we might come out openly in the Branch against the leadership's line.'

'I doubt whether the Branch would be ready for that yet.'

'No, perhaps they wouldn't. We might do better to wait until

I've given the last of my talks on *State and Revolution*. But before then we could persuade them to pass a resolution which without suggesting the line is wrong would deferentially ask the Executive to make it clearer. That might force a revelation of where the leadership really stands in relation to Lenin.'

'I can imagine the kind of answer we'd get,' Elsie said. 'The Executive would be most surprised that in spite of all the statements it has issued on policy, we could still be in any ignorance about the Party's theoretical position, but would assure us that everything would be made absolutely plain in a book by comrade McNarney, to be published this autumn, which we must study with the greatest care.'

'Yes, I'm afraid that's all we'd get. And the Branch would be quite satisfied with it. Perhaps we shall have to postpone our attack until after McNarney's book has come out.'

'That seems a very long time to have to wait,' Elsie said.

'Only three months. And we can try to make sure before the autumn that every Branch member appreciates the depth and force of Lenin's theory sufficiently to regard any ambiguity in McNarney's attitude towards it as intolerable.'

'But perhaps his book will be Leninist after all.'

'How I wish there could be some slight hope of that,' Alan said.

3

They could not get to sleep. Earlier in the evening they had discussed the speech Elsie would make next day at the Borough meeting which was being specially called to hear how she, as secretary of her Branch, could justify her refusal to sell Mc-Narney's book, *Britain's Way Forward*, now published at last; but long after they had come to bed the meeting remained on their minds and they continued talking about it. They lay side by side close to each other – Alan's left arm was pressed lightly against Elsie's right, though neither he nor she was conscious of the contact – upon the bumpy double mattress they had been so glad of at the end of the war when it had been given them, together with the brass-ornamented black iron bedstead, by her uncle Sid after his wife had died. The light from a street lamp just outside the window shone quite strongly into the room – through pale green damask curtains made to measure for their pre-war maisonette but not ample enough here after Elsie had stitched them together in pairs to lengthen them for the taller windows of this house. Though she and Alan were talking quietly and almost calmly, they kept on repeating themselves and reaching the same conclusion: that she must say as little as possible about the Party's policy, which she had made the mistake of criticizing point by point in the statement she had read out against *Britain's Way Forward* at the Branch meeting a week before, and must concentrate on the unLeninist theory, or lack of theory, behind the policy. No wonder the Branch comrades, to most of whom her criticisms had come as a surprise, had been unable to believe all at once that so very many things in the book could be wrong, and they had been shocked by her objection to the Party's industrial production drive 'without which', so Bill Whiddett had said in the subsequent discussion, 'Britain's crisis could never be solved.' In her speech at the Borough meeting tomorrow she must limit herself to exposing, with the utmost simplicity and clarity, the one basic error underlying all McNarney's other errors, his assumption that the transition to socialism was beginning in Britain now while capitalism still held State power here. But she must avoid the mistake made by Alan whose own separate statement to the Branch, although it had rightly concentrated on McNarney's basic theoretical error, had stressed Lenin's view that the capitalist State needed to be violently overthrown. No wonder the Branch comrades, who had been accustomed by the leadership to regard violent revolution as belonging to past history, had paid little attention when Alan at the end of his statement had expressed the emphatic hope that no one there would think he was advocating revolutionary action immediately or in the near future. 'Tomorrow you'd better not even mention revolution,' Alan advised her again, as he had already done more than once since they had come to bed. 'You can put our main point over quite adequately without touching on that at all.'

They became calmer, each of them being strengthened by the complete agreement they found themselves in. How dreadful it would have been, Alan imagined, if one of them had believed McNarney to be fundamentally wrong and the other had been certain he was right. But throughout their marriage they had not once had a serious disagreement, either about politics or about anything else. They had never really quarrelled, and when they had had a minor tiff now and then they had always made it up soon in kisses and had never slept on it overnight. And the persistence of the harmony between them, Alan thought, though it was no doubt helped by temperamental compatibility, was primarily due to their trust in reason, which they regarded not as something they could use to subserve their wishes but as the arbiter that would set them right if they appealed to it disinterestedly. While he was thinking this he became aware of the contact of Elsie's arm against his, and at the same moment he felt desire for her. Although his consciousness of the feeling was sudden he knew that the desire itself was not, that it had been growing in him for many minutes past, as if their political talk had been nourishing it but also masking it, and now he had abruptly found it. He sensed that she too had simultaneously become conscious of a desire already grown in her, and he was sure of it when he slid his arm over hers and she instantly turned to embrace him. Soon they were closed in a moving closeness as complete as it could physically be.

He moved with her away from themselves and far away from any thought of tomorrow's meeting, away from his identity as a Party member, as a schoolmaster, as a father and a husband. Away also from the family into which he had been born, from his own father and mother whom he momentarily and strangely remembered now with the feeling that he was severing himself from them and forfeiting their protection. Away from his class origin, his nationality, his epoch, away from Elsie as an individual person. This act linked him with men and women of every race all over the world, in the past as well as in the present. It carried him back to humanity's earliest times, and beyond. It carried him back into animality. Yet he still kept a conscious and civilized control over himself, wilfully postponing the climax, wanting to pleasure his partner to the utmost. Then he whispered to her and she took control of him and he abandoned himself to her ecstasy. And he moved beyond animality, became one with the earliest and most elementary forms of life, was as though swaying in the primeval salt lagoon, was carried beyond all life and assimilated into the earth's hydrosphere, became inert, became part of the lithosphere, of the solar system, of the universe, became negligible, became nothing. The whole human race was nothing, was negligible. Neither the martyrs who had died for human progress nor the nuclear warmongers and fascist genocides had any importance. But this feeling soon passed, and he thought of humanity as an emanation of the universe. In us the universe had become self-conscious, and that was our greatness. The thought brought an exaltation with it. A boundless power seemed to flow into him. The difficulties that had loomed so mountainously in front of him not long before – his disagreement with the Party, his exhausting daily work at school, his failure so far to start writing poetry again in spite of the seven weeks' freedom he had had during the summer holidays – were trifles which he felt he would surmount with soaring ease. He even knew now exactly what had been wrong with the poem he had been trying to write: its theme, that the life in and for the Party was the finest life, lacked strength at a time when the Party seemed to be straying from Marxism. He knew too the poem he ought to try to write: it would revive the appeal of the Party life by foreseeing the glory of the future world-wide victory of communism which only the devotion of Party members to the Party could bring about. He felt no need to investigate this new theme further, his confidence in it was so strong. Abruptly he became aware again of Elsie in his arms, and he covered her face with his kisses.

When they were lying side by side once more, he said:

'Oh darling, what a wonderful marriage ours has been.'

'Has been?'

'Has been, is and will be.'

'Don't be too confident about the "will be", dear.' She laughed. 'You may have sowed your wild oats long ago but I haven't started sowing mine yet.'

'For all I really know, you sowed them with Jim Brunton two years before we were married.'

'No, I didn't, though I could have done. He was nice – intelligent and handsome, and I daresay if I'd married him I could have lived very happily with him.'

'I think you could. What's more, it's just an accident you didn't. If I hadn't been offered a job in London and narrowly avoided the sack from it at the end of my first year you would never have got to know me. And no doubt there were thousands of other possible partners whom either of us could have been quite happy with – though I must admit that none of my actual old flames would have been likely to tolerate me for long as a husband.'

'I can believe that.'

'How wrong the romantics were in their idea that for every person there exists somewhere a unique soul-mate.'

'Yes, and in practice it's an idea that doesn't go at all well with monogamy.'

'Perhaps under full communism there will be a return to group marriage. Engels seems almost to favour that.'

'I suspect it rather appeals to you too.'

'I confess I do have a sentimental hankering after it, because it would be so much fairer to everyone, especially to the less attractive ones. And it might bring back a kind of matriarchy on a higher level, which would compensate women for their biological disadvantages.'

'You always were a loyal feminist, dear.'

'But at present monogamy seems best.'

He put his arm gently around her. She said:

'To be perpetually looking for new sex-partners must be such a drain on energy when there's so much else to do.'

'Some people seem to enjoy it, and it may even increase their energy. It's all right for the young.'

'But for the not-so-young it must often be more of a misery than an enjoyment – especially for women who have lost their charms and can't look around as hopefully as their husbands can.'

'I couldn't look around if you lost your charms. I really couldn't. I could never enjoy myself if I knew I was making you miserable. But anyway, how mad it is for married couples in these vile times to add domestic wretchedness to the horrors that threaten them from the world outside.'

'They can't always help it.'

'No, that's true. We mustn't get conceited. We've been lucky.'

'Yes, though we were prudent too. We mustn't be ashamed to give ourselves credit for that. We didn't rush into marriage. We'd been having loves together for two years before we risked going to the Registry Office, and even then we both had very serious doubts.'

'I was so unstable. My whole outlook was coloured by my middle-class upbringing, and I had moments when your not being middle-class made me find you unattractive. But now you seem uniquely beautiful to me.'

'That's an exaggeration in the opposite direction.'

'No. I often look at you during Party meetings when you're

not looking at me and I think that your face is the most beautiful on earth.'

'And I look at you, too, when you're not looking, and I think the same about you.'

They avoided returning to the subject of the special Borough meeting. They talked for some while longer – about their lives before the war. Sleep must have come almost simultaneously to them and so suddenly that when they woke in the morning they could not remember at what point in their talk they had fallen asleep.

Twenty-five minutes before Alan and Elsie were to set out from their house for the Borough meeting, he was standing in the back sitting-room listening to sounds from upstairs and trying to guess what stage Elsie might have reached in her supervision of the children's preparations for bed: he would have liked to talk over with her once again, even at this late moment, the speech she was going to make – because, good though he felt sure it would be, they might yet manage to think of some point which would improve it and which would make it impregnable. But he would have liked still more to have been able to have a few conciliating and explanatory words now with one of those comrades who had seemed bewildered if not antagonized by the statements Elsie and he had read out at the last Branch meeting. Sometimes when a Party meeting was to be held locally elsewhere than in this house, one or other of the Branch comrades living near them would call here first in order to accompany them to it, and just possibly one might call this evening. Alan sat down on a chair facing the open doorway of the sitting-room, and, with his back to the curtainless windows that divided the room from the conservatory and from the October evening darkness of the garden beyond, he looked out into the hall passage, which was lit by an unshaded electric bulb, and watched the opaque-seeming coloured panes of the front door.

The comrade he would most of all have liked to speak to at this moment was perhaps Alec Murrayfield, who with his wife

Iris had called in here before the last Branch meeting – which had been held at the house of Ken Pollock, the Borough organizer. Alec and Iris were comparatively new members of the Branch, having moved into this district only eight months ago, but what Alan and Elsie had so far got to know about Alec's life – he was the son of a French actress and a rich Anglo-Egyptian cotton merchant, had studied medicine, had become an actor, had given up acting and taken to archaeology and then to gliding, had been landed in occupied France from a submarine during the war, was now working for a degree at the London School of Economics – suggested that he was an independent-minded comrade who wouldn't automatically object to criticisms of the Party's theoretical line. When Alan had criticized *Britain's Way Forward* in conversation with him and Iris here before going with them to Ken Pollock's house, Alec, and Iris perhaps even more so, had seemed on the point of being convinced, but by the time the Branch meeting had ended Alec had become suspicious – alarmed perhaps by the denunciatory tone in which Alan and Elsie had read out their statements against the book – and he had looked at Alan as at someone he didn't know well and who might conceivably be a clandestine enemy of the Party. If Alan could have a few unexcitable words with Alec before this evening's meeting he might still be able to predispose him favourably towards Elsie's speech. However, Alan would have been almost as glad to see any other member of the Branch who might knock at the front door now – even Rose Barlow, though he would have to be very untheoretical in trying to predispose her to accept Elsie's attack on McNarney's theoretical position. He had never felt more warmly towards rank-and-file comrades, or needed them more, than at present when he had lost his confidence in the leaders.

An illuminated shape came up to the suddenly translucent coloured panes from outside the house. Alan, hurrying into the hall passage towards the front door, could see that the shape was of a man – and not of Miss Sims who lived up the road and with whom they had arranged, as they customarily did when both of them were to go out together in the evening, that she should come and sit in the house so that the children would not be left alone here. The comrade outside the coloured panes seemed short and slight in build and might be Bert Alldiss. Alan, turning the door latch, hoped so, because Bert at the last Branch meeting had shown less opposition than any other comrade there to the statements read out by him and Elsie and could perhaps be won over completely now before the Borough meeting began. Alan opened the door and was startled to see a fair-haired shiny-faced man of about forty-five, unknown to him, who wore a clerical collar and who said after a smiling pause:

'I wrote to Mrs Sebrill. I'm Maldwyn Pryce.'

Alan remembered. Elsie, as secretary of the Branch, had had a letter some days before from a Swedenborgian minister who wanted to join the Party and she had written back asking him to call here on any one of several evenings when she would be at home.

'Oh, of course. Come in – comrade.'

The disappointment which Alan wondered if he'd succeeded in hiding was quickly modified by a return of the eagerness he had felt, after reading Maldwyn Pryce's letter, at the prospect of being able to recruit such an unusual member into the Party.

'Very glad to see you.' As soon as Alan had said this he realized he must get Pryce out of the house again within five minutes. To have him present while Alan tried to persuade some Branch member who might yet arrive here at any moment that an authoritative book written by a Party leader was un-Leninist might give Pryce a bad first impression of the Party. Alan, bringing Pryce into the back sitting-room, added: 'I'm afraid that at the time when my wife answered your letter she didn't know we would have to go out to a special Borough meeting this evening – '

Pryce's wide-open eyes, fringed with short fair lashes, had a look in them which reminded Alan of something – though he didn't immediately know what – and which checked him.

'That's quite all right,' Pryce said with comprehension and humility. 'I can easily come along again some other evening.'

Then Alan knew that the look, diffident and at the same time strangely exalted, reminded him of his own feelings years ago when, in the vacated shop premises which the Party had used as committee rooms during a Parliamentary election, he himself had first made contact with Party members. Perhaps the room here – with its fleur-de-lis-patterned copper hood over the fireplace, its large plaster cast of a sea shell above the doorway, its china-knobbed bell-pull signifying that this semi-detached house had been built at a period when every lower-middle-class family expected to have a servant in the kitchen – was for Pryce a holy place, just as the committee rooms had been for Alan.

'We shan't have to start out for twenty minutes yet,' Alan said. 'You must stay until my wife has met you – she's seeing the children to bed at the moment.'

And suppose Bert Alldiss or the Murrayfields or all three did turn up now, why shouldn't Alan discuss *Britain's Way Forward* with them in front of Maldwyn Pryce? To want to conceal from an intending member the fact that the Branch secretary and her husband disapproved of a book written by a Party leader was to be as dishonest as Digby Kelsall had been when instead of answering Elsie's criticisms he'd objected to their being made at all. And why shouldn't Alan invite Pryce to hear Elsie speak this evening? He decided he would invite him.

'Could you come along with us to the Borough meeting?' Alan asked.

'I should like to very much, if you're quite sure that as a non-member I wouldn't be intruding,' Pryce said diffidently.

'Yes, quite sure – after all, you are going to be a member.'

Some of the comrades at the meeting might not approve but they probably wouldn't go so far as to say so, and in any case letting an intending member see what the Party was really like had now become for Alan a principle which he would be prepared to defend against any comrade who objected to Pryce's presence.

'You've not been in touch with the Party before?'

'No. I've been a sympathizer for some time but I decided not to apply for membership until my two youngsters had more or less grown up, which they have now.'

Alan showed himself puzzled, and Maldwyn Pryce explained:

'My work as a minister has been my sole source of income. If I'm admitted to the Party I shall leave the ministry.'

Alan's shocked response had the instantaneousness of a conditioned reflex:

'But you mustn't do that!'

Maldwyn Pryce didn't answer, because at this moment Elsie came quickly downstairs. Her movement along the hall passage was so lively that it seemed about to become a run. No doubt she had heard Pryce announce himself at the front door. Alan introduced her to him, and mentioned having invited him to come to the meeting.

'Good,' she said without the least uncertainty, and added: 'We were excited when we got your letter. We don't have a clergyman wanting to join the Party every day of the week. And a clergyman of the New Church at that.'

'Her parents were both Swedenborgians,' Alan said.

'Were they?' Pryce's smile showed pleasure. 'That's interesting. And it bears out a pet notion of mine that Swedenborgianism leads on naturally to Marxism.'

This remark, in spite of the suggestion of parsonical playfulness which the phrase 'a pet notion' gave it, seemed seriously meant, and Alan might have questioned it if he had been less concerned by what Pryce had said just previously. Alan told Elsie:

'Comrade Pryce wants to leave the ministry after he's joined the Party.'

'Oh, what for?' Elsie was as shocked as Alan had been.

'Well, if I didn't leave of my own accord my congregation would insist on my going.'

'Do you mean you would tell them you had become a communist?' Elsie asked.

'Yes.' Pryce seemed a little surprised at the question. 'I shall announce it from the pulpit.'

Alan, anxious lest Pryce should think him machiavellian, hesitated before saying:

'The Party wouldn't be in favour of that. You could do

far more effective work for communism if you didn't leave the ministry. We need as many comrades in influential positions as we can get.'

Pryce did not seem to find Alan's suggestion ethically repellent. He rejected it on other grounds:

'I'm afraid I just couldn't bring myself to go on with my present work as a minister.'

He sounded so firmly final in saying this that Elsie, though Alan knew she would argue with Pryce against it later, chose to evade it for the time being.

'Having to preach something you no longer believe in must be unpleasant.'

'Oh, that wouldn't be the trouble. I don't disbelieve in what I've been preaching.' Pryce added unassertively: 'There's something to be said for Swedenborg's ideas, I feel, even from a Marxist point of view. What I don't think I could do would be to continue putting up with the pettinesses and narrownesses of a minister's life. I've had more than twenty years of that.'

'You're still a Swedenborgian?' Elsie was openly amazed for a moment. 'But how can you reconcile –' she became aware she was about to be guilty of a Party cliché, and avoided it – 'but don't you find dialectical materialism awkward to accept?'

'No,' he said easily, and Alan was at any rate relieved of the brief suspicion that he might not have heard of dialectical materialism. Pryce, obviously glad to have been given the opportunity of clarifying his position for them, went on: 'From the time when I was a biology student at Manchester University I have always felt that Swedenborg's Christianity is the only kind really adapted to a scientific age.'

At this Alan very nearly grinned, because he happened to remember how once in a secondhand bookshop he had opened at random Swedenborg's *Spiritual Diary* and had read that the odour which prunes have when they are cooked signifies the delight experienced by married people in just lying next to each other. He had not bought the book, which in other passages seemed less interesting. Pryce looked at Alan and said:

'As I expect you know, he was a scientist with a European reputation before he took up theology. And his theological writings never ask us to believe anything anti-scientific. For him the scriptures are allegorical, not literal – they have a spiritual meaning which was known to the Most Ancient Church and afterwards forgotten, but which he is able to reveal to us again through the study of what he calls "correspondences".'

Alan didn't try to avoid exchanging glances with Elsie, and he felt confirmed in his assumption that she too must be thinking 'What kind of recruit is this we're going to be responsible for getting into the Party?' She said bluntly:

'Swedenborg isn't the only Christian who has tried to get round science by arguing that the Bible doesn't mean quite what it says.'

'No,' Pryce agreed mildly, 'but he is consistent. He isn't one of those who claim that the gospels are literally true except where they're scientifically incredible.' Pryce looked at Alan again. 'His Christianity doesn't lay itself open to the kind of attack Dryden makes on Anglicanism in *The Hind and the Panther*: "To take up half on trust, and half to try, / Name it not faith, but bungling bigotry".'

That Pryce should quote from Dryden was almost as startling to Alan as his arrival at the front door had been a few minutes before. How had Pryce come to know those lines? Perhaps he'd found them in a theological text-book. Alan for some reason couldn't suppose him to be a man widely read in English poetry for its own sake. And yet Pryce did not speak the lines mechanically but with emphasis as though he felt they would be of special interest to Alan. And he suddenly added:

'William Blake was a Swedenborgian.'

Did Pryce perhaps guess that Alan had been a poet? Certainly the references to Blake and Dryden had the effect of disarming Alan's scepticism and of making him enter imaginatively with such sympathy for a moment into Pryce's Swedenborgian ideas that he could almost believe them to be politically innocuous. Elsie however reacted as Alan would probably have done if the poets hadn't been mentioned; she asked with scarcely disguised suspicion:

'What made you want to join the Party?'

'I was a supporter of the Labour Party for many years,' Pryce said. 'I never had any illusions about its leaders, but I did believe that sooner or later the rank and file might be able either to force them to adopt a socialist policy or to replace them with other leaders who would. Recently I've come to see that the Labour Party is of its very nature pro-capitalist, no matter who leads it, and can never be anything else.'

A knock at the front door prevented Alan from getting Pryce to enlarge on the interesting phrase 'of its very nature'. No doubt for Elsie too, Alan thought as he went out into the passage, this phrase would indicate that Pryce had a better knowledge and understanding of Leninist ideas than they had guessed, and she would question him further. The solitary shape that showed through the coloured panes now was a woman's — and she couldn't be Iris Murrayfield, who was broader and would anyway have had Alec with her. Alan opened the door to Miss Sims. Her thin and gentle face, seeming as always to be thrust forward a little — because of a disabling curvature of the upper part of her spine which bowed her neck and was bad enough to make her unfit for most kinds of work other than baby-sitting — had a hint of nervous inquiry in its smile of greeting, as though the agitation and distraughtness she might have noticed in Alan and Elsie during the past fortnight had caused her to fear some worse manifestation from them this evening. She was not much surprised when Alan, bringing her into the back sitting-room, introduced her to a clergyman: other equally unusual things had happened here lately. Alan immediately went on to say, trying not to sound at all anxious:

'Well, perhaps it's time we thought of starting out for the meeting now.'

'Did you arrive by bicycle or on foot?' Elsie asked Pryce.

'By bike. I've left it outside against the fence.'

'I hope it hasn't been stolen,' Alan said with a slight laugh. 'I ought to have got you to put it at the back of the house with mine and Elsie's. But assuming it's all right, the three of us will be able to ride together.'

'It won't have been pinched. I've padlocked it.' Pryce laughed also, but perhaps a little guiltily as though conscious of being caught out in an excessive concern for his private property.

They said good-bye to Miss Sims, and Elsie added the hope that she wouldn't mind having to sit-in here a little longer this evening than usual but that they didn't expect to be later than half-past ten. Outside in the street they rode off in single file, with Elsie leading. There was not much traffic, far less than there would have been before the war at this time of the evening, but the street lights were not good – though at least there wasn't a complete power cut as there had been more than once recently. The Nonconformist chapel hall which had been hired for the Borough meeting was a mile and a half away, and their quickest route to it was at first winding and then zigzagging, leading them across two major roads and along working-class side streets where at intervals boarded-up windows and gaps between houses were reminders of air-raids. The chapel itself seemed at first sight very little damaged externally, and so did the hall next to it. They wheeled their bicycles into the passageway between the hall and the chapel and left them there – unpadlocked, not because they thought them safe there but because the prospect of the meeting made Maldwyn Pryce as well as Alan and Elsie forgetful. Alan, coming out of the passage-way before Elsie or Pryce, found himself facing two short broad advancing figures, a man and a woman, the man no taller than the woman: they were Alec and Iris Murrayfield. The look he got from Iris, though less decidedly unsmiling than the look he got from Alec, did not seem to promise openmindedness towards the speech Elsie would make at the meeting. But perhaps Alan had misinterpreted their looks – yes, these were directed not so much at him as at the clerical stranger who was emerging from the passageway behind him and whose presence here with him and Elsie must puzzle the Murrayfields. Alan greeted them, warmly, and explained that Elsie and he had brought along a new comrade who was going to join the Party. Their looks, after the briefest of hesitations, changed, and they came forward keenly to shake hands with Pryce. But quite soon they turned away and moved quickly towards the entrance doors of the hall. There were two entrance doors, so close to each other as to be almost contiguous, and Iris stood momentarily at one of them while

Alec stood at the other, and Alan was reminded of the figures of the rain man and the sunshine woman at the miniature doors of a Swiss weather-house, but then he had the uncomic thought that the Murrayfields might be hurrying because they didn't want to give an impression inside the hall of having arrived in company with the Sebrills.

At least thirty of the local comrades were already here, seven minutes before the meeting was due to begin, Alan noted when he came into the hall with Elsie and Maldwyn Pryce. A pile of rubble, as yet unremoved by the war-damage repairers and lying just below a lead-latticed window which had a pointed arch, contributed towards making these Party members seem for an instant to Alan like a Christian congregation from Nonconformism's earlier, less respectable and more fervent days. Several comrades, and not only at the back of the hall, showed an immediate awareness of Elsie's arrival. One of these was Bill Whiddett, who was sitting not far from the entrance with his girl Rose Barlow and his sister Annie and whose stare suggested that he hadn't become any more sympathetic to Elsie's views than he'd been at the last Branch meeting when he'd defended the Party's production drive as essential if 'Britain's crisis' was ever to be 'solved'. But perhaps the stare might be aimed at Maldwyn Pryce rather than at Elsie, Alan thought, and he went up smilingly to Bill Whiddett and told him that Elsie and he had brought a Swedenborgian minister along with them who was going to join the Party. Bill however had not noticed Pryce, and when Alan beckoned Pryce over to introduce him to the Whiddetts and also to Rose Barlow, Bill was undisguisedly startled – for more than a moment and in spite of having been forewarned – by the actual presence of this parson wearing a clerical collar. Alan, turning away from the Whiddetts, caught sight of the face of Bert Alldiss on the other side of the hall, and was heartened when Bert – who appeared to have been interestedly watching the incident of the introduction – gave him a cheerful wave of the hand which seemed to imply not only that anyone the Sebrills brought with them had his full confidence, but also that he had become still less unfavourably disposed to their theoretical line than he had been at the Branch meeting.

Elsie began to walk up the hall towards the platform. Faces on either side of her turned to look at her as she walked. Alan, taking Maldwyn Pryce with him to sit down at the back of the hall from where there would be a good view of everyone who spoke this evening, remembered a meeting before the war at which a Party member named Mike Bainton had been expelled from the Party. At that meeting, too, comrades had arrived early – and had waited avidly for Bainton to arrive. But there were no grounds whatsoever for expecting expulsion this evening, Alan soon reassured himself. And even though Elsie might not succeed in fully persuading this Borough meeting that she and he were right, there was a good chance of her being able to put over their point of view clearly enough to make the comrades here thoroughly understand if not agree with it yet.

He was more nervous for her than she seemed to be for herself. Her walk, however, which was less bobbing than usual, told him of the conscious effort she must be making to control herself. The comrades watching her go up the steps to the platform and across it to take her seat beside the chairman, Danny Scrivener, who was already there at the table, would surely think she was unperturbed. She was no doubt encouraged to find that the Borough committee had chosen Danny Scrivener to chair the meeting. He, certainly, should understand the theoretical issue which she was going to concentrate on this evening. A communist of the old type, he really knew his Marx and Engels – and his William Morris too. At times he'd seemed almost old-fashioned even to Alan and Elsie, as though he belonged to the socialist generation that had done such things as founding a 'communist' colony in wooden shacks at Whiteway in Gloucestershire. But he was probably under sixty; and, except for the fact that he kept hens in his back garden and was a craftsman whose hobby was making and playing violins, he showed little resemblance to those pre-1917 utopians. On the other hand, though a modern communist, he seemed not to belong entirely among comrades who had joined the Party during or after the 1939 war and who had never paid their monthly dues to the Third International. With this thought there came also to Alan the hope that Danny Scrivener would not merely understand

Elsie's argument but might even support it. The wholly un-hostile, almost welcoming look on Danny's high-cheekboned face, and the way his lean tweed-jacketed torso turned and inclined civilly towards her as she sat down beside him, increased the hope.

Three minutes before the meeting was due to start most of the members of all the four Branches in the Borough, Alan estimated, were already in the hall. Danny Scrivener brought a large half-hunter watch out of his pocket, looked at it and then laid it on the table in front of him. An affection for him came suddenly alive in Alan, and not only for him but for all the comrades who were here. There wasn't one of them, no matter how new to the Party or for how short a time the comrade had been known to Alan, whom he didn't feel more intimate with than with almost anyone outside the Party. And he would have felt much the same if he had never seen any of these comrades before. Wherever a communist went he was at home when he was with other communists. This thought brought with it the memory of a bleak town which Alan had lived in during part of the war and which had been transformed for him from the moment when he had met members of the Party there. He remembered a pleasant young soldier who was a communist and whose offer to bath the children one evening, so that Alan and Elsie could go out together, Elsie had gladly accepted – justifiably without the least misgiving even though they had known him for less than a fortnight. The close friendliness and the trust that Party members felt for one another were something Alan hoped never to be excluded from. He had an impulse to go up to the platform and to ask Elsie not to attack McNarney's book after all this evening; but though she would perhaps have agreed not to do so, assuming he must have some very good reason for asking her which he hadn't time to explain, and though by withdrawing their objections to the book they would avert the risk of alienating the Branch members from them, eventually the relationship with his rank-and-file comrades which Alan so much valued couldn't survive if it was no longer based on a common acceptance of Marxism. Elsie and he must take the risk and she must make the speech they had planned together.

Danny Scrivener looked again at his watch and then stood up, thin and tall, to say:

'Comrades here will know that comrade Elsie Sebrill has stated her unwillingness to sell copies of *Britain's Way Forward*. This Borough meeting has been called so that she can explain the position she has taken.'

He sat down. His brevity and his quiet tone of voice could both have been interpreted as indicating neutrality. But all Alan's hope now, and anxiety, became centred on Elsie, who stood up slowly, her fingers leafing over the pages of a small notebook on the table as she did so. When at last she raised her head and looked fully at the audience, Alan had the quick fear that she might forget everything she wanted to say, even though she had discussed her speech with him in detail on the previous evening and had made notes for it in her notebook. She might continue standing there behind the table in her dark green overcoat, her wide face staring out from beneath its triangle of wild curls, and be unable to speak a single word. However, when she did begin he knew from the emphatic and unusual slowness of her voice that her long pause beforehand had been deliberate too. She meant to make sure that every word went home to her hearers.

'Comrade chairman, comrades. There is one major point on which I want to express my views. I think it is a point of fundamental political importance. In *Britain's Way Forward*, at the end of the first paragraph on page one hundred and four, comrade McNarney makes the following statement.'

She put down her notebook and picked up McNarney's booklet, conspicuous in its rather arty-looking brown and green paper cover, from the table. As she read out – pausing after each of the more important words – the sentence which Alan and she had selected as showing more blatantly than any other McNarney's abandonment of Leninism, 'I have no hesitation in declaring that the period we are now in is that of a transition stage towards socialism,' Alan for the first time had the suspicion that what seemed to be a muddled repetitiveness in its language might be due less to McNarney's clumsiness as a writer than to his political wiliness. Perhaps, though fully intending to persuade the workers that by working harder they would be help-ing to construct a socialist society under a Labour government, he knew quite well he was disagreeing with Lenin's theory of the State, and he had worded the sentence in such a way that he could if challenged deny he had said the transition to socialism was taking place in Britain now. He could pretend he had not been referring just to Britain or to the immediate present but had meant that the world as a whole had ever since the Bolshe-vik revolution been in an historical period of transition. Even when Elsie went on to say, 'And on page eighty-seven, at the end of the last paragraph but one, comrade McNarney writes of "the British road to socialism which now opens so gloriously before the people of this country",' Alan couldn't feel altogether assured that she had pinned McNarney down, since the phrase 'road to socialism' was ambiguous and could if necessary be said to imply that there was some way still to go before the ac-tual building up of socialism could begin.

But then Elsie, after reading out another of McNarney's more revealing sentences – a real revisionist gem, 'We want our own workers to have confidence in their own land, to take a pride in building it up' – repeated her first two quotations slowly and with a yet stronger emphasis on the words 'transition', 'social-ism', 'now opens', 'the people of this country' and Alan be-came convinced that no comrade listening to her could remain in any uncertainty about McNarney's intention of making his readers believe Britain to be in transition to socialism now. And Alan's conviction was not weakened at all when Elsie, having added that McNarney habitually used the word 'our' in refer-ring to Britain's economy, quoted the phrases 'our basic industries' and 'our exports' with the comment that she wondered why he hadn't mentioned 'our armaments' or – as another Executive Committee member, comrade Baxter, had recently done – 'our foreign investments'.

'According to Marxist writings, as every Party member knows,' she continued, 'socialist construction cannot begin in any country until *after* the workers there have created their own State machinery, until *after* they have established their own armed forces, police, courts of law, civil service, etc.' She quoted a sentence from Lenin's *Left-wing Communism*, written three years after the Russian workers had won power. 'We in Russia are now taking the first steps in the transition from capitalism to socialism.' Alan's brief uneasiness lest her hearers might suspect Elsie of sarcasm when she said 'as every Party member knows, was soon superseded by an admiration for her ingenious use of the word 'created' to by-pass the question whether the capitalist State would first have to be violently overthrown. His and her choice of *Left-wing Communism* as the book she should quote from seemed to him admirable also, because comrades who might be disposed to think she was leftist wouldn't expect her to be able to support her argument from a book in which Lenin had attacked leftism as 'an infantile disorder'.

'Non-Marxists believe the State exists to serve the interests of all the people under it, but Lenin in *State and Revolution* takes the view – as comrades will remember – that every State whatever its form, whether autocratic or democratic, is in essence a class dictatorship, and that the workers before they can begin to build socialism must impose their own dictatorship to prevent a capitalist comeback.'

Her 'as comrades will remember', spoken with extra emphasis, was meant to remind the comrades in her Branch of the course of six talks Alan had given to them during the summer. Now she went on to summarize in more detail, though as briefly as the need to make herself entirely clear to comrades from other Branches would allow, Lenin's argument in the first two chapters of *State and Revolution*. As she spoke he knew that, like the competent schoolteacher she had been before she had resigned from teaching to have children of her own, she was constantly aware of her hearers as individuals who were at different levels of educational attainment, and was trying to adapt her presentation of Lenin's theory accordingly. When, after referring to 'the judiciary', she said synonymously 'His Majesty's judges', he could have guessed without seeing her glance towards Rose Barlow that it was for Rose's benefit she had added this; and when she said, 'Lenin stresses the irreconcilability of class antagonisms because some Mensheviks in 1917 had been arguing that the State exists 'to reconcile classes, whereas it exists precisely because they can't be reconciled,' Alan knew she was speaking particularly to Iris Murrayfield, who worked for a Party research bureau and was an historian.

Now Elsie was coming to the last of the three parts into which she and Alan had planned that her speech should be divided. After reading out for the third time – or perhaps it was for the fourth time but even so it wasn't too often – and with no less emphasis than before, McNarney's unhesitating declaration on on page one hundred and four about the transition to socialism, she said, 'Circumstances alter cases, we know, and no Marxist imagines that all of Lenin's views will remain correct for all eternity. But why should we suppose that Lenin's teachings on the State are no longer valid? Post-war developments provide excellent proof of their validity. In no country do we find socialist economic construction unless the State machine is firmly in the hands of the people. Why should Britain be an exception?'

She made a long pause, then concluded: 'I do not believe the road to socialism now opens gloriously before us as McNarney says it does. I believe that in Britain today we have a capitalist government helping to operate a capitalist State machine in the interests of Big Business, and that this State machine cannot be made to operate in the interests of the people, although the government can be forced to grant concessions if popular pressure is strong enough. *Britain's Way Forward* can only encourage hopes which when proved false will leave the workers with no political party they can turn to.' She put down the green-and-brown-covered book on to the table, with a final slight propulsive movement of her wrist as though she was throwing something away from her. 'I think that what I have said should explain sufficiently why I cannot take any part in selling this book.'

The anxiety Alan had felt before she had started speaking had never quite gone, he realized, until the moment when it gave place to a certainty that she had spoken well. He turned to Maldwyn Pryce at his side, eagerly, wanting to discover how the speech had impressed him; but Pryce was still looking, with what seemed a rapt interest, towards the platform where Danny

Scrivener was now standing up to ask for comrades' views on the criticisms of *Britain's Way Forward* they had just listened to from comrade Elsie Sebrill – did Danny's use of the word 'listened' instead of 'heard' carry with it a partisan implication that the audience had been exercising patience while she had been speaking? – and before Alan could say anything to Pryce, Alec Murrayfield had quickly risen from a seat near the front of the hall, so quickly that Alan wondered whether he'd prepared, since the start of this meeting or perhaps much earlier, a speech which he thought could have its full effect only if it was delivered immediately after Elsie's.

Alec's opening sentences made Alan begin to hope he might not be going to oppose her. Every comrade, he said, should recognize how important it was for the health of the Party that there should be *real* discussion among members at Branch level and that no member who felt any doubts at all about the Party's policy should ever hesitate to come out with them frankly. With a hint of humorousness in his voice he spoke of Branch 'discussions' which, owing to the total acceptance of current policy by all the comrades who contributed to them, were really no more than summarizings of articles from the Party press. Alec's face, with its arched almost semi-circular eyebrows like a comedian's, though it did not actually smile showed a confident pleasantness that was wholly different from the near-panic it had seemed to show after Elsie and Alan had read out their statements at the Branch meeting. However, what he said next was less promising. 'As for comrade Elsie Sebrill's objections to *Britain's Way Forward* I should like to begin by playing the part of devil's advocate.' This suggested that he was going to support Elsie's argument only in order to attack it all the more strongly afterwards, though he was far from sounding condemnatory yet. 'Let us admit that this country doesn't appear to be making any great headway towards socialism at present.' He went on to survey very capably, for two or three minutes, the government's record since it had been elected, its continuation of the aid that Churchill had given to the reactionary forces in Greece, its sending of British troops to Indonesia, its hostility to the Soviet Union and its deference to U.S. Big Business, its steady retreat before capitalism at home. Then his tone changed. 'But Jimmy McNarney, though comrades might not suppose so from listening to comrade Elsie Sebrill, makes quite clear again and again in *Britain's Way Forward* that he's very well aware of the pro-capitalist tendencies among the right-wing Labour leaders – as for instance when he says that the government has "whittled down the real effects of nationalization" by leaving the old capitalist elements in key positions on the Boards and has "paralysed its own policy".'

These two quotations were so naïvely revelatory of the depth of McNarney's wilful delusions about the true intentions of the Labour government, and about nationalization under capitalism, that Alan could hardly believe Alec to be unconscious of their vulnerability. Perhaps he was very conscious of it, and his bringing them out with such effrontery was a kind of pre-emptive defence against any use Elsie might have intended to make of them when she spoke again at the end of the meeting. Now, it seemed, he felt able to move on with greater assurance to the attack. 'Jimmy McNarney, however, unlike comrade Elsie Sebrill, recognizes that 1947 is different from 1917' – this struck a cruder note than Alan would have expected from Alec – 'and in chapter six, though he says "a Labour government does not inevitably mean progress towards socialism", he also says "the advance of democratic and Socialist forces throughout the world has opened out new possibilities of transition to socialism by other paths than those followed by the Russian Revolution, and in a number of countries where popular democracies have been established the people will move towards socialism without the dictatorship of the proletariat".' Alec, who was quoting from memory, had evidently made himself a great deal better acquainted with the contents of *Britain's Way Forward* than he had appeared to be when Alan had talked to him before the last Branch meeting. 'On page ninety-three Jimmy McNarney shows he fully understands – though comrade Elsie Sebrill has tried to give the impression he doesn't – that "today in Britain the State has been unchanged" and "is operating in favour of the ruling classes". But he believes' – Alec at this point, probably in order to give special emphasis to what he was about to quote and not because his memory had for the moment failed him, opened the copy of *Britain's Way Forward* which since the beginning of his speech he had been holding up in front of him and occasionally gesturing with, and he read out: 'that "in the measure to which the Labour movement is united, in the measure to which it presses forward energetically for the fulfilment of its programme, for the development of a general economic plan, for democratization of the Armed Forces, for increased working-class control of industry, for the new recruitment of personnel from the Labour movement into every part of the State machine – to that measure it will reduce the power of the capitalist class and carry Britain along a new road to socialism in which British institutions will be preserved and strengthened."'

Alec closed the book, and repeated significantly, '"In the measure to which it presses forward energetically."' He paused. 'Comrade McNarney does not expect socialism to be handed to the British people on a plate. He knows that socialist construction will require a very great effort, even greater than the effort called forth during the war at the time of the evacuation from Dunkirk. It will require sustained enthusiasm. But comrade Elsie Sebrill is trying her utmost to damp down enthusiasm.'

Why couldn't Alec frankly admit that he considered Lenin out of date, Alan thought with anger. Perhaps because, like Digby Kelsall and like McNarney himself, while rejecting Lenin's theory of the State he still needed the kudos that came from being regarded as a Leninist.

'Some comrades might think that her attitude is due to a genuine difficulty in understanding the theoretical basis of the Party's policy, but what makes me more than a little suspicious of her motives is that she – and this goes for comrade Alan Sebrill too – has attacked the Party leadership.'

For the first time in his speech Alec had said something which caused Alan momentarily to feel a frightening doubt whether Elsie and he were right to have come out against McNarney's book. Wasn't democratic centralism a Leninist principle, and wasn't loyalty to the elected leadership essential if the Party was to function as a communist Party? Lenin had once compared the Party to a modern army; and an army could hardly achieve its objectives if the rank-and-file were constantly criticizing the High Command. Elsie and Alan could have tried taking their 'difficulties' once again to a member of the Executive, possibly even to McNarney himself, and could have waited loyally for the Executive to decide at last that its theoretical line had been wrong. Weren't they by their present behaviour undermining the Party? But suppose the Executive persisted in its wrong line to a point where disaster was imminent for the Party, surely the duty of a rank-and-file communist then would be to come out openly against the Executive? Alan reached this strengthening conclusion just as Alec was bringing his speech to a close. 'The Borough will have to take a very serious view of the disruptive line that the Sebrills have been trying to put over in the Party.'

Alan was protected from feeling the full menace of these words by the sudden malicious thought that perhaps Alec knew Elsie to be in the right about *Britain's Way Forward* – he had seemed to accept most of the criticisms Alan had made of the book in conversation with him and Iris just before the last Branch meeting – but that supporting the Party, however wrong the Party's policies became, might be necessary to him as a salve for a bad conscience about his inherited money. This uncomradely supposition, for which Alan had no real grounds, almost compensated him for his disappointment about Alec's speech, and occupied his mind sufficiently to make him fail to take in at first the significance of the fact that the next comrade who stood up to speak was Ken Pollock.

As Borough Organizer, Ken Pollock was more influential in the Party than any other comrade here, not excluding the Borough secretary, comrade Alice Newton, who hadn't his drive or political ability; and his choosing to be the second speaker, instead of waiting to weigh in with an authoritative summing-up after everyone else had spoken, suggested that if he was going to come out in opposition to Elsie – as he had done at the Branch meeting – he wasn't going to make an all-important thing of it. He stood up very straight, very stocky, his stance and posture seeming to present an immobilized and statuesque version of the brusqueness that was customary to him, and Alan remembered how whenever Ken came to a meeting at Alan and Elsie's house he had the habit of striding into the hall as though the house didn't belong to them, a habit which Alan found flattering rather than irritating since it could imply an assumption on Ken's part that whatever was theirs was dedicated to the Party. He wore steel-rimmed glasses with noticeably thick lenses and the flesh of his cheeks below the rims was reddened as though he had been rubbing it with his knuckles. The side of his face was as straight as a cliff, with stiff slightly curly hair jutting out at the top of it like wind-contorted hawthorn at the top of a cliff. His first words made clear he was going to oppose Elsie, even if not with his full strength. He said he had listened very carefully for any mention in her speech of what practical policy she advocated, but there had been no mention of that. Was she suggesting that the Party should go out and talk to the workers about the dictatorship of the proletariat? What sort of reception did she suppose this would get? She had said the effect of *Britain's Way Forward* must be to encourage illusions among the workers. Were the fourteen thousand homeless families in this Borough an illusion? Or the present shortages in industry? Was it an illusion that we must produce food to live? What comrade McNarney's book aimed at encouraging was action, not illusions and not abstract discussion of Marxist theory either, action to force the Labour government to fulfil the programme on which it had been elected. The Party must give the government critical but *constructive* support. 'We mustn't get ourselves branded as destructive critics sitting back and watching. We can't afford to let the Labour government fail.'

Evidently Ken Pollock had no intention of answering Elsie's theoretical argument, which he seemed honestly to find irrelevant just because it was theoretical. He ended by imputing to her an attitude of doctrinaire superiority, of wanting to opt out of the actual political struggle for fear of soiling her hands. 'She has had a great deal to say about Lenin' – there was an impatience in the way he spoke the word 'Lenin' – 'and I would like to remind her of a literary quotation which Lenin himself was fond of: "Grey is theory, but green is the everlasting tree of life." Our main trouble now is that we haven't yet succeeded sufficiently in getting the Party's policy out among the people. Let us give our energies to this, not to theoretical quibbling.'

The quotation startled Alan into remembering that Ken Pollock, who earned his living in the dispatch department of a publishing firm, not only knew something about books but had a genuine interest in literature. Alan, though relieved that Ken Pollock hadn't attacked Elsie's speech more heavily, was at the same time depressed that the first two speakers had been against her, and his depression wasn't immediately alleviated even when Bert Alldiss, who earlier on had waved to him so encouragingly from the other side of the hall, got up to speak next.

'There is a bit here near the end of the book I want to read out,' Bert began. He thumbed through the pages, not at all deftly, till he found the passage he wanted, then after folding the book right back so that its covers touched he held it under his arm while he fetched out his glasses from his pocket and carefully put them on. Reading, as well as writing, was always a bit of a business for Bert and required preparation and concentration: the propaganda work that he did orally and ebulliently among his fellow-workers at the electrical factory where he was employed and among the tenants on the housing estate where he lived came to him much more easily. 'On page one-two-one comrade McNarney says' – Bert's following Elsie's example in being precise about the whereabouts of the quotation was a promising sign – '"I know good trade unionists who argue: 'That's all very well, Jimmy, but what good is it having a production drive if we have a wrong foreign policy which is going to land us in the soup, no matter how much we produce?'"' This passage was one which Alan had pointed out to Bert after the Branch meeting but which hadn't seemed to make much of an impression on him at the time. Bert's quoting it now showed he must have given further thought to it, and Alan became hopeful that he might have changed his mind about the book as a whole. 'These good trade unionists have got a point there, I think,' Bert continued, making Alan still more hopeful. 'Comrade McNarney answers them by saying "I would like to remind these comrades that just the same arguments were used when the Communist Party launched its great wartime drive for increased production and the opening of the Second Front." But isn't the situation a bit different now? At that time British capitalism – for its own purposes, of course – was an ally of the Soviet Union against the Nazis and was sending arms and supplies under convoy to Archangel. Now – since Churchill without any disapproval from the Labour government made that speech at Fulton in 1946 attacking the Soviet Union – British capitalism has shown it wants to break the alliance, with the aid of the right-wing Labour leaders, and I wonder whether this is the time to demand as comrade McNarney does that the government should take emergency powers and introduce direction of labour like during the war. And when he says on page sixty-eight that if we could export thirty to forty million tons of coal, as we did before the war, we would begin to see the end of our present difficulties and face a bright and happy future, I wonder what the old style Marxists would have thought of this idea of socialism through exports.'

He paused, then brought out from an inner pocket of his jacket a flat oblong metal object, somewhat resembling a child's paintbox, which he held up for everyone to see. 'Talking of the Party's production drive, here is one of the products of a certain factory not a hundred miles from where I work – a hearing-aid, retail price ten guineas.' The movement of the heavy creases in the skin of his forehead while he spoke – creases that would have given him a look of tiredness if seen wholly in repose, as Alan had never seen them – animated his face, although it was unsmiling. 'I won't ask you to guess the cost of producing this, but I will say that someone, not the workers on the shop-floor nor the old people who've been kept waiting for deaf-aids during the war, isn't doing at all badly out of it. You can imagine I'm not exactly handed any bouquets by my mates when I try in accordance with Party policy to persuade them that they ought to produce to their utmost.' However, Bert, just as Alan was beginning to expect he would go on to say he supported Elsie, ended his speech by seeming to retract his objections to *Britain's Way Forward*. 'But these deaf-aids are needed, and coal and textiles and steel and building materials are needed still more. Unless we step up production the whole nation will be in the soup, workers as well as bosses. I can't see how Elsie can get round that.' His referring to her as Elsie and not as comrade Elsie Sebrill was friendly, and indicated that though he couldn't agree with her he didn't think she had done anything outrageous or uncommunist in attacking McNarney's book. As he sat down, an admiration for him was strengthened in Alan, and a conviction that his good sense and honesty would never allow him to accept trickery from any Party leader, if only he could be brought to recognize that it was trickery. But the recognition might take time, since he was less strong on theory than on practice, and since the leadership's line – just because it was opportunist – appeared plausible enough in Britain's immediate economic situation.

Alan was lulled by his warm feeling for Bert into a temporary unawareness of how unpromising the opening words of the next speaker, Bill Whiddett, were. 'The Sebrills are barking up a very wrong tree,' Bill said. Alan took this statement in almost the same spirit as he had taken the alarmed amazement Bill had shown in being introduced to Maldwyn Pryce: it was one of those involuntarily comic lapses which made Bill likeable. But for such lapses, Bill – with his perky cocksureness and with his fondness for showing-off the knowledge of economics which, though he had left school at fifteen, he had very creditably acquired in the main by his own private reading – might at times have seemed conceited and even priggish. He began to seem so now as he went on, in lecturing tones, to accuse the Sebrills of adopting an attitude which had nothing in common with 'creative Marxism'. This phrase, which made sense only if it was taken to imply a distinction between creative and ordinary Marxism, angered Alan, who would have liked to retort that, judging by *Britain's Way Forward*, 'creative Marxism' had nothing in common with Marxism. But what Bill Whiddett came out with next was still worse. 'Elsie Sebrill has said that the advance to socialism cannot begin until after the workers have established their own State. For some reason she has not told us, this evening, how she thinks they ought to set about establishing it. But those of us who heard the statement she read out to the Branch last week haven't forgotten that then she was advocating – and so was Alan Sebrill – the immediate revolutionary smashing up of the capitalist State machine.' Alan, stung by the obvious deliberateness of this falsehood, was on the point of standing up to object that neither Elsie nor he had said anything about an 'immediate' revolution and that on the contrary he had emphasized the impossibility of a revolution now or in the near future; however not wanting to seem to the chairman to be committing a breach of order he hesitated to interrupt Bill Whiddett, who very soon made a far uglier accusation. He said that the Sebrills were indistinguishable from Trotskyites. This ominous word might have been more daunting to Alan if he hadn't been protected against it by the indignation he felt at Whiddett's dishonesty or stupidity in applying it to him and Elsie. He stood up as soon as Whiddett's speech, the rest of which he was not calm enough to listen to properly, came to an end.

'Comrade Chairman, one reason why comrade Elsie Sebrill hasn't mentioned revolution,' Alan said, 'is that she does *not* think there is any immediate possibility of bringing it about in Britain.' What Alan most urgently needed was to refute Bill Whiddett's charge of Trotskyism, but he didn't want the meeting to sense how much this had disturbed him, so he decided to deal with his and Elsie's views on revolution first. 'Another reason is that she wanted to concentrate attention not on the question whether the workers will have to face and overcome violence from the bourgeois State before they can build up a socialist society – she knows well enough that in certain circumstances a peaceful taking-over of power might be possible – but only on the question whether the transition to socialism can begin, as comrade McNarney assumes it can, before the bourgeois State has been replaced by a workers' State.'

Alan noticed while he was speaking that Les Gatten, who was sitting in the front row at the other side of the hall next to the gangway, had turned on his chair and was intently looking back at him. The look was enigmatic, might be either disapproving or approving. Les Gatten had been out of London at the time of the last Branch meeting, and Elsie and Alan did not yet know how he would react to their rejection of *Britain's Way Forward*; but as long ago as that evening in the summer when

Alan had given his first talk to the Branch on *State and Revolution* Les had shown himself aware that the Party's post-war line disagreed with Lenin's theory of the State, and they were optimistic about him. He gave the impression now that he was smiling slightly, though his lips were straight and his eyes unmoving and the smile seemed to have no physical location in any of his features. Alan, going on to deal with the dangerous accusation which had been the main cause of his getting up to speak, felt and resisted an influence to look exclusively at Les Gatten.

'As for the suggestion that we are Trotskyites' – Alan tried to sound as though the suggestion had not given him the least uneasiness – 'I need only point out that all Trotskyites without exception are opposed to Stalin and to the Soviet government, whereas we support Stalin and the Soviet government.'

Les Gatten was still looking steadily at Alan. Big-built, sitting low on his chair almost as if it was an armchair, his face roundly childlike beneath fair hair which even though closely cut showed signs of a natural waviness, Les resembled a physically precocious but very well-behaved boy keeping his inexpressive eyes attentively on his teacher – the sort of boy, nevertheless, whose extreme respectfulness might be a blind and who might suddenly commit some act of indiscipline outvying anything that the more obviously unruly members of the class had thought of attempting. But what grounds had Alan for feeling like this about Les Gatten? None, except that when Les had come to see Alan and Elsie at their house one evening just before the summer holidays and they had had a very friendly discussion alone with him about their objections to the Party's theoretical line, he had called Alan Mr Sebrill – not even Comrade Sebrill, though that too would have seemed over-formal – on saying good-bye. However, as Elsie tried to persuade Alan at the time, this was less likely to have been due to hostility than to the fact that 'young as you still look, you may have acquired a certain, let's say, dignity in the eyes of yet younger comrades'.

Alan now stopped gazing back at Gatten and, immediately forgetting him, went on:

'The present period in Britain is not one of revolution, nor is it one of socialist construction; it is a period of continuing struggle against capitalism. At least, that is what it should be, and can be if the Party remains true to Marx and to Lenin. We are living not in a new and progressive Britain, not in a people's Britain, not in "our" Britain, but in a monopoly-capitalists' Britain, an imperialists' Britain, a reactionary and pro-fascist Britain which is doing its damnedest to destroy every decent progressive movement all over the world. We are living in a pro-fascist Britain, and unless we wake up fully to this fact pretty soon we may find ourselves living in a pre-fascist Britain.'

Alan suspected that he was using words which might cause even a sympathetic listener to think he was overstating his case, but he was not sure what words he was using. His apprehensiveness about the political future was so strong that he couldn't concentrate on his manner of expressing himself, though he vividly knew what he needed to communicate to his comrades here. His voice sounded remote to him as he went on to try to convince them that the capitalist powers were once again grouping against the Soviet Union, much more unitedly than before the war; and that the world far from being 'One World' as the Party leadership, adopting a phrase used by the American Liberal Wendell Wilkie, were still proclaiming it to be, had already started heading towards what would be its most appalling disaster yet, unless the working-class intervened in time — but instead of rousing the workers to the danger all the Party did was to lull them by complacently parroting a phrase coined during a quite different situation when the U.S. and the U.S.S.R. were in alliance against Nazism. Alan's feelings so dominated him by now that he not only ceased hearing the words he was using but began to find that even his sight of the hall and of his comrades in it was becoming unsteady. The horror of the international prospect came increasingly upon him, ousting his immediate surroundings from the forefront of his consciousness, dissolving the walls of the hall, placing him in the blackness of an outer world where the crimes committed against humanity at Auschwitz and at Hiroshima had been repeated on a huger scale. As he ended his speech and sat down he vaguely knew that Maldwyn Pryce had turned towards him and was about to say something, had perhaps actually said something, but Alan was too disturbed to pay attention to Pryce, who soon turned away to look towards the platform again. And Alan paid little attention, either, to what was said by the comrades who spoke to the meeting from now on : he heard them only for so long as he remained in any doubt about their attitude to Elsie; and one by one, some more downrightly than others, they came out against her.

The comrade who was least downright and who kept Alan in doubt for longest was Pete Naylor. Alan had always felt a special liking for him. A comrade keen on poetry, unhappy in his job as a quantity surveyor, unassertive and habitually amiable, his voice as now having a gentle burr in it – which Alan had once described to Elsie as a 'butter-burr' and which reminded them that he was the son of a Northumberland farmer – Pete was obviously distressed at the general disapproval the Sebrills were bringing down upon themselves, and he tried to mitigate it by suggesting that their disagreement with *Britain's Way Forward* might turn out to be mainly about words; however, he eventually showed whose side he was on when he said that socialism in Britain would have to be achieved by parliamentary means – though he gave no reason for assuming so except the implied one that any other means would be unthinkably unpleasant. Immediately after he had sat down, Annie Whiddett, as if outraged by his mildness, stood up to make the most vehement and unqualified attack that anyone had made on Elsie yet. Her big handsome face heavy with indignation, she spoke much more impressively even if less knowledgeably and less showily than her brother Bill. She had the powerful sincerity of an unwavering Party loyalist who saw the world in black and red and to whom political problems appeared as simple as to an average woman Tory – a sincerity which carried all the greater weight because, though she had to look after a war-disabled husband besides going out to work every day, she was untiringly active for the Party. Only one other speech disheartened Alan more than hers – Sybil Pollock's, which was the last before Danny Scrivener, the chairman, asked if Elsie wanted to reply to any points that comrades had made. Sybil spoke with a quiet severity to which her finely-featured face, in spite of the suggestion of voluptuousness conveyed by a slight plumpness of the flesh beneath her chin, gave an added chilliness. She had the profile of a fourteenth-century Florentine aristocrat, frighteningly beautiful, how different from her proletarian-looking husband Ken's, though he was the son of a solicitor while she was the daughter of an L.C.C. ambulance driver. She ended her speech by saying that Elsie Sebrill should immediately resign from the Branch secretaryship, and by repeating Alec Murrayfield's suggestion – though with an emotionless firmness which made her seem far more intimidating than Alec had ever seemed – that not only the Borough but the District too would have to consider whether further action to deal with the Sebrills might not be necessary.

Elsie's final speech was short. She said there was one point she would like to reply to. Comrade Ken Pollock had found fault with her for not mentioning what practical policy she was in favour of, but her reason for not mentioning it had been that in her view McNarney's main error was theoretical rather than practical, and she had wanted to concentrate on this main error. However, she would state briefly now the short-term policy she thought the Party should put forward: cut the armed forces; no conscription either by law or by hunger; trade with Russia and the New Democracies; slash profits – cut prices; soak the rich. There was nothing in her tone of voice to suggest that the attitude of the meeting had discouraged her, but Alan thought he could see in her face a dazedness, an almost incredulous amazement at the inability of the comrades here to begin to understand the simple theoretical point which she had so clearly and so repetitively made this evening about the transition to socialism. She did not try to answer any of the speakers other than Ken Pollock. She said she agreed with Sybil Pollock's demand that she should resign from the Branch secretaryship, and she finished by adding that she would give full and loyal support to her successor. It was good tactics for her to have added this, Alan felt, and would help to mollify certain comrades who might be inclined to question her right even to remain within the Party – though how she could give support to a new Branch secretary whose main immediate task would be pushing the sales of *Britain's Way Forward* wasn't obvious to him.

There was still the possibility that the Chairman, who now stood up, would not join in with the others against her. The fact – rather unexpected at a Party meeting specially called to hear an explanation from a comrade who had expressed strong disagreement with the leadership – that Danny Scrivener had invited her to reply to the attacks made on her speech was promising; and, at worst, Danny in his summing-up could not totally reject an explanation which he as a knowledgeable Marxist must know to be based on elementary Marxist principles. But Danny did not sum up; leaning forward for a moment with his knuckles on the table in front of him and with his long thin arms rigid beneath their brown tweed sleeves, he declared the meeting closed. A bitterness arose in Alan, such as the silence of two other comrades who ought to have supported Elsie – Iris Murrayfield, the historian, and Les Gatten – would not have been sufficient to make him feel. Iris had the excuse that to come out openly in opposition to her husband Alec, who had already spoken against Elsie, would have been embarrassing, and Les might have the excuse that though he had been aware months ago of the irreconcilability of the leadership's line with Lenin's theory of the State he still wasn't entirely sure that the leadership was wrong; but Danny Scrivener, who must have fully understood and recognized the Leninist correctness of Elsie's argument, could only have been deterred from supporting her by a cowardly reluctance to oppose the Party leaders no matter how unLeninist they might become. However, Alan would force him to declare himself. Now, immediately, before Scrivener could leave the hall.

About to get up and walk towards the platform Alan remembered Maldwyn Pryce at his side and told him: 'I just want to have a quick word with the Chairman.' Comrades were already moving out from the rows of chairs into the gangway as Alan made his way towards the front of the hall. Though they did not ostentatiously avert their eyes from him, they did not look at him. The chill realization came to him that now not only was he at odds with the Party leadership but had become estranged from the rank-and-file too. Within a few yards from the platform he found himself facing Iris Murrayfield who, however, did look at him, though expressionlessly. He blurted out to her: 'You didn't speak this evening. But surely *you* at least did know what Elsie was getting at.' With a meekness of voice which was habitual to her but which was ill-suited to her words now, she answered: 'I thought she was splitting hairs. It was an exercise in scholasticism. And she seemed to have forgotten that Marxism is above all a *method* – not a body of unalterable doctrine.' Alan had a sudden vivid understanding that for her the question whether Lenin's analysis of the economic and political forces at work in the modern world still corresponded to reality or not was irrelevant, and that she thought his writings – and no doubt Marx's writings too – should be valued not for the conclusions they embodied but for the 'scientific' manner in which the conclusions had been reached. He would probably have expressed to her his contempt for this misconception of Marxism, but before he could say anything more Danny Scrivener stepped down from the platform and approached them. Alan didn't have to ask him what he had thought of Elsie's speech, because as soon as Danny came up to them he said to Alan – and he gave the impression of having come up to them especially in order to say it – 'I do feel rather concerned about Elsie. I'm afraid if she goes on like this she will be running the risk of a mental breakdown.'

Danny's solicitude seemed absolutely genuine. Alan was too astounded to protest against what he'd said. Danny, who knew more about Marxism than any other comrade here and who ought not to have had a moment's difficulty in grasping the main point Elsie had repeatedly made, had apparently found even less sense in her speech than the others had. Alan stared at him, and as he stared became aware that Ken Pollock had come up from behind Danny to stand at the side of Iris Murrayfield. Ken's face was solemn. Through his thick glasses his magnified brown-green eyes began to watch Alan with a cold calmness which, like the tone of Sybil Pollock's voice when she had suggested in her speech that not only the Borough but the District too would have to consider whether further action to deal with the Sebrills might not be necessary, seemed to arise from a total confidence in the unhurrying processes of Party discipline. Ken

85

had no need to become excited. But agitation got the better of Alan, who uncontrollably said to him. 'So this is the Party I have given sixteen years of my life to. It's no longer Marxist – it's reformist. This is the Party I have sacrificed my career to.'

What had lured him to use such a word? He had by implication accused himself, falsely, of careerism, had presented himself in just the light that the Party leaders would want the rank-and-file to see him in. Ken Pollock, however, surprisingly did not take advantage of his self-condemnation, but said:

'I could say that I have sacrificed my career to the Party too. There's nothing unusual about that.'

Alan suddenly knew what he had really meant when he had used the damaging word. He had wanted to say that he had sacrificed poetry to the Party; but he had preferred to be thought a careerist rather than expose his tenderest ambition to the possible ridicule of Ken Pollock.

He abruptly turned and walked away from Ken and Iris and Danny. He was surprised to see Elsie standing ahead of him, near the back of the hall. She was arguing with Bill Whiddett, not at all heatedly it seemed. As Alan came up to them he heard enough of what she was saying to guess that she was trying to make Bill admit how unjustified he had been in accusing her of Trotskyism. Alan was too despondent to want to take part in the argument, or even to stand and listen to it. He moved on past them. She didn't need his support anyway, as Bill was already showing signs of being much less hostile towards her than when he had spoken to the meeting. Alan, coming to a stop near the last row of chairs, all at once found himself facing Maldwyn Pryce whom he had completely forgotten since leaving him in order to speak to Danny Scrivener. Pryce had put on his trouser-clips ready for cycling and seemed to be on the point of walking out of the hall. He gave Alan a look of understanding, and said:

'The British working-class movement never has been very strong on theory.'

This generalization, so calmly and so sympathetically spoken, was consoling to Alan. Maldwyn, already turning to begin to go towards the doors at the back of the hall, added a little hesitantly:

'I suppose the new Secretary will notify me of the next Branch meeting.'

Alan felt compunction at having almost entirely ignored Maldwyn ever since they had arrived in the hall.

'Oh of course we'll make sure you're notified,' Alan said, 'And I hope you'll come to see us at our house again, often.'

'I hope so.'

Maldwyn sincerely meant it. His turning away, with a brief 'cheerio', to leave the hall now did not indicate that he wished to separate himself quickly from two Party members whom he'd discovered to be at odds with the Party, but was due, Alan felt sure, to a considerate awareness that Alan and Elsie must want to talk with each other alone as soon as possible about what had happened at the meeting this evening.

When Elsie finished arguing with Bill Whiddett, which she soon did, and came to join Alan, he said to her:

'Not one of them really knew what your speech was about.'

'No, not one of them. I still can't get used to what happened. I was flabbergasted. Only Bert Alldiss seemed to come anywhere near understanding us.'

'Danny Scrivener has just said to me he's afraid if you go on like this you'll have a mental breakdown. He meant it kindly, not spitefully. How can he, of all people, have forgotten what Marx and Lenin wrote about the transition to socialism?'

'Perhaps we *are* mad,' Elsie said, 'or at any rate, just a bit simple. And perhaps all the others are merely showing commonsense and reasonableness.'

They came to the nearest of the two darkly-varnished shammedieval arched doors that led out of the hall. It had for an instant an insane, hallucinatory look, as though it couldn't really belong to a hall in which communists had held a meeting.

'We're not mad,' Alan said, as she opened the door and he followed her outside into the darker open air. 'It's we who are being reasonable, and Marxist.'

'I know we are.'

They went down the passage between the hall and the chapel to get their bicycles. Elsie didn't ask where Maldwyn Pryce was and had evidently forgotten all about him. She added:

'What I don't know is how I can carry out my offer to give full and loyal support to my successor as Branch Secretary.'

'You obviously can't, without withdrawing your refusal to sell *Britain's Way Forward*. I'm afraid the whole prospect of our going on with day-to-day Party work gives me a feeling of utter revulsion. But we must go on. There are still some activities we can take part in which won't be tainted with McNarneyism – the housing campaign, for instance, and we can recruit new members for the British-Soviet Friendship Society.'

'Yes, but also we mustn't give up trying to persuade comrades in the Branch that the Party needs to be brought back to Leninism. We should regard this as our most important Party activity of all.'

They were wheeling their bicycles out from the passage. They glanced towards the entrance doors of the hall, expecting to see other comrades leaving, but they saw no one. Some of the comrades would have left already, but many must still be in the hall, talking, holding an informal meeting after the formal meeting, and Alan could guess what they must be talking about. His guess did not worry him for long. As he and Elsie brought their bicycles out on to the road he thought of how much more leisure he would have in the evenings from now on. He felt a relief which only briefly had something of guilt in it, and he quickly justified it by assuring himself that his becoming freer in future from ordinary political activities would enable him to give more time to the work he was by nature best fitted to do for the Party – the writing of poetry. And remembering the poem he had conceived last night, which would reaffirm the desirableness of the life in and for the Party by dwelling mainly on the future victory of communism that only the Party could bring about, he realized that its theme had been made even more appropriate by what had happened at the meeting this evening.

Elsie was riding ahead of him and they had already gone fifty yards along the road when he noticed that the rear lamp of her bicycle had not been switched on. He called out to tell her. She found she had not switched on her front lamp either. Only after she had dismounted from her bicycle and had switched on both lamps was he aware that he too had been riding without lights.

4

On the last morning of the summer holidays it became clear to
Alan that the poem he had first thought of nearly a year ago now
during the night before the Borough meeting, but had been unable to write satisfactorily in spite of all his attempts since then,
could never be any good, and that he must try to think of a new
one. He had just finished helping Elsie wash up the breakfast
things and had come upstairs to sit alone here in their bedroom
where he would have quiet for writing. He did not feel despondent. An optimism which had been created in him by happen-
ings outside his poetry helped him to be confident that his next
poem would not be a failure. At the beginning of August the
Party periodical *World News and Views* had published – and no
doubt the time of publication had been chosen just because many
comrades would be on holiday then and wouldn't get their usual
Party literature – a letter sent four months before by the Political
Committee of the Communist Party of Australia criticizing the
British Executive on the grounds that its whole line was a revi-
sion of Marxism-Leninism. Alan had duplicated this letter
(though not the lengthy and trickily evasive reply to it from
the Executive which *World News and Views* had also printed)
and he and Elsie had distributed a copy of it to every member
of the Branch, with the result that two members – Bert Alldiss
and Les Gatten – were already saying that the Sebrills had been
right all along in their objections to the Party's recent policy.
And Elsie had written to the Australians and had received from
them a week ago a parcel containing twelve copies of the Sep-
tember issue of the Australian *Communist Review* in which
were printed not only the letter from the Political Committee
and the British Executive's reply to it but also an overwhelmingly convincing reply to that reply. During the past six days he

and she had been busy taking round copies of this *Communist Review* to comrades who they thought would be most likely to make good use of them. But he must not let the excitement of being freed at last from political isolation prevent him from continuing to try to write poetry. Only if he succeeded in writing it would he be giving what he felt to be the best of himself to the Party. He must stop staring out of the window at the gables and chimney cowls of the houses across the street, as though this bedroom were a detention cell from which he longed to escape into the external world of political action. He must start trying to think of a new poem immediately.

Or at least he must start not later than ten minutes from now. And during those minutes he would do well to make sure he understood exactly what had been wrong with the poem he was abandoning, because otherwise there could be a danger that its faults might be repeated in the new one. His intending it to convey a political message had certainly not been wrong. What other motive could he justifiably have for wanting to write a poem ? If, in this age of Auschwitz and Hiroshima and of the still greater horrors imperialism was preparing to inflict on the world, he wanted to write poetry for its own sake, or for his own sake, or in the contemptible and ridiculous hope of making himself famous, or for any purpose except to support the struggle against imperialism – then he was little better than those bandsmen who when new batches of victims were brought to the Nazi extermination camps welcomed them with classical music in order to lull their fears and to keep them docile. And since the Party, in spite of having lapsed temporarily from Marxism-Leninism, was the only organization which could eventually lead the struggle through to success, his poem had not been wrong to aim at celebrating the life in and for the Party as the finest life. But he had a suspicion that there was something inadequate about the vision of worldwide future victory which the poem would have offered as an encouragement against the frustrations to be met with in the Party life at present.

He could not at first give precision to this suspicion. He stood up from the armchair in which he had been sitting, and he put down on the end of the bed the notebook he had been holding, and he began to move about the room in the hope of accelerating his thinking. He came close to the window beyond the dressing-table and he stopped moving for a while. Gulls were in the London sky above the chimney cowls; scavengers. They reminded him of a phrase describing them which had pleased him poetically when he had found it recently in a natural history book: 'ecological homologues of the medieval kites'. They reminded him also of the fortnight at the seaside he had had with Elsie and the children this August. Glimpsing in his mind now the village where they had stayed – a village whose cottage post-office with pierced barge boards and whose small pebbly bay had made it strangely resemble the one where almost seventeen years before he had gone to live the poetic life at his friend Richard's invitation – he suddenly knew what would have been wrong with the vision of victory in the poem he was abandoning. It would have been a negative vision, would have shown the absence of war and of imperialism but not the life that could be lived after the victory. However, before he turned away from the window to pick up his notebook from the bed and to go back to his chair, he remembered that there was something much worse about his poem than its vision of the future. Every beginning of it he had made in his notebook – and during the months since the Borough meeting he had made at least a dozen different beginnings – had been totally lifeless as poetry. The words he had written down had had no colour except as pale blue ink marks on the paper, had been virtually invisible, had been toneless, had been words that had long ago shouted themselves dumb in the newspapers. His next poem, which he oughtn't any longer to delay starting to think of now, must aim at conveying its political message in non-political, or at any rate non-newspaper, words.

Sitting in the armchair again he opened his notebook. Perhaps he would be helped to concentrate on thinking of a new poem if he wrote down any ideas, however unpromising, that came into his head about it. He was turning over the pages of the notebook when he caught sight of an uncompleted poem in which both the words and the theme were non-political. It was one of seven or eight fragments of varying lengths that, during evenings of the summer term, he had written as an exercise and in the hope of reviving his poetic inventiveness. He had not bothered about their content, had written them quickly and with as little forethought as possible, and aimed mainly at making them less unlike poetry than the many cancelled beginnings of his political poem had been. Probably he had half-hoped they might provide some clue that would lead him to discover how a political poem could be made to come alive as poetry. They had not provided a clue. Nevertheless he wouldn't be wasting his time if he re-read them now, he assured himself, because they too could remind him of certain faults he must at all costs avoid in his next poem.

What caused the first of these fragments, which he had produced during the free evening of a working Monday in London after a Sunday in the Kentish countryside around Trottiscliffe, to be so repulsive? Perhaps, almost as much as anything else, its diffidence about being in verse, a diffidence made evident both by its flatly prosaic rhythm and by his having written it down in the form not of verse but of prose, with vertical dashes to indicate the ends of lines.

Buried in tiredness as in a long barrow/whose mound surrounded by fallen ragstones / has suffered the attrition of four thousand years / the local vicar came and collected my bones / for show in a stone coffin under the porch / of the village church

No, there were unpleasanter faults in this than diffidence – its copycat modish lack of punctuation and its decadent slovenly syntax, for instance. But its content was even more objectionable than its style and revealed a quite sinister inclination on his part towards adopting the attitude of those once pro-communist intellectuals who, although they had never become active accomplices of imperialism, had allowed their disillusioning experience of politics to lead them into a philosophic despair or into the acceptance of some kind of religion not excluding pre-Christian magic or even Anglicanism.

The next of these exercises was as obviously uneasy as the first about being in verse, though it showed its uneasiness not by trying to resemble prose but by using a verse rhythm that was assertively doggerel-like. This exercise self-contradictorily began by asking why he couldn't write, and then – after two lines which appealed for help to 'mania' as 'the only unequivocal liberator' and after another two which were surrealistically unintelligible – went on to indulge without disguise in the sheerest reactionary pessimism.

> Whom in the world can I wish to address
> Except the dead and men in the mass
> And both are as far out of my reach
> As a day of summer on childhood's beach.

No wonder that when writing these lines he had become aware at this point how blatantly uncommunist they were and in the quatrain that followed them he had changed the first person to the second in order to suggest that the sentiments expressed were not his own but were those of some bourgeois tempter.

> Why be intelligible if there's no one cares
> Better go smug and rest on your oars
> Smile with despair like Lermontov's hero
> And live for your meals and your comfortable Norah

So he had even stooped to implying here that Elsie – 'Norah' being the pseudonym for her which had been dictated to him by his need of a word that would give both a consonantal rhyme with 'hero' and a vowel rhyme with 'oars' – was an a-political philistine who would be quite content to live a life of mere domesticity for his sake. However, in the final quatrain of this exercise he did consider the possibility that he might after all be able to write a pro-communist poem –

> Could I use a metre like this
> If I were writing of the lures and lies
> Of the terrible dwarfs in the high places
> Who are beckoning us on to the last crisis?

– though the trivializing doggerel rhyme at the end suggested a negative answer to the question. But neither this exercise nor the one about the long barrow near Trottiscliffe was as pernicious as the one he began to read next. The first two exercises had been only half serious in the feelings they expressed, had been trying on attitudes like clothes which he didn't really intend to buy: there had been a kind of sickly playfulness in that line about the collecting of his bones by the local vicar, and also in the flippant rhyming of 'crisis' with 'places'. Whereas every word of the third exercise gave the disgraceful impression of being in deadly earnest. No, not every word, perhaps: verbally, because of certain literary echoes and poetic clichés, it did not seem so sincere. But there could be no doubt that the emotion behind the words was only too genuine.

> All's lost, and so deeply, so irrecoverably / that I'm not even sure what it is that is lost. / Sometimes a hint of it when I'm walking on a Sunday / in the country will glint from a hedge as I go past, / enough to assure me that there has been joy once / but not to resurrect it except in the abstract / a ghost of feeling, autumnal clematis in the sun's / warmthless light.

Nor could there be the least doubt that this fragment, like the poem he'd conceived and rejected more than a year ago in the garden on the evening of his first talk to the Branch about *State and Revolution*, had been inspired by a longing for the life he had tried to live before coming into the Party – the poetic life, as he and Richard had called it, which had eventually brought him, though not Richard, to the verge of madness and suicide. The possibility that this longing might find its way into his next poem was something he must be alert against; all the more so because several times during his recent fortnight at the seaside he had been snared by nostalgic remembrances of the years when he had aimed at living for poetry. However, the most important thing now wasn't to think what he must keep out of his next poem but to get some idea of what he could put into it.

The telephone rang from downstairs. Elsie was out shopping, but Stephen would answer it and would perhaps take a message. No. The door of the back sitting-room was soon opened and Stephen called out: 'It's for you, Dad.' As Alan went from the bedroom towards the stairs the expectation that someone wanted to talk to him about his and Elsie's campaign against the leadership's line aroused an excitement in him which put poetry completely out of his mind. Coming into the back sitting-room he asked who was on the phone, and Stephen said: 'He didn't say.' And the voice which Alan heard after picking up the receiver was at first unrecognizable. Its tone was formal. 'Is that Mr Alan Sebrill?' – 'Yes.' – 'Is that Mr Alan Sebrill?' it repeated. 'Yes.' About to ask who was speaking, Alan became suddenly certain the voice was Les Gatten's. Why didn't Les address him just as Alan? Perhaps because he had something to say which he wanted to be sure of not saying to the wrong person. 'Oh good, it's you, Les. You sounded quite unlike yourself for a moment.' After Alan had said this the voice relaxed a little as it went on:

'About this Australian *Communist Review* with the two letters in it attacking the Executive of the British Communist Party – how many copies of it have you given out so far to Party members?'

'Seven.'

'Who have you given them to?'

Alan was slightly surprised that Les, after taking precautions to ensure that he was not speaking to the wrong person, should ask – over a phone line that might possibly be tapped – these not very discreet questions. Nevertheless Alan answered:

'Well, besides the three copies you –'

Before Alan could add the word 'took', Les interrupted him:

'Did you give any to the Murrayfields?'

'Only one copy, because Elsie and I are a bit doubtful how favourably they'll react.'

'You gave one copy to the Murrayfields. What about Comrade Bert Alldiss?'

'We gave him two. And we gave Maldwyn Pryce one.'

Alan waited for Les to say something which would explain why he was asking these questions, but Les said: 'Can I come and see you this evening?'

'Yes, do.'

'I've got some interesting news for you.'

Alan restrained himself from asking what the news was.

He remembered, as soon as Les had rung off, that Elsie had arranged to go and see the Murrayfields this evening and that the arrangement couldn't be changed because both Alec and

Iris were fixed up with meetings for the rest of this week. Elsie wouldn't want to miss Les; but her visit to the Murrayfields must not be postponed, because they had begun to vacillate in the opposition they had at first shown to the Australian line and if they were pressed now they might be won over entirely. He couldn't ring Les back and ask him to come tomorrow evening instead, since Les was not on the phone at home and had presumably rung up from a public call box. As Alan was thinking this he was moving towards the door of the sitting-room, and only when he had taken a step into the hall passage did he realize that he was going out of the room without saying a single word to Stephen. He quickly turned back and went over to the table at which Stephen was sitting with an open exercise book in front of him drawing a map of an imaginary country. The names of the towns were neatly written in, and there were many railways, harbours and mountains. Alan asked questions about various details on the map and Stephen gave him an account of the products and then of the recent history of the country. Alan stayed listening for longer than he might have done if he hadn't felt sorry that his preoccupation with Les had almost made him ignore Stephen. He didn't listen as attentively as he wanted to, however, both because he couldn't stop remembering his telephone conversation with Les and because he was becoming increasingly conscious that he should be upstairs again thinking of his next poem. At last he told Stephen: 'I ought to get back to my work now.' Then he added, 'Where is Christina?'

'Playing next door with Sandra,' Stephen said.

As Alan came out into the passage he knew he was going to have difficulty in getting his thoughts back to poetry, and almost as soon as he was in the bedroom again he decided that too much of the morning had already gone by for him to hope to make any progress with a new poem before lunchtime, and that he would gain nothing by trying uselessly to stop thinking about politics.

At half-past seven, soon after Elsie had gone off to see the Murrayfields, Alan was in the back sitting-room with the children when he heard a not very loud knock on the front door, and he said to them: 'That's Les Gatten. I expect he'll be here quite a while so I'd better say good night to you now. You'll take yourselves off to bed when it's time, won't you?' They said they would, and Alan went to the front door. Though the sun must have set, there was still enough daylight outside the house to outline Gatten's shape darkly against the coloured panes. He looked even taller, and his shoulders seemed broader, before than after Alan opened the door to him.

'Hullo, Les.'

'Good evening.'

Though Les smiled, and though he didn't call Alan 'Mr Sebrill', there was an odd suggestion of deference and even perhaps of nervousness in his tone, as though he was a very young man arriving to be interviewed for a job. His face looked extraordinarily young, soft-skinned and rosy beneath golden hair which if it hadn't been so closely cut might – to judge by a waviness surviving in it here and there – have been as curly as little Lord Fauntleroy's. Alan brought him into the front sitting-room where he remained standing with his back to the bookcase until Alan, after switching on the light, invited him to sit down in an armchair. Alan couldn't help feeling a brief disappointment that, in spite of their being united now by their common opposition to the leadership's line, Les could still sometimes seem unable to be on easy comradely terms with him. However, as soon as Les had sat down, Alan said eagerly:

'What is this interesting news you've got for me?'

'You remember my asking whether you thought it would be a good idea if I sent a copy of that Australian *Communist Review* to a friend who is a Party member and who lives in Manchester?'

'Yes, I remember. Did you send it?'

'I did, on the morning after I'd talked to you about him, and by return of post I got a letter from him saying he fully agrees with the Australians and is going to get their criticisms of the British leadership discussed at his next Branch meeting.'

'That's very good.'

'And I also sent the Australian *Communist Review* to a Party member I know in Birmingham. I didn't mention him when I last talked to you because at that time I hadn't yet thought of him as a possible sympathizer.' Les was apologetic. Alan gave him a look of the warmest encouragement. 'I heard from him this morning,' Les added, 'and he's not only willing to be active on our behalf in his local Branch but he offers to cyclostyle at his own expense as many copies of the two Australian letters as we want.'

'That's marvellous. You've certainly done some useful work in the five days since we last saw each other.'

Les seemed gratified by this praise and he sounded wholly at ease for a moment as he went on:

'I'm specially pleased that my Birmingham contact will be getting busy there, because –' he became hesitant, as though afraid that what he was going to say next might offend Alan – 'but I'd better explain why I haven't told you anything about this before. To be quite frank I knew nothing about it myself till a day or two ago. The fact is that the Insurance firm I'm working for wants to transfer me from London to Birmingham.'

Alan felt very surprised, though the feeling was not so strong as to prevent him from noting distastefully the phrase 'to be quite frank' – a phrase which in his experience was most often used by people who intended to be the opposite of frank.

'Do you mean you'll be going to live in Birmingham?'

'It would amount to that. Though of course I could refuse. And I could try to get another job, if necessary.'

Les gave the impression of hoping for advice from Alan who, however, refrained from offering it, although he would have liked to tell Les to stay in London.

'I would keep in touch with you from Birmingham,' Les went on, 'so that we could co-ordinate the two prongs of our attack, as it were.' He seemed to smile slightly. 'And I shall still be here to support you and Elsie when you're called up before the District.'

'Do you think we shall be?'

'I rather expect we shall all be, all of us who've had anything to do with distributing the Australian material. Quite soon – within two or three weeks from now, I would say.'

'I doubt it. A year ago after Elsie criticized *Britain's Way*

Forward at the special Borough meeting, we were expecting the leadership to take disciplinary action against us but all that happened was that Digby Kelsall was sent down to give a series of lectures to the Branch on Creative Marxism.'

'There was a good reason why the leadership didn't act against you at that time,' Les said mildly, as if reluctant to disagree at all with Alan. 'The ground was more or less cut away from under their feet by the Nine Party declaration.'

'Yes, wasn't that wonderful. And it came only three days after the Borough meeting.'

'I suspect that it took them quite by surprise.' Les's tone ventured to be almost as triumphant as Alan's had just been. 'They may have known that a conference of Communist Parties to which they hadn't been invited was meeting somewhere in Poland but they can't have expected it to declare that the world had become divided into two opposed camps, socialist and imperialist, with Britain in the imperialist camp.'

'That put a stop pretty quickly to all McNarney's talk about Britain's being a great progressive country on the road to socialism. But the funniest thing was the way Max Dunstable, who just before the publication of the Nine Party declaration had written an editorial insisting that the world was One World, began to try to slide inconspicuously round to an opposite point of view by writing in his next editorial that the world was One World but there were now two camps in it.'

Les smiled at this, then said unsmilingly: 'But McNarney didn't change his views quite so quickly as Max Dunstable. It's true he admitted in his report to the E.C., two months after the Nine Party conference, that the British Party had made mistakes – though he didn't clearly specify what these were – and also that increased production would not benefit the British people but would only help to subordinate Britain to Wall Street; and yet in this same report he contradictorily added that the Party's production drive *had been* absolutely correct and was something to be proud of and that the drive for increased coal production was still correct.'

Alan was impressed by Les's remembering these details.

'By the time of the 20th Party Congress here last April,' Les went on, 'McNarney was no longer defending the production drive, not even in coal-mining, but he was still – and is still – calling for a new Labour government based on the forces of the Left within the Labour movement.'

'Yes, as the Australians point out, he has forgotten Lenin's warning that Social Democrats whether of the Right or of the Left who accept ministerial office under capitalism are "Labour lieutenants of capital". I'm afraid Elsie and I didn't clearly recognize that McNarney's continuing to call for a Labour government of the Left showed him to be just as much a revisionist as ever. We thought he and the E.C. as a whole were gradually coming round to a Marxist-Leninist position. That's why we more or less stopped criticizing the Party line during the past few months.'

'But you mustn't forget the letter you sent as a contribution to the pre-Congress discussion in *World News and Views* last February,' Les said with quiet admiration. 'No wonder it wasn't printed. It was far too good and quite unanswerable.'

'We were rather proud of it,' Alan admitted, pleased, and remembering that Les hadn't been so enthusiastic about the letter when he'd been shown it at the time. 'Especially of that quotation from Lenin's *Left-wing Communism* which we included at the start of it: "to admit a mistake openly, to discuss its reasons, to study attentively the means of correcting it – these are the signs of a serious party".'

'And then there was that devastating quotation you gave from an article that Comrade Fred Hurley wrote before the Nine Party declaration: "the workers must bear cuts to solve the crisis".'

Alan laughed exultingly, and said: 'Yes, that letter of ours must quite have got under the skin of the editorial board. Our only mistake was to slack off afterwards and stop our criticisms; but we'll do our best to make up for that from now on.'

'The E.C. is going to find itself in a difficult situation, I think,' Les said, echoing Alan's exultation.

'They'll be furious, but what can they do to us? After all they did publish the first Australian letter in *World News and Views*, so they can hardly condemn us for circulating it. My guess is they may try more or less to ignore us, as they did in the end after our attack on *Britain's Way Forward*.'

'I don't think they'll ignore you,' Les said slowly. 'As a matter of fact I've had some pretty reliable information that they won't.'

Les stopped, as though he needed to be assured, before continuing, that Alan wanted to hear more about this information.

'Who told you?' Alan asked.

'Well, recently I've got to know a comrade who works at Headquarters and hears a good deal of what is being said there. His name is White. He would like to meet you.'

'I should like to meet him.' Alan's impatience to know exactly what White had told Les didn't prevent the thought coming to him that Les, so intelligent and with all these well-placed contacts he evidently had, was going to be a very useful ally indeed.

'It was from him I heard that the District intended to call us up before them very soon,' Les said. 'Furious isn't the word for the E.C.'s feelings towards us. White says that if they were in power in this country they would undoubtedly have us shot.'

'I can well believe it.' Alan managed to grin.

'The name they're using for what we've been up to is "international factionalism".'

For some reason this phrase was more disturbing to Alan than the news of the District Committee's intention to summon him before them very soon. In order to combat his uneasiness he said jeeringly:

'What a beauty.'

Les showed no sign of understanding his meaning, so Alan added:

'What a gem of Party jargon.'

As he said this he was able to generate within himself such an indignation against Party jargon in general that the words 'international factionalism' lost all their power to make him feel apprehensive.

'Of course, it's no worse than plenty of other samples you could pick out from any speech or article by almost any leading Party member nowadays,' Alan went on. Les still made no comment, and Alan tried to think of some actual sentence of Mc-Narney's or Max Dunstable's which he could quote in order to make himself clearer to Les, but though recently in a notebook of his he had started a written collection of such sentences, he couldn't immediately think of any. 'The kind of thing I object to is the pretentious use of abstract nouns that add nothing at all to the sense of a sentence – I mean nouns like "situation" and "aspects" and "basis" and "issue" and "position" and, of course, "perspectives" – "perspectives" is a special favourite of theirs, and is used as a long-winded substitute for "prospects".'

'I came across a sentence of Max Dunstable's the other day which I think you'll appreciate,' Les suddenly said. He quoted: '"It is essential to face the issue squarely as positive and negative features of the total situation in which we live." '

Evidently Les had not only understood from the start what Alan meant by Party jargon but was well up in the study of it. The discovery that they shared a concern about the use of words made Alan feel closer to Les than before, and helped to stimulate his memory.

'That reminds me of a sentence of Frank Baxter's I read recently,' Alan said. '"Here is the crucial point which has not yet become the central issue in the discussions about the future position of the labour movement."'

'Then what about this from McNarney – "The Congress was never given a real analysis of the actual economic situation, particularly in relation to the perspective of increased shortages."'

'Or this, also from McNarney,' Alan said, keen to do still better than Les. '"The situation is being accentuated and I have no hesitation in saying that a crisis position is being reached."'

'Or' – Les easily kept up with him – '"There are two other aspects arising from the position of an imminent American slump." That's McNarney's too.'

'And there's another type of jargon – if jargon is quite the right name for it – which McNarney is specially fond of: I mean out-of-date figures of speech.'

'Such as "plain as a pikestaff",' Les suggested.

'Yes, that's one of them. And "spiking the Tories' guns". And "it wouldn't matter a tinker's cuss".'

'And "the wigs would be on the green with a vengeance".'

Alan laughed. 'Yes, he actually uses that in *Britain's Way Forward*. Also "the bloated financiers of Wall Street and their ilk are already gloating over our situation".'

'And "the Tories will gloat like the ghouls they are over the difficulties of the nation".'

'But McNarney's most characteristic absurdity is his use of proverbial or idiomatic sayings which he doesn't get quite right. Rather in the manner of –' Alan was going to say 'in the manner of Bill Whiddett's remark at the Borough meeting that Elsie was "barking up a very wrong tree"', but he was checked by the feeling that to poke fun at a rank-and-file Party member would make a bad impression on Les, so he had quickly to think of an illustration from McNarney's own writings.

'One example that occurs to me is "the *Daily Worker* will never trim its sails to fit a prevailing wind".'

Les immediately capped this with:

'"The government's foreign policy is being challenged from increasingly wide quarters."'

Alan laughed loudly, and asked:

'Were you reminded of that one by the "prevailing wind"?'

'It's quite authentic.' Les grinned modestly.

'I've thought of another, but it will come as an anti-climax after yours. "The U.S.S.R. is to a considerable degree alone in condemning the cold war."' Then Alan remembered a better one. 'But perhaps this from *Britain's Way Forward* is pretty good: "They will use the stomachs of hungry men and women as bargaining counters."'

Les easily matched this with:

'"The government must solve the bottle-necks of production."'

Suddenly Alan felt ashamed of himself. Wasn't he, in sneering at McNarney's solecism about the stomachs of hungry men and women, behaving like the worst kind of pedantic snob for whom the 'grammatical' correctness of a sentence is more important than its meaning? Wasn't his whole attack against Party jargon just the type of thing that could have come from any bourgeois-minded academic who believed that his education made him superior to the working-class? Alan's doubts were only momentary, however. He was soon assuring himself that the leadership's pretentious and redundant use of abstract nouns was not due to a lack of academic training. It was a product of political degeneration. Meanwhile Les remained silent, and was perhaps having doubts also, though his silence might simply be in response to Alan's. In their talk about the leadership's language Alan had so far not only been the one to start the attack but he had been the one to keep it going; Les had been no more than his follower.

'I'm not objecting just to clumsiness in the use of words,' Alan felt the need to explain, 'but to the underlying confusion of thought which the clumsiness arises from. Party leaders with working-class origins aren't the only offenders. Digby Kelsall, who must know better, has taken to using the ridiculous expression "self-study" when he means "private study".'

Les said downrightly: 'I think the leadership's jargon in general shows their contempt for the people it's addressed to.'

Alan, in spite of Les's support and of his own conviction that Party jargon was a vice that needed to be seriously combated, felt a lingering guilt about having sneered at certain sentences of McNarney's which were inept rather than pretentious. He tried to rid himself of this guilt by saying:

'Of course, McNarney sometimes uses colloquialisms quite effectively. I remember one good one: "Those persons who so patronizingly say with their hands in the wrong place, 'You young people don't understand.'"'

Les smiled, but he didn't – or couldn't – cap Alan's quotation with another of the same type. Alan, having now said something favourable about McNarney, felt free to attack the leadership again, not this time for their jargon but for a related vice of theirs which he all at once thought of.

'Talking about hands in the wrong place reminds me of the gestures that the Party leaders go in for now when they're making speeches at public meetings – so stagey, like the gestures of very bad actors.'

But a renewed feeling of guilt checked Alan as he was about to go on to describe more fully what he meant. There seemed something far more personal in his criticizing the leaders' gestures than there had seemed in his attacking their jargon — something petty and even malicious, something uncommunist. Les looked at him, showing interest, waited for him to continue, then said:

'I think I know the kind of thing.'

Alan still did not continue. Les, after hesitating as though he too felt a little guilty, slowly raised his right hand, clenched it and brought it ponderously down on to the open palm of his left hand. Alan, encouraged by this demonstration, overcame his own scruples and said:

'Yes, or if they're standing by a table while they're speaking, they'll thump that instead. I remember once when Elsie was chairing a meeting for Fred Hurley he thumped so hard that he stopped her watch which she'd put down on the table in front of her.'

'And I've noticed that the thumping is very seldom related to what they're saying. It's just mechanical; it provides a background rhythm.'

'That's true,' Alan said admiringly, impressed that Les had been so observant. He thought of another gesture which several of the leaders were fond of, and he gave way easily this time to the temptation to mock it. 'Then there's this,' he said, holding his hand stiffly out in front of him and chopping the air with it strongly yet precisely as though he was a butcher using a cleaver.

'And this,' Les said, jabbing jerkily and repeatedly downwards with his forefinger as if to puncture a series of taut invisible membranes.

They were both grinning broadly now.

'And there's the sideways pointing gesture,' Alan said, 'with the forearm bent like the neck of an aggressively-intentioned swan.'

Alan briefly tried to give Les an illustration of this, but he couldn't make his fingers resemble a swan's beak at all.

'And there's the backwards pointing gesture,' Les said.

He got up quickly from his chair and, his wide-opened eyes giving the impression that they were fixed on a huge audience in a public hall, he raised a rigid right arm and swinging it backwards at shoulder level through an angle of thirty degrees he pointed threateningly as though towards something unseeable far beyond the wall of the hall. His extended hand, which was just so far back that he was able to keep sight of it from the corner of his eye, vibrated as it pointed.

Alan laughed outright, then said:

'I can't believe that when I first came into the Party the leaders used to go in for these antics.'

Perhaps McNarney had always been given to gesturing when speaking to a crowd, Alan thought, but in the old days his gestures had not made him seem like a ham actor trying to put over the words of a bad play. He and Max Dunstable and Frank Baxter and Fred Hurley and the other comrades on the Central Committee (as the Executive had then been called) had been proper communists, not reformists and opportunists. During the years when they had led the struggle against unemployment and against fascism they had been leaders whom their rank-and-file could love and be inspired by. Alan, in attacking them as they now were, was defending them as they had formerly been, was being loyal to what had been best in them and to what might even yet, as a result perhaps of his and Elsie's and Les Gatten's present efforts, be brought to life in them once more. With this thought a powerful confidence arose in him which not merely rid him of all remaining apprehensiveness about what the District would quite soon have to say to him, but made him look forward to what he would be able to say to the District. Meanwhile Les, who had sat down again after his unconstrained demonstration of the backward pointing gesture, was talking about his own early impressions of the Party leaders. Alan, though trying at least to appear to be keenly interested in what Les was telling him, was too much occupied by his new feeling of confidence to pay full attention. Everything external which he was conscious of, including the quietness of Les's voice and his forward-leaning posture in the armchair and also, especially, the books visible on the shelves behind his head, helped to intensify this feeling. The sight of the books gave Alan the thought that in his struggle for truth against the Party leadership he had the support of the best minds in all the ages. And the books reminded him of his poetry; and suddenly he was able to solve the problem of what his next poem would be about. Like the poem he had been working on during the past year and had abandoned finally this morning, it would aim at reviving the appeal of the Party life and it would show day-to-day Party work in the light of the future world-wide victory of communism, but unlike that poem it would foresee the life that could be lived after the victory. And the life it would foresee would be the poetic life. His new poem would hold out the promise of a time when everyone would be free to follow his or her own inborn bent, and when the poet would give himself primarily to poetic creation. But wasn't this an idea he had thought of years ago, just before the war, and why hadn't he tried to make a poem out of it long before now? Had it perhaps not been wholly convincing to him emotionally?

Before Alan could think of an answer to this question, Les Gatten said something which put it wholly out of his mind. There was no change in Gatten's tone of voice. While he had been describing to Alan his early impressions of the Party leaders he had at last seemed — as he perhaps hadn't even when he had stood up to demonstrate the backward pointing gesture — totally at ease, and he seemed so still as he told Alan now: 'Before I joined the Party I was a private detective.'

For a moment this statement had no emotional effect on Alan. His consciousness was exclusively occupied by the hard clear certainty that he had not misheard what Gatten had said, and then by the conviction that it was true. It was true because only it could explain everything Alan had found puzzling about him, both today and ever since first meeting him two years ago. Gatten, as though the revelation he had just made had been of not much importance, continued to talk about his early experiences in the Party. Feeling was abruptly brought to life in Alan. Like someone who coming into a kitchen sees a joint of cooked meat on a white dish in the middle of a table and sees also on the same dish and in contact with the meat something which is not meat, greenish-grey, part liquid, part solid, and which he instantly knows to be dog's vomit though it does not make him begin to retch until his mind has willy-nilly formed an idea of what the solid (fishy, spool-shaped, shaggily stringy) might have been before the dog's stomach rejected it – Alan did not feel nausea until after he had comprehended fully what Gatten was. But the nausea was brief, was soon transformed into loathing and anger. He had an impulse to shout into Gatten's face: 'Get out of this house this instant you treacherous swine.' However, he restrained himself. He decided that he must not say or do anything precipitately. Otherwise Gatten would be prevented from revealing himself further. It was important that Gatten should not see in Alan's face any signs of mistrust or hostility whatsoever. Apparently he had not seen any yet. He was sitting comfortably back in the armchair – not, as during most of the time since he had first sat down, almost on the edge of it. He was talking of the anti-fascist demonstrations which the Party leadership had so effectively organized before the war. Perhaps he was a genuine communist who had formerly been a detective but had been brought to communism by disgust with his vile job. Would a man who was still working as a detective have risked rousing Alan's suspicions by admitting he'd worked as one before joining the Party? Perhaps what had made him reveal himself had been a desire to be absolutely honest with Alan, and the uneasiness he'd shown before telling him might have been due to shame and to anxiety about how Alan would react. Or on the other hand the revelation might be a special kind of confidence trick, intended to forestall a possible discovery of Gatten's past by Alan on his own account. And if Gatten was a genuine convert to communism, wouldn't his proper place be as a counter-agent within the capitalist security system rather than as an ordinary member in a Party Branch? No, he was still a detective, an agent of the ruling class, and Alan was confirmed in this conclusion by something else which he suddenly heard Gatten say:

'Of course, a private detective has to work in with the police. And they keep a check on me even now.'

There could no longer be any doubt at all. Gatten was a spy within the working-class movement, a provocateur, almost the vilest thing – to Alan's mind – that a human being could be. Far viler than any open enemy, than any fascist. Almost as vile as those Social Democratic leaders who while claiming to be socialists give their support to imperialism. But if Gatten was certainly a police spy what could his motive be in revealing that he was one? He might hope to scare Alan into political inactivity. Probably Gatten's masters regarded Marxist-Leninists in the Party – even though there were few at present – as more of a menace than the revisionists and opportunists. 'Yet he must know,' Alan thought, 'that anyone who has been in the Party for any length of time takes for granted spies will get into it, and is unlikely to be frightened of them.' Yes, but perhaps he saw Alan as someone who by his disagreement with the leadership had isolated himself and had forfeited the Party's protection and was therefore more susceptible to intimidation. Gatten would be unable to understand that internationalism really meant something to Alan and Elsie and that with the Australian Party on their side they could not feel alone. What Alan next heard Gatten say seemed to confirm the supposition that his hope was to intimidate.

'The British Secret Service is one of the best organized in the world, as I daresay you know. Not much goes on that they aren't aware of.'

'Yes,' Alan said, without thinking what he said. During the past few minutes since Gatten had revealed himself as a detective Alan had made several other would-be noncommittal interjections in order to keep him talking, but this time Gatten looked surprised for an instant; and then he went on to give his ideas about the tactics they should adopt when they were interviewed by the District committee.

Alan only partly listened. He was still trying to decide why Gatten had revealed himself. Was it really likely that the Secret Service thought Alan important enough, Marxist-Leninist though he was, to be worth their attempting to frighten him into inactivity? They would probably prefer to use him to subvert the Party, revisionist though it had become. Gatten's aim might be to blackmail him into working for the police within the Party. To blackmail him by threatening to let the Party leaders know that one of his supporters, his main supporter, in his campaign against their line, was a police agent. This idea didn't disturb Alan much, because there seemed to be a logical flaw in it, but it gave rise to another idea which alarmed him deeply. Suppose the Party leaders got to know without being told by Gatten – who surely would not want to uncover himself to them – that Alan was being helped by an anti-communist spy. Suppose they already knew; and were waiting to use their knowledge to the greatest effect against him, perhaps on the day when he came up before the District committee, perhaps at the very moment during his interview with the committee when he was making his most telling attack against the leadership's revisionism. They could smear him as an associate of out-and-out enemies of the Party. They wouldn't be incapable of that. In their reply to the first letter from the Australian Political Committee, a letter which had been written some weeks before the Eight Parties had denounced Tito as a renegade from communism and which had quoted with approval something he'd said, they had strongly hinted that the Australians were Titoists. They could smear Alan and, worse, they could smear through him the truth he stood for. But the truth would eventually be vindicated, whereas he might be dishonoured permanently. No calumny against him from capitalist sources could be as lasting as one from the leaders of a Party which would control the world of the future. A poet might be able to vindicate himself in the end through his writings if they survived, but not a poet who had written so little and so badly as Alan up to now had done. How many true communists who had been wrongfully accused during their lives would go down to history as traitors for ever? And might there not be among the heroes of the Revolution buried below the Kremlin wall perhaps one undiscovered potential traitor who would remain a hero for as long as history continued to be written?

This last thought had the surprising effect of lifting Alan out of the mood of horrified helplessness into which he had begun to fall. He told himself that to be a true communist yet to be regarded for ever as a traitor to communism would be better than to be a police spy yet to be mistakenly immortalized as a communist hero. To act like a communist was more important than to have the reputation of being one. A true communist now must fight against revisionism, whatever the consequences for his reputation. And Alan might still be able to prevent the leadership from accusing him of collaboration with an anti-communist agent. He would go up to District headquarters tomorrow, would report that he had discovered a detective within the Party, would emphasize that he was making the report as soon as possible after he had made the discovery. He wished he could go up tonight, at once; but he might not find any member of the District committee there at this time. Luckily tomorrow would be a half-holiday and he could get there early in the afternoon.

Gatten was no longer talking about what tactics they should adopt when they came before the District committee, but was outlining the practical policy, as distinct from the theoretical line, which he thought the Party ought to have in place of its present one. He did not, as previously, seem to be modestly offering suggestions whose worth only Alan could pronounce upon, but to be expressing opinions he was already very sure of. Alan heard him say: "The Party instead of advocating that conscription into the imperialist armed forces should be for one and a half and not for two years ought to campaign for its total abolition, and ought to spread propaganda for this inside as well as outside the forces.' 'There speaks the provocateur,' Alan thought with hatred. He made very little effort now to prevent his feelings from showing in his face; but Gatten seemed unaware of them. Or was he actually very well aware of them, and had he been aware of them ever since he'd revealed himself as a detective? All at once he said, though without any special significance in his tone, that he had better go. He stood up, and Alan stood up too. Gatten was the first to move towards the sitting-room door. Alan followed him, not from automatic politeness but consciously in order to prevent his changing his mind and turning back into the room again. Every yard of the floor that Gatten yielded Alan quickly occupied, and as soon as they were out in the hall passage Alan shut the door of the sitting-room behind them. He still followed Gatten, letting him open the front door for himself, seeing with revulsion the sideways-curving hair at the back of his neck and the neat clean cloth of his grey suit covering his broad shoulders and his narrow rump. Now Gatten had stepped over the doorstep, and was outside this house which he might not yet guess he would never be allowed into again.

'Cheerio,' he said.

Alan would have liked to shut the front door without answering, but he was checked by the vague thought that if at this stage he allowed himself to show outright hostility he might in some way be giving Gatten a future advantage over him; and after a rather long pause he said:

'Good-bye.'

He did not watch Gatten walk down the path to the front gate. He shut the door quickly and turned round to go and tell Elsie immediately that Gatten was a spy, but then he remembered that she was out seeing the Murrayfields. He went back into the sitting-room which Gatten had just left. Having to wait for Elsie was almost as agitating to him as having to postpone until tomorrow the visit he would make to District headquarters. He tried to begin to think how he would word the report he would give about Gatten when he got there. He did not sit down. Moving around the room, stopping now at the curtained window and now at the bookcase without seeing its books, he could not think of the words he would use tomorrow but only – again and again and with a feeling of rising tension within him – of what had just happened here. At last, though actually not much more than ten minutes after Gatten had gone, he heard Elsie's latchkey turn in the lock of the front door.

He was out into the hall passage before she had fully opened the door. Her face as she came in seemed to promise good news, but he didn't ask her about the Murrayfields. He began at once to give her an account, so hurriedly that it became jumbled and he had to begin again, of his conversation with Gatten. When he had finished she said she didn't think Les could still be a detective, because if he were he wouldn't have disclosed that he'd once been one. She gave the impression she wouldn't be greatly worried even if they discovered for certain that he still was one. But she agreed that in any case they must stop taking him into their confidence and that it would be a good precaution for Alan to make a report on him to the District tomorrow. Her attitude calmed Alan a little, though even now he didn't think of asking what success she had had with the Murrayfields. There was a further slight improvement in his morale when she eventually told him:

'Iris already knows we're right, and she admits she knows. Alec knows too, and almost admits it. But neither of them is quite ready yet to go to the length of disagreeing openly with the Executive – though I'm sure both of them soon will be.'

5

It was not till more than a week after Gatten had revealed himself as a detective that Alan thought of poetry again.

He was coming back from a day's teaching, which had gone smoothly enough, and he was walking along the pavement of his home road. He was within fifty yards of his own house. He saw, though only vaguely and without interest, behind the front garden fence of a house about ten doors away from his, the small-leaved and always closely-clipped Japanese honeysuckle hedge whose top surface, undulating a little here and there, had the smoothness almost of snow when it has lost its powderiness and is just beginning to thaw. He saw too along the outer edge of the pavement ahead the silver birches and the brown-barked prunus trees alternating at intervals that seemingly diminished farther down the road; yet though an afternoon sun was shining there was between his perception and the trees something like a faint dark haze which he could almost believe to be external while he nevertheless knew it originated from his state of mind. For the past nine days — in spite of his having gone up to the District as soon as possible to report what he had discovered about Gatten — he had never quite been able to come out from the shadows of an anxiety lest the Executive might still decide that the most effective way of putting a stop to his and Elsie's attack on revisionism in the Party would be to accuse them of collaborating with a police agent. Beyond and above the birch and prunus trees at the far end of the road there was a railway bridge, and he looked at this just before he reached his front gate. It was an iron bridge, elegant, of an early type, with what appeared like a balustrade along the top of it, and through the interstices between the uprights of the balustrade the greenness of a small hill, unbuilt-on and used for allotments, was visible.

As he looked he realized that the faint dark haze had dispersed, and that he was seeing the bridge and the hill beyond it with the utmost vividness. At the same moment he was abruptly freed from his anxiety. He knew that he and Elsie would not be accused of intentionally accepting support from an enemy of communism. It was true that when he had gone up to the District to report about having discovered a spy in the Party the District committee member whom he had spoken to, Mike Tarrant, had not thanked him and had almost seemed displeased at his having made the report. But the point was that even if the Party leadership would have been quite capable of using Alan's association with Gatten to discredit his criticisms of their political line, his interview with Tarrant had put an obstacle in the way of their doing so. The fear that he had felt for nine days, and that the sight of the railway bridge had released him from, had been unreasonable. He looked again at the bridge. The rounded space below it which it overarched, and the rounded solid hill beyond it which was arched against the space of the sky, were topped by the round of a big cumulus cloud summer-white in the autumn afternoon sun. He remembered the poem he had conceived more than a week ago in the front sitting-room just before hearing Gatten admit to being a former private detective, a poem that would justify his longing for the poetic life by seeing that life not as something in the past, everlastingly lost, but as a shining future possibility inspiring him to persevere in the political struggle through which alone it could eventually be realized, for others, if not for him. This poem now seemed more appealing and more promising than any he had conceived during the past eight years.

His enthusiasm for it was not due solely to the attractiveness of its theme. At the same time as the sight of the railway bridge made him remember the poem, there came to him the exciting idea that from now on he would adopt a totally new attitude towards the writing of poetry. He decided that his failure just before the war to produce a poem on an almost identically similar theme which he'd thought of then was to be explained not by any weakness in the theme but by a wrong view of what his main aim when writing poetry ought to be. Nearly every poem he had written or tried to write ever since he had joined the Party had been primarily a political statement and only secondarily a poem. His awareness that for a communist the political struggle must take precedence over everything else including poetry had led him to suppose mistakenly that if he was to serve communism as a poet his starting-point when writing a poem must be a political message, which he must then try to translate into poetry. He had believed that poetic quality, though it was essential as a means of getting the message across more effectively, ought not to be his first concern. Consequently his poetry had been constricted and pauperized, had become etiolated, and even the political message had always been less effective than if he had not tried to poeticize it but had given it in the plain prose of a pamphlet or of a newspaper article. From now on he would put poetic quality first, and the politics in his poems would subserve the poetry: his aim would no longer be to use poetry to make political statements but to use his political experiences and feelings to make poems. 'At last I shall be poetically free,' he thought with elation as he opened his front gate and began to walk up the short path towards the house. Then he had a doubt: wasn't there something a little suspect about this idea of using politics to make poetry – didn't it savour of bourgeois aestheticism, of poetry for poetry's sake? Didn't it belittle politics? He had no time to resolve his doubt. Behind the front door, whose coloured glass was not bright now as when seen from inside but was hardly less dull overall than the mazy lines of lead that held its separate pieces in place, there was a quick dim movement, and before he reached the door it was opened to him by Elsie. She must have been watching for him from the window of the front sitting-room.

She was holding two letters in her hand.

'These came ten minutes ago,' she said, immediately giving him one of them. 'This one is from the District. They're asking us to come up before them next Thursday, a week from today.'

He had a sharp chill feeling in the stomach. He fumbled to get the letter out of its envelope into which she had put it back after reading it. It was typewritten and quite short, and it made him feel calmer as he read it. Its language did not convey the slightest hint of a threat, was as if giving a reminder of a routine meeting. At the end of the letter there was the signature of the secretary of the District Committee, Sid Noaks. The calming effect the wording had on Alan was not entirely dispelled when the thought came to him, after he'd finished reading, that the unthreatening tone could be due to a conscious intention on Noaks's part of not putting into the letter anything which might make the Sebrills hesitate to attend the meeting.

'I'm glad they've fixed the date at last.' Saying this he really was glad. He remembered how good, how irrefutable, the arguments were that he and Elsie would be able to put to the Committee. He felt even more confidence in these now, after having taken steps to prevent the Committee from accusing him and Elsie of being accomplices of a police spy, than he had felt before he had discovered what Gatten was.

'Yes,' Elsie agreed. 'And this other letter is from Australia.'

He eagerly took it from her. She added: 'But it's not from the Australian Party. It's a very peculiar letter.'

He began to read it. It was typewritten but had no address or date at the head of it.

'Dear Comrades,

You may be somewhat surprised to receive this communication from a Party comrade who is unknown to you. I am a merchant seaman on a ship which has just put in at Sydney, Australia, and while here I have taken the opportunity of paying a visit to a certain Mr Sharkey who has given me your names.'

At this point in his reading Alan already recognized a stylistic resemblance between this letter and the letters printed in a book called *Anti-Soviet Forgeries* that the Party had published during the late nineteen-twenties. In this letter as in those forgeries there was the same blatant conspiratorial tone which, though it might seem typically communist to the kind of reader who accepted as true that capitalist daily-newspapers' view of communism, would at once be detected by any communist reader – or by any politically educated reader for that matter – as coming from an anti-communist source. And in the phrase 'a certain Mr Sharkey' the very word 'Sharkey', which was the actual name of a leading member of the Australian Party, adventitiously heightened the conspiratorial effect.

'This is written by an anti-communist agent,' Alan said. 'Someone much more noxious than Gatten, since Gatten as far as we know isn't working on an international level.'

'We aren't certain that Gatten is still working as an agent at all, even on a local level,' Elsie said calmingly. 'I agree, of course, that this letter does seem pretty suspect. But you haven't read to the end of it yet, have you?'

Alan continued reading and his feelings now competed for his attention with the words of the letter. A sense of menace made rational judgement of what he read more difficult for him. 'Mr Sharkey,' the letter went on to say, 'has informed me of your views and I am in the fullest agreement with them.' Alan was for an instant, though only for an instant, unreasonably gratified by this statement of support. Next the seaman said that he had been given some idea by Mr Sharkey of what had been going on since the war in the Communist Parties of countries under British colonial rule in south and south-east Asia, and that his eyes had been opened wide to the appalling damage caused to these Parties by the advice which the leaders of the British Party had pressed upon them. (He didn't say what the advice was, but there was certainly a possibility that the leadership – which regarded Britain as a 'great progressive country' now – had urged these Parties not to campaign for the full independence of their countries from Britain.) Because of what Mr Sharkey had told him, as well as because of his own conviction beforehand that the Party's home policy was not revolutionary but reformist, he had reached the conclusion that immediate and decisive action against the leadership was imperative. He and the Sebrills would not be alone in undertaking this. He had certain friends in the Party who took the same view of the situation as they did and would be happy to help. Alan, as he read this, briefly remembered an incident that Wal Hannington, leader of the National Unemployed Workers' Movement during the nineteen-thirties, had described in his book *Unemployed Struggles*. Hannington was speaking at a session of the Hunger Marchers' central council in London when another member of the council, arriving late for the session, handed him a sealed envelope received from a stranger outside the hall who had said that Hannington would be expecting it. Hannington was about to put the envelope in his pocket and to go on speaking but something made him decide to open it without delay, and inside it he found a terrorist letter beginning with the words 'Concerning the direct action activities which we have already discussed, the plans now are . . .' It proposed waylaying cabinet ministers and setting fire to various government buildings. Hannington then read it to the council, pointing out that it was a 'plant' and was intended to incriminate the council, and they agreed that to leave the building with it in their possession would be too dangerous and that however useful it might be as evidence against agents provocateurs it had better be burned immediately. Next morning he was arrested and very thoroughly searched by the police, who seemed to be looking for something in particular and to be disappointed at not finding it on him.

'This look like a frame-up,' Alan said excitedly.

'How could it be?' Elsie's tone was correctively rational.

'Some act could be arranged by this provocateur against a member of the Executive, perhaps. Some violence. And this letter would be found on us and we could be implicated.' Alan increasingly felt the improbability of what he was suggesting as he suggested it, but like someone unable to wake up from a nasty dream he persisted. 'For the authorities this would have the double advantage of enabling them to incriminate us while at the same time putting one of the Party leaders out of action.'

'That's utter nonsense,' Elsie said. 'I think you're far too prone to exaggerate our importance in the eyes of the authorities. They'd hardly go to those lengths in order to suppress us – even if they thought they could get away with such methods, which they couldn't in England, yet – and as for suppressing McNarney or any other leading revisionist, what need would they have for that?'

'I suppose you're right.' Then Alan swung to a new and opposite extreme. 'Perhaps this seaman is a perfectly sincere socialist but politically inexperienced and that could be why he uses the kind of language and makes the kind of propositions he does.'

'I don't think any sincere socialist could write like that.'

'Then what *is* the purpose of his letter? Is it to try to scare us – like those two phone calls we got yesterday from someone who wouldn't speak when you lifted the receiver?'

'Those could have been a coincidence – they could have come from two different callers who'd both been given the wrong number and hadn't the manners to apologize to me. One purpose the seaman obviously has is to get us to visit the woman he mentions.'

'What woman?'

'So you still haven't read to the end of the letter.'

Alan continued reading: 'Unfortunately I shall not be back in England until the end of next month, but in the meantime you could get in touch with a friend of mine, a woman comrade who has a cottage in Sussex and who has recently returned from Italy where she has been active along the same lines as ourselves.' Then came the woman's name and the address of her cottage, but Alan read these with so little attention that if he had had to put the letter away somewhere at this moment and had subsequently been unable to find it again he would have been totally incapable of remembering them. The seaman ended: 'With very good wishes and looking forward to calling on you soon after I arrive in London. Yours fraternally, Tom Bowling.' The very obviousness of the presumably false name would have prevented Alan from forgetting it even if he'd decided to burn the letter immediately.

'His aim is to involve us in an anti-communist conspiracy,' Alan said.

'The style of his letter doesn't seem very well calculated to do that.'

'It may seem crude and incompetent to us, but no doubt it was taught to him by his employers who must have found that it worked in other cases.'

'Well, it won't work with us, and we needn't let it worry us.'

But Elsie did not succeed in making Alan any less uneasy.

'Suppose the Executive were to get hold of this – with our name on the envelope,' he said.

'I don't see how they could, unless we were foolish enough to give it to them.'

'It might eventually find its way to them somehow. And then we could be smeared as accomplices not just of the British police but of an international anti-Soviet spy ring.'

Alan became aware how very dangerous a thing this piece of typewritten paper was that he still held in his hand. The consequences for him and Elsie if it came into the possession of the Executive could be such that even though the chance of the Executive's getting hold of it might be no more than one in a million, this chance ought to be eliminated.

'We ought to destroy it,' he said.

'I don't think so.'

'Why not?'

He was startled by a sound from the kitchen. The door into the house from the side passage was being opened.

'It's one of the children back from school,' she said. 'I shall have to start getting tea ready.'

He put the letter into his pocket very hurriedly, as though harm might come if one of the children were merely to catch sight of it in his hand. Elsie went towards the kitchen, and he followed her, but before they got there Stephen came out to them. He looked as though he had news for them, not good, no doubt to do with the Grammar school at which he had just begun his first term, a school whose uniform – black jacket, diagonally-striped tie and grey flannel trousers – he was now wearing. However, what he told them wasn't about school:

'I'm afraid I've just broken our side gate.'

'How did you manage that?' Elsie asked.

'I was leaning on it as I came in with my bike.'

'I suppose you had your right foot on one pedal,' Elsie said, 'and your left forearm and most of your weight on top of the gate which swung nicely as you freewheeled in.'

A slight embarrassment was combined in Stephen's look with a surprise that his mother, who was not rated highly in the family for mechanical flair, should have so clearly visualized the mechanics of the situation. Alan too was surprised – at her ability to joke without the least sign that she had the seaman's letter on her mind.

'Yes,' Stephen admitted.

She laughed; and said, 'The gate wasn't exactly in a first-class state of repair anyway. If you hadn't broken it someone else – the greengrocer's boy, or Christina – soon would have. Now we shall have no excuse for not getting a new one.'

Stephen, who looked relieved, went to hang up his school cap on one of the pegs near the front door. Alan followed Elsie into the kitchen. She said, quietly so that Stephen wouldn't hear:

'It's good the way Stephen told us at once about the gate.' Alan, preoccupied still with his feelings about the seaman's letter, did not say anything, and she added: 'We've got so used to our children being honest with us that we've almost come to take it for granted.'

The door leading into the kitchen from the passage-way outside the house had been left open by Stephen. Christina bouncingly appeared in the doorway, asking with a smile:

'What's that you were saying about Stephen?'

Her hearing had always seemed preternaturally good. Stephen came back into the kitchen. Elsie said:

'Nothing for the ears of either of you. It was complimentary.'

'Now you've got to tell us,' Christina said.

'If you must know, I was talking about what a good thing it is you've both acquired the habit of owning up promptly when you've caused breakages.'

Both the children looked pleased. Elsie added: 'You haven't always been models of truthfulness, however.' She wasn't going to sow any seeds of complacency in them. 'There's a story I could tell about Stephen.'

Stephen showed signs of having guessed what story she meant, and she could see that his wish to hear it again was stronger than his wish not to hear it. She began it now by reminding him that there had been a time during the war, some while after they'd been evacuated into the country from London, when he was always telling lies. 'We supposed at first that you'd caught the habit from the Wilkinson boy next door, who certainly was a remarkable liar, but then we remembered that parents are often only too ready to blame the misdoings of their own angels on the bad influence of other people's children.' She went on to describe how one evening in the house where they were living then the wooden-framed brown-paper blackout fell down from the window of the landing outside Stephen's bedroom. 'We assumed you must have been playing about with the metal catches which held the frame up against the window, and you said you hadn't been, but we couldn't be sure you were telling the truth, and you were very upset.'

Alan made himself join in:

'You weren't too young then to know that a fallen blackout could have got us summonsed by the police, or, worse, that it could have shown a light to Nazi bombers.'

'An evening or two later,' Elsie continued, 'the blackout fell again, but luckily this time we discovered that the wind had blown it down and that the catches weren't tight enough. When we apologized to you and explained that we hadn't been able to believe you because of the lies you'd recently been telling, you saw the point.'

'And have never told a lie again,' Christina said, grinning.

Elsie, not giving Stephen time to retort to Christina, said to her seriously: 'Never to tell a lie could be as bad as never to tell the truth.'

'How could it be?' Christina asked.

She knew quite well the kind of explanation she would get, having heard it from her parents several times before, but she was as keen to hear it repeated now as, in earlier childhood, she had been to be told over again stories that were already familiar to her in every detail.

'Suppose you're saying good-bye to someone you've been to tea with,' Elsie said, 'and she asks if you've enjoyed yourselves, and you haven't, you would be very rude if you told her the truth.'

Alan's feelings about the seaman's letter, combining with his wish not to seem to the children to be uninterested in what she was saying, influenced him to add an instance which in its grimness was very different from the one she had given:

'Suppose the Nazis had occupied this country during the war

and you had known where a Jewish girl and her family were hiding and the Nazis had asked you whether you knew, you would have done a very wrong thing if you had told them the truth.'

'There are some people who think that all lying is wicked,' Elsie said, 'but they need to think harder.'

'Yes,' Alan said, trying to make his tone more like hers, 'when I was nine I had a very pious headmaster who used to preach to us that there can be no such thing as a "white" lie, but I'm sure that anyone who tried to live up to his standards would soon find himself failing very badly.'

'All the same,' Elsie said lightly, 'as a general rule lies are not a good thing. Now go upstairs and get your hands washed before tea.'

They went; and as soon as Alan and Elsie were alone again in the kitchen his apprehensiveness about the seaman's letter surged up in him once more. But the conversation with the children about lying was not instantly blotted out from his mind: instead, it took on a new and embittering significance for him.

'This "morality" we believe in and have taught to the children – isn't this just what has got us into our present mess? Isn't this what has made us vulnerable to twisters and provocateurs?'

'I don't see how you make that out,' Elsie said resistantly.

'If we'd been less "honest" and outspoken in opposing the leadership's line, if we'd been more underhand and subtle, we shouldn't have laid ourselves open to political blackmail as we have done. Has our behaviour been very different from Maldwyn Pryce's when he insisted in the name of honesty on telling his congregation that he'd become a communist and as a result has had to leave the ministry and to lose the influence for the Party he could have had among Swedenborgians?'

'That was quite different, and we were absolutely against it and tried to dissuade him.'

'I wish I could feel that we hadn't behaved like bourgeois humanists in bringing our children up to think they ought to be truthful and modest and considerate towards other people.'

'We've also brought them up to be on the side of the working-class and the oppressed peoples of the world,' Elsie objected. 'And we've not taught them that being truthful and mild is always preferable to being violent and cunning.'

'We've taught them it normally is.'

'Well, it is, isn't it?'

'It may not usually be preferable during a period of intensifying struggle such as they are likely to have to live in.'

'Ought we to have taught them that they should be quite indifferent whether they tell lies or the truth and that the only way for them to decide which to tell in any situation is by asking themselves which would be the more helpful to the fight against imperialism? That would have been quite meaningless to them.'

'So we taught them instead that they ought to be truthful in order that their parents should be able to trust them. What sort of morality is that?'

'It's commonsense morality. It's a morality for people who have to live together.'

'I'm afraid it may be bourgeois morality,' Alan said reluctantly.

'Would we have been better Leninists if we'd neglected the children and lied to them and not loved them and they'd had to work out their own morality through hard experience?'

'No, because if we'd done that we would have shown a preference for lies and harshness, and the morality the children would have been most likely to pick up would have been imperialist and fascist.'

'We're forgetting to get the tea.'

Elsie went to fill the kettle from the tap above the sink. Alan lit one of the burners on the gas cooker and she put the kettle over it. She said, 'Truthfulness and considerateness are needed not only between members of a family but still more between supporters of the struggle against imperialism.'

'Yes, but how can we justify our feeling that communists even in their relations with the enemy should be truthful and humane, as far as they can be without betraying the interests of the struggle?'

'Trickery and ruthlessness are more necessary to the imperialists, who can't maintain their rule without deceiving and repressing the people,' Elsie said, 'whereas the revolutionary movement needs to combat lies and cruelty in order to win the people over to its side.'

Suddenly Alan thought of an argument which seemed more convincing than this.

'Certainly truth and humaneness can be a weapon against imperialism,' he said, 'but I think there's a more fundamental reason than that for preferring them to their opposites. I think we should prefer them because they will be necessary in the really human classless society of the future.'

Elsie couldn't at once accept this.

'Why should what will be preferable in the future be preferable now?' she asked.

'Of course there can't be any question that whatever helps the present struggle against imperialism is moral and whatever hinders it is immoral,' Alan said, 'but if communists now *feel* no preference for truth and humaneness – even when the situation requires that they should choose craftiness and retaliatory violence – then they are likely to commit excesses which besides weakening the struggle may transform it into a struggle for something quite other than socialism or communism.'

He felt he had discovered the answer to a bourgeois humanist accusation which had recently often troubled him – that communist morality is merely 'relativist' and based on expediency. But the satisfaction his discovery gave him was ended when he abruptly remembered the letter in his pocket, and the remembrance was all the blacker because of its contrast with the satisfaction it had annihilated. He brought the letter out of his pocket. The children had gone into their rooms upstairs and there were no sounds to suggest that either of them might be about to come down again immediately.

'Why don't you think we ought to destroy this?' he asked.

'We might need it later to expose the provocateur who sent it.'

'It might get into the hands of someone who would take it to the Executive.' Then Alan thought of a way in which without destroying it he could lessen its dangerousness. 'We could write in something – not at the top or bottom of the paper where it could be torn off but between the lines of the letter – which would be evidence that we disapproved of what the seaman is proposing. I mean something like "This is the work of a provocateur".'

'We might want to show the letter to comrades in the Branch who are nearest to agreeing with our criticisms of the leadership, such as the Murrayfields and of course Bert Alldiss, and if we'd written in the sort of thing you suggest I think it might look a bit silly to them.'

'I suppose it might,' Alan had to agree. 'And we *ought* to show it to them – if only to disprove accusations that might be made against us later of being in league with spies. But as soon as possible after showing it to them I think we ought to write something in between the lines and then lock the letter up in a drawer here.'

She did not disagree. Then what seemed a better idea came to him: as there was always the risk that what he wrote between the lines could be erased if he wrote it with ordinary ink, he would write it with the indelible ink which Elsie used for marking clothes. He did not tell her of this new plan, because he suspected that if he were to she might think the seaman's letter had momentarily upset his mental balance. Nevertheless the idea gave him comfort, until he remembered the last sentence in the letter. He said agitatedly:

'This man will be calling on us as soon as he arrives back in London.'

'If he does call, all we'll need to do is tell him we're not interested and close the door on him.'

She wasn't in the least disturbed, and again he felt comforted, but as he glanced through the letter for a second time he became aware of another and more horrifying aspect of it which hitherto he had wholly overlooked.

'Even if we can prevent ourselves from being smeared as accomplices of this man and his "friends",' he said, 'they could still do harm to the Party. That's something we've hardly thought of. Our only concern – or at least my only concern – has been to prevent harm being done to ourselves and of course to our campaign against the leadership's revisionism.'

'There have always been agents trying to injure the Party, and while capitalism lasts there always will be. A Leninist Party must take that into account as a matter of course.'

'Yes, and Lenin said that the best way of limiting the damage they can do is by demanding the strictest obedience to Party rules from all Party members. But we have deliberately broken Party rules. And as a result we've objectively been giving help to out-and-out enemies of the Party.'

'But we shall ignore this letter and have nothing to do with this seaman if he turns up.'

'That won't stop him and his friends from carrying on with their conspiracy. Nor will it stop Gatten, or his contacts in Birmingham and Manchester and elsewhere, who are probably linked up with the seaman, or if they aren't they soon will be. And we shall be responsible for all this.'

'No, we shan't.'

'We shall have made it possible. And we can't guess how widespread and formidable it may become. We shall have been the soil from which this poisonous creeping plant has begun to grow. And, by not telling the Executive what we know, we shall be acquiescing in whatever injury this man may inflict on the Party. Yet we daren't tell the Executive. Oh if only I knew what we ought to do.'

'I think you're making this letter out to be far more important and sinister than it is.'

'I wish there were someone we could get advice from.'

Elsie made a concession to his anxiety.

'You could go to the National Council for Civil Liberties. They're probably experienced in dealing with this kind of thing.'

'Yes, I'll do that.'

However, he couldn't do that till tomorrow at the earliest, and what he needed was to do something immediately.

'And this evening I could take the letter to Maldwyn Pryce,' he said. He was aware of not fully knowing why Maldwyn should suddenly seem to be the right person to consult.

'I doubt if he could help us much,' Elsie said. 'After all he's only just joined the Party.'

'That's one reason why he might be able to see our problem more clearly than we can.'

A sound from the landing above the kitchen ceiling told Alan that one of the children was on the move towards the stairs. He put the letter back into his pocket again, and added:

'I'll go to Maldwyn as soon as we've finished tea.'

Only when Alan arrived outside the front door of Maldwyn Pryce's house, ten minutes after starting out from home on foot (he'd decided not to trust himself on a bicycle in his present pre-occupied state) did he believe he recognized what the main reason had been for his wanting to consult Maldwyn rather than any other comrade in the Branch: it had been that the troubles Maldwyn had just gone through in his Church, as a result of having told his congregation he'd become a communist, would be likely to give him a sympathetic understanding of the troubles Alan and Elsie were going through in the Party. Maldwyn's situation was in a material sense far worse than theirs: his resignation from the ministry had deprived him, at forty-five, of his livelihood, and would soon deprive him and his wife of this house which belonged to the Church and which would be needed for the new minister. Alan took hold of the scalloped metal knob of the bell beside the front door, and as he pulled it he simultaneously thought that this bell being a Victorian one would most probably no longer be in working order; however, after the lapse of almost a second the bell jangled from the base-ment of the house. While he waited he stood sideways to the door – a habit unconsciously retained from his middle-class up-bringing during which he had at some time been taught that it is rude for a visitor to be found staring straight at a door when it is opened to him – and he looked towards the corner of the bay window where there was an ornamental Corinthian pillar top-ped by an indistinctly moulded and paint-clogged acanthus capi-tal. He realized as he looked that he had come here wholly un-prepared for the possibility that Maldwyn might not be in.

But quite soon Maldwyn came and opened the door. At see-ing Alan he showed the kind of warm pleasure that, ever since he had first visited Alan and Elsie's house wanting to join the

Party, he had given signs of whenever he had met either of them. As if he had been expecting Alan he showed no surprise at all – though he could only have been expecting him in the way that any Party member expects to be visited at any time by some other Party member on Party business. Alan, however, did feel a moment's surprise: just before Maldwyn opened the door Alan had pictured him wearing a clerical collar with the black triangle of a clerical 'vest' showing below it, but in fact he wore a soft collar and a dark red tie. He led Alan towards the door of the sitting-room. The hall-passage had a strangely appealing smell, reminiscent – of what? Of the faint metallic-seeming smell in the house where, when Alan had been a child, his grandparents had lived. After they had died the basement there had been discovered to be infested with cockroaches, but the smell had remained pleasant in his memory, and the similar smell here – together with Maldwyn's gladness to see him – helped to lessen a little the intensity of the unease that the sea-man's letter had caused in him. Maldwyn's movement along the hall-passage was quick-footed, and Alan briefly saw in him the amateur teacher of boxing he had been at the youth club that he had run in connection with his church. Alan followed him into the sitting-room, which in spite of its big windows was rather dark – both because of its dark brown wallpaper and because immediately outside one of the windows there was a full-grown rowan tree. Maldwyn asked:

'Do you want a bookcase?'

He pointed to the only bookcase in the room, a long tall one which was filled, so it seemed to Alan at a glance, mainly with theological books. Alan did want a bookcase; and he wanted one like this, not like the miniature modern ones which were all he'd been able to find in shops since the war. But he felt almost that if he were to offer to buy it he would be taking advantage of the misfortune which was compelling Maldwyn to try to get rid of it.

'Wouldn't you rather keep it?' he asked.

'No,' Maldwyn said, without revealing any regret. 'It's far too large. My wife and I will be moving into lodgings. You can have it for five pounds. Together with the books if you like.'

'That's far too little.' Alan avoided mentioning the books.

Conscious of how he himself would have felt if he'd been forced to sell his bookcases, let alone his books, he was distressed for Maldwyn, who however said easily:

'I should get less than that from a secondhand dealer. You would be doing me a good turn. Anyway, think about it. There's no hurry – the move from here is still three weeks off.'

'Have you had any luck yet in your –' Alan tried to think of an unembarrassing word – 'in your inquiries after a new job?'

'None at all. I've been to the Labour Exchange. They seemed rather taken aback when I told them my previous occupation, and my age.' Maldwyn laughed. 'I doubt whether they'd come across a case quite like mine before.'

Alan, realizing that Maldwyn's lightheartedness was due not simply to courage but also to relief at being freed at last from the life of a minister, remembered his own situation which he could not take lightly. He brought the letter from the seaman out of his pocket and, handing it to Maldwyn, said:

'I would like your opinion on this. It came this afternoon.'

Maldwyn took it and went to sit down in the leather-backed swivel-chair in front of the bureau by the window – a bureau at which he had perhaps been used to sit when writing his sermons. He still wore the clerical-grey jacket he had worn at the time of his first visit to Alan and Elsie's house. The armchair that Alan sat down in was upholstered in faded bottle-green moquette, and, together with the other furnishings here, made the room seem to him like a Nonconformist minister's study in the nineteenth century, far removed from modern politics. For an instant he had a feeling of safety, of having found refuge. Then he became sharply conscious again of the letter. Watching Maldwyn read it, Alan wondered whether he would grasp its significance, whether he mightn't think that the seaman genuinely agreed with Alan and Elsie and wanted to help them. Maldwyn himself more or less agreed with them, though he had been in the Party for so short a time that he might not understand how fundamental their theoretical differences with the leadership were. He looked ingenuous now, and almost boyish in spite of his thin hair, as he sat in the swivel-chair holding the letter up in front of him, his short fair eyelashes unblinking. But what he said as soon as he'd finished reading made clear that he had not been deceived:

'It's very unpleasant.'

Alan, needing to be quite sure that the unpleasantness Maldwyn saw in it was the same that he himself saw, asked:

'What kind of person do you think this seaman is?'

'An anti-communist agent, I would say.'

'Yes, Elsie and I think so too. I wish I knew what we ought to do about it.'

Maldwyn looked again at the letter, not in order to re-read any of it but – so Alan felt – to avoid appearing too ready with the advice he was going to give; then he said:

'In your place I would take it up to the Executive straight-away.'

Alan did not know quite how to word his fear that if the Executive got hold of this letter they might use it against him and Elsie. Maldwyn, as a new and keen Party member, would possibly be unable to believe the Party leaders capable of such tactics.

'The fact that this agent chose Elsie and myself as suitable people to approach might be thought to reflect badly on us.'

Maldwyn, not seeming to get Alan's point, said:

'I should put it into the Executive's hands and make it their responsibility. Let it be their worry, not yours.'

Might he, in recommending this, be intending to serve the interests of the Party leaders rather than of Alan and Elsie? Alan, in order to put his sudden misgiving about Maldwyn to the test, risked coming out a little more explicitly with his fears of what the Executive might do if they got hold of the letter.

'It could be used to make us appear to be collaborating with enemies of communism.'

Maldwyn's look showed that he understood what Alan meant, and that whether or not he found the imputation against the Executive credible he at least did not resent it. Alan's misgiving about him was immediately removed.

'At one time I wouldn't have thought for a moment that the Executive could adopt the kind of methods I'm implying,' Alan said, 'but I've changed my mind since reading the answer they published to the first letter of criticism from the Australian Party. They tried to smear the Australians as Titoists, and they based their ridiculous accusation on one sentence of the letter – a sentence which had been written before the Jugoslav Party had been denounced by the other eight Parties and which referred with approval to some politically unobjectionable statement that Tito had made at that time.'

'The accusation is rather a double-edged one,' Maldwyn said. 'It might have the effect of making some readers of the Australian criticisms realize that as a matter of fact the British Executive's line is much nearer to Tito's than the Australian line is.'

This comment seemed not only to show political acuteness but also to suggest that Maldwyn didn't think the Executive incapable of using the seaman's letter to smear Alan and Elsie. Alan added to what Maldwyn had said:

'They may be accusing the Australians of Titoism in order to forestall being accused of it themselves.'

The thought suddenly came to him that the Executive might, in all their actions and pronouncements, be a great deal more cunning than he had hitherto supposed. He impulsively went on:

'Perhaps the seaman is *their* agent, not the government's.'

Though Maldwyn gave no sign of finding even this suggestion inherently improbable, Alan was aware of having no evidence for it, and he wished he had, and then he thought of a piece of evidence which had been available to him ever since he'd read the seaman's letter but which he had up to now overlooked. He said:

'There are phrases in this letter that are almost identical with phrases used by Mike Tarrant when I went up to report to him about Gatten.'

Actually Alan could think of only one such phrase. The seaman had written that Mr Sharkey 'has informed me of your views', and Mike Tarrant at the end of Alan's interview with him had said frigidly something like 'I'll make a note that you have informed me of your views.' The coincidence might not seem very remarkable to Maldwyn if Alan told him of it. However Maldwyn did not ask what the phrases were. He said, with no apparent scepticism:

'You mean that this seaman may be acting on instructions from Mike Tarrant?'

'It's possible.' Having said this Alan began to doubt whether it was possible. How could there have been time, since his interview with Tarrant not much more than a week ago, both for Tarrant to get the instructions out to Australia and for the seaman's letter fulfilling them to arrive in England? Tarrant would hardly have gone to the expense of sending a cable to Sydney. All the same, assuming that he hadn't and that the similarity in phrasing was accidental, this didn't mean that the seaman couldn't be an agent of the Executive. Alan was about to go on to say that Gatten too might be a spy of theirs whom they employed to nip in the bud any movement against them among the Party rank-and-file; but he remembered that when a few days ago he'd told Maldwyn about Gatten's having admitted to being a former detective, Maldwyn – like Elsie – while regarding Gatten as someone whom it would be wiser not to continue trusting had doubted whether he was still a detective. Therefore Alan hesitated to mention Gatten now; but, as he hesitated, a new and yet more sinister idea about the Executive occurred to him, and he couldn't restrain himself from coming out with it to Maldwyn:

'Another possibility is that at least one of the Party leaders may himself be a police agent.'

'As communists we can't afford to refuse to be suspicious,' Maldwyn said, not committing himself to accepting the particular possibility Alan had suggested. He looked with sympathy at Alan. 'And there are times when suspicion becomes very great. I have just been reading an account of what happened in the German Communist Party when Hitler came to power. No comrade could be sure that another comrade wasn't a concealed Nazi. Party members found themselves in such a murky web that many of them lost the will to struggle.'

What Maldwyn said about the German communists helped Alan momentarily to see his own situation in proportion. He recognized how unbalanced he must have seemed to Maldwyn in suspecting that the seaman might be carrying out instructions from Mike Tarrant or that the Executive might be directed by a police agent. He had allowed himself to indulge in persecutory imaginings. And as a result he had probably defeated his own main intention, which had been to convince Maldwyn that if the Executive got hold of the seaman's letter they couldn't be trusted not to use it against Elsie and himself. But now Maldwyn said:

'I do see what the objections are to taking this letter up to Party Headquarters.'

A gladness at having after all apparently convinced Maldwyn came and quickly went in Alan. He remembered that if he did not take the letter up to the Executive he would be shielding an enemy of the Party. He would be betraying the Party. An intolerable despair uncontrollably arose in him and he began to express it to Maldwyn without being fully conscious of the words he was using. He said the Party had been everything to him – and but for it he would have killed himself long ago, as a young man. It had taught him that his personal unhappiness had been due ultimately to the same external evil which was the cause of the immeasurably greater wretchedness of the oppressed and exploited all over the world, and that the only freedom for him as for them was to be found in the struggle against this evil, and that only the Party could lead the struggle successfully. But his very wish to do all he could to strengthen the Party had led him now into actions which would make it more vulnerable to its anti-communist attackers. Alan, aware that his voice was becoming shaky at this point, paused and then said, 'I don't know what right I have to pour all this out to you.'

'You must tell me whatever you want to.' With gentle seriousness, though perhaps also with the very faintest of apologetic smiles, Maldwyn added: 'Look on me as though I were your minister.'

How strange it was that Maldwyn who had been glad to leave the ministry should say this to Alan whom he knew to be an atheist. Perhaps he sensed that Alan wanted him to say it. Maldwyn's face, the skin a little shiny on its broad forehead and slightly flattened nose, reminded Alan all at once of the face of the minister who used to preach in the chapel to which his grandparents had taken him when he had stayed with them during summer holidays as a child Now, in the shadowiness of Maldwyn's sitting-room, he felt the appeal of religion much more strongly than he had then, or since then. He was aware of an aspect of Christianity which he'd given no thought to before – its mercy. It rejected no one. Its churches did not refuse membership to the weak, or even to the vilest of criminals. It offered forgiveness to all who asked for it. But where would he – who in spite of himself had got into the position of aiding the enemies of a Party which meant more than anything else on earth to him – find forgiveness? Maldwyn was waiting for him to speak. Alan said:

'Did you see, before the war, that film called *The Informer*?'

'No; I'm afraid I wasn't able to be much of a film-goer.'

'There is an episode near the end of it which I shall never forget. The main character is a member of the Irish Republican Army who has been betraying his comrades for money, and they have found him out, and he knows they have condemned him to death. The authorities who have employed him are aware that he can be of no further use to them and they don't care what becomes of him. He has no one to turn to. He goes into an empty church and sees, high up on the wall, an image of the Virgin Mary. He comes towards it and kneels on the stone floor beneath it.'

Maldwyn did not say anything, looked steadily and mildly at him.

'But in the Party there can be no forgiveness for those who betray their comrades,' Alan went on.

He stopped, realizing that he might seem to be inviting Maldwyn to offer him Christian consolation and that if Maldwyn were to offer it – even in a comparatively unhackneyed Swedenborgian form – it would be both embarrassing and unacceptable to him. But Maldwyn surprisingly said:

'The Christian hell is not a very forgiving place.'

Had he, in the year since his first visit to Alan and Elsie's house, turned against the Swedenborgianism which he had then thought to be compatible with Marxism? Alan was strangely impelled to come to the defence of Christianity:

'Isn't it Swedenborg's doctrine that God does not send men to hell, and that those who are in hell are there of their own choice, because it suits their natures and because they prefer it to heaven?'

'Yes, though a Marxist might make the point that the human beings whom Swedenborg's God does not prevent from going to hell inflict appalling torments there eternally on one another.'

An ambivalence was detectable in Maldwyn's attitude: he didn't seem wholly to identify himself with the Marxist who might make this point against Swedenborg. He continued:

'Christianity holds men totally responsible for their actions. Whereas Marxism takes the view that men are moulded by their social circumstances and that in the last analysis it's these which are to blame even for the actions of imperialist genocides or of ex-communists who denounce their former comrades to the fascist police.'

In saying this, didn't Maldwyn show himself to be a better Marxist than Alan who had been thinking that there was more mercy in Christianity than in Marxism? And yet Maldwyn gave the impression that at heart he was still a Swedenborgian. He seemed to have accepted Marxism intellectually but not emotionally. Might this be because the Party as it was at present had not given him the opportunity to engage in practical Marxist activity, and because only through such activity can anyone become emotionally a Marxist? Unlike Maldwyn, Alan had joined the Party at a time when it did not seem to have begun to deviate from revolutionary Marxism, and emotionally he had never ceased to be a Marxist, but loyalty to the Party had led him for a while during and after the war into a confused intellectual acceptance of the reformist ideas which the leadership were adopting. Maldwyn, by making him recognize the mercy in Marxism, was helping him towards becoming intellectually a Marxist once again. And Alan, although he felt no nearer to discovering how he could avoid shielding an anti-communist agent, was no longer in despair. And now Maldwyn was saying:

'Suppose there were nothing at all you could do about this

letter, you would still be in a very different position from the I.R.A. man who betrayed his comrades for money.'

'That's certainly true.' Alan was ashamed of having compared himself, by implication, with a man condemned to death.

'But I think there is something you could do,' Maldwyn said. Alan looked at him with doubt and hope.

'You could let the Executive know the contents of the letter without actually putting it into their hands. You could make a summary of it, interspersed with your own comments, and give them that.'

'Then they might demand to see the letter itself.'

'I don't think they will, but if they do you can explain quite firmly to them that you're not prepared to risk having it left lying about at Headquarters.'

Maldwyn, who was evidently confident that Alan, though still hesitant, wouldn't be so for long, added:

'I am sure you would be right to let them know what's in the letter – especially the address of the woman with the cottage.'

'I'll do that.'

Alan felt a great relief, and at the same time a wish to get back to Elsie as soon as possible and to have her opinion about this decision that Maldwyn had helped him to reach.

'I'm very glad I came to have a talk with you,' he said.

He stood up.

'I'm glad too,' Maldwyn said. He carefully folded the letter and returned it to Alan.

As they came out of the room into the hall-passage Alan said:

'I forgot to tell you that besides this letter we've had one from the District Committee – asking us to go up before them next Thursday.'

'That's good news. And I am sure neither of you will allow any worries about this seaman to discourage you from making out the strongest possible case to the Committee for the political stand you've been taking.'

Alan realized with shame that, ever since Elsie had handed him the two letters this afternoon on his return from work, all his feelings of militancy against the leadership's line had been in abatement. Maldwyn, opening the front door for him, added:

'You know that I am on your side. I shall be thinking of you both next Thursday.'

He laid his hand lightly on Alan's elbow.

On the way home Alan's mood was so much less unhopeful than it had been before he'd talked to Maldwyn that it allowed him, when he turned into his home road and saw the railway bridge again, to remember the idea he had had this afternoon for a wholly new approach to the writing of poetry – the idea of using his political experiences and feelings to make poetry instead of trying to use poetry to make political statements. He was even able, before he reached his front gate, to think about the idea sufficiently to convince himself that his previous fear of being led by it into bourgeois aestheticism was groundless, because the political experiences and feelings which he would use to make his poems would be pro-communist and anti-bourgeois.

But he knew that until his and Elsie's meeting with the District Committee was over there could be no hope at all of his being able to start to write a poem.

6

On his way in the bus with Elsie to meet the District Committee Alan did not think about what he and she would say in defence of their opposition to the leadership's line. They sat, without talking much, on a front seat on the top deck; and staring through the broad window he hardly noticed how towards the end of their journey the street lights, though less powerful than the hard pale blue mercury-vapour ones he had seen along a main road half an hour earlier, were brighter against the darkening evening than those had been against the sunset's smoky crimson. He thought about his need to help the Party to frustrate the anti-communist agents he'd unwittingly encouraged. He had not yet followed Maldwyn's advice that he should let the Executive have a summary of the seaman's letter, but he had written a summary, interspersed with his own comments, which was in his pocket now and the first thing he would do when he came into the presence of the Committee would be to hand it to the Chairman. As for any pseudo-Marxist theoretical argument the Committee might produce to rebut his and Elsie's criticisms of the Party's policy, Elsie would certainly answer it with vigour. He would answer it too, but his first duty would be to come to the defence of the Party against anti-communist subversion rather than to defend himself and Elsie who, however Marxist their theoretical views were, had facilitated this subversion by breaking Party rules.

Neither he nor Elsie had previously seen the building where they were due for the meeting; but they were sure they had found it from the moment when, having got off the bus and walked for some while alongside a grimy wall behind which a sunken railway threw up echoes and steam, they first sighted its clean concrete-and-glass front shining in the light of the street lamps. It was new since the war, and had only recently been finished, and it looked like ordinary modern business premises, a box of offices. How different in every way it seemed from the old building in Worship Street which had been destroyed during an air-raid and which, thanks to War Damage compensation money, it had now imposingly replaced. Or was he really remembering the building in Tabernacle Street where the *Daily Worker* offices had been originally before being moved to Worship Street? He had gone there one afternoon in the early nineteen-thirties when he was not yet a Party member. He had intended to buy a copy of the paper but his main purpose had been to find himself, however briefly, among Party members, even if he didn't presume to try to get into conversation with any of them. That former building, with a horse-drawn van from Liverpool Street station moving along the roadway in front of it, had made him think poetically about the history of the London working-class movement – and about his own situation as a young bourgeois, who by daring at last to come to the movement, would extricate himself from the misery of the failure that his upbringing had led him into. He had opened the outer door, had glimpsed a room through the glass panels of another door which he had funked opening, had gone on up the wooden stairs to see if he could discover a room with its door already open, had been given a look of not unfriendly curiosity by a dark-blue-shirted young man passing quickly down the stairs, had soon turned to follow the young man and had been unable to find him again, had then walked out of the building in a state of elation without having gone into any room at all and with a poem beginning to form in his mind about this experience of his. But the present building that he and Elsie were approaching had no poetic appeal for him and would have had none even if he hadn't been on his way to meet the District Committee inside it.

As he looked up towards its bleak front he was not only empty of all poetic emotion but suddenly, with a disappointment so bitter that it temporarily quite overcame his apprehensiveness about confronting the Committee, he knew he would never write the poem he had conceived during his conversation with

Gatten a fortnight before. At the time of his visit to the earlier building he had felt he was beginning to free himself from a life in which he had disastrously made self-fulfilment his main aim, from the poetic life, and to move towards a life in which the cause of the exploited and oppressed would come first for him; yet this poem he'd been hoping to write would have tried to rehabilitate the poetic life, would have assumed that though that life had proved totally unrealizable in the past it would be realizable in the communist future, and that the prospect of it could inspire him to persist in the present anti-capitalist struggle, and that it was the finest life. This poem would have been worthless, an attempt to justify his wholly disgraceful nostalgia for the days before he joined the Party. And the new attitude to the writing of poetry that he'd thought of a week ago when looking at the railway bridge – an attitude that wasn't really new but was very similar to one he'd had in his pre-Marxist days – was worthless too, because if poetic quality rather than political content became his chief concern what guarantee was there that he would use in his poems the political material which could help the Party most at this stage, or even that he would use political material in his poems at all?

The new attitude, he thought just before he and Elsie arrived at the entrance to the building, was nothing more than a return to bourgeois aestheticism. An instant later he forgot about his poetry. Awareness of the imminent encounter with the District Committee overwhelmingly came back to him as Elsie pushed open the outside door and he followed her into the building. They met no one in the entrance hall. They did not know on which floor the meeting was to be held. The doors on the ground floor were all closed. Elsie went towards one of these but Alan said it probably led to where the printing machinery was, and they decided to go upstairs to the first floor. The stairs had concrete steps. Alan thought of the well-worn wooden treads of the staircase of the converted warehouse in Tabernacle Street where the *Daily Worker* had had its first offices. What a pride such a building as this present one would have aroused in him before the war if it had existed then. But now, though he had been a Party member for sixteen years, he could not think of this one as belonging to him at all. He seemed more of a stranger in it than he had seemed in the Tabernacle Street building even during his first diffident visit there; and his estrangement made him afraid. When they reached the top of the stairs he saw a woman with typewriting paper in her hand who was coming towards them along a passage, and he was about to ask her if she knew which room they should go to, but her look showed a remoteness and a faint haughtiness that deterred him. She had the drawn-back glossy black hair and fine features of an aristocratic Victorian beauty. She must have produced a similar impression on Elsie, who said nothing to her either but watched her go into a small office-like room from inside which a voice with an upper-class accent that he assumed to be hers made itself heard immediately afterwards. Possibly she knew why they were here, and perhaps she saw them with contempt as a middle- or lower middle-class couple reverting to the anti-working-class outlook which was typical of the bourgeoisie but which she believed the aristocracy had historically often been free from. They walked on down the passage. A half-open door gave them a glimpse of Sammy Hollingworth, a leading member of the National Executive of the Party, who was standing sideways to them and talking to someone hidden by the door. Though Alan had lost his former admiration for the Party leaders he still could not be quite without awe at the sight of one of them, and neither he nor Elsie thought for a moment now of interrupting Hollingworth to ask him which room the meeting would be in. They went on and came to a wide-open door that revealed a room with several rows of chairs in it; and Alec Murrayfield and Bert Alldiss were sitting alone there next to each other in the middle of the middle row, not talking, like two schoolboys awaiting an awkward interview with the headmaster whom they expected to appear at any moment. Elsie said to them:

'We didn't know you would be here.'

Her tone asked why neither of them had told her and Alan about this beforehand.

'Nor did we until today,' Alec said, in a voice noticeably less animated than usual. 'We both got a note from the District this morning.'

'It was marked "Important".' Bert spoke with a significant grin; and he no longer seemed like a guilty schoolboy – as Alec still did.

The reason why the District had given them such short notice might be, Alan thought, to prevent them from consulting with him and Elsie in advance. But their being summoned to this meeting was a good sign: it meant that not only Bert Alldiss but more unexpectedly Alec Murrayfield too must have been expressing disagreement with the leadership's line more strongly and openly among Party members than he and Elsie had been aware of, strongly and openly enough to make the leadership take notice.

'Have you seen anything of the District Committee yet?' Alan asked, attempting a lightness of tone he didn't quite achieve.

'We're not going to have a meeting with the Committee,' Bert said. 'Only with Sammy Hollingworth. So we were told by the woman comrade we spoke to when we came upstairs.'

'Why Hollingworth?' Alan asked, surprised. 'He's not on the London District.'

'If they need to bring in such an important member of the National Executive to deal with us,' Bert said, 'that just shows what a dangerous lot they think we are – with our stick of Australian dynamite.' He grinned again, while Alec seemed to wince.

The slight relief Alan at first felt on hearing that the meeting would be with Hollingworth alone gave place soon to a disappointment that now he and Elsie would not have the opportunity of putting their case to a Committee which he was sure must include at least one or two members who would have been capable of recognizing that he and she were right and who would have been honest enough to support them. He had little hope that Sammy Hollingworth would be open to persuasion at all. However the essential thing this evening, he remembered as he and Elsie sat down next to Bert and Alec, wasn't to justify himself but to submit to the Party which he had harmed through his indiscipline. Elsie he knew was in no mood to submit, and he illogically couldn't regret this. He wouldn't be sorry either if Bert and Alec were to show some obstinacy. He couldn't help hoping that the silence in which they had been sitting together, and into which they had now relapsed, didn't signify that Alec felt contrition and that his feeling had to some extent infected Bert. Elsie was silent too, from tenseness before the confrontation with Hollingworth and certainly not from contrition. Alan looked round at the walls of the room, which were bare except where strips of white paper with current Party slogans printed on them were stuck along the upper line of the dado. One of these slogans had long ceased to appear in the Party press but it was evidently still current here in this building that the Party leaders frequented. It consisted of the three words 'Produce or Perish'. Alan's own contrition would not have overcome an impulse he had to point this slogan out triumphantly to Elsie, and to Bert and Alec, but before he could do so Sammy Hollingworth walked into the room.

The skin on Hollingworth's forehead and cheeks was slightly brown as though he had just had a long open-air weekend in the autumn sun. His expression was not at all grim. His clothes were neat, and he seemed like an office-worker about to start on a merely routine bit of work. Someone else walked into the room immediately after him, whom Alan did not look at until Hollingworth had come up to the table in front of the rows of chairs, and whom then with revulsion and alarm he saw to be Les Gatten. Gatten must have been the person Hollingworth had been talking to in the room with the half-open door which Alan and Elsie had passed on their way along the passage. From this assumption Alan leapt to the suspicion that there must be complicity between Hollingworth and Gatten, and that Hollingworth too was possibly a police agent. He tried to calm himself with the thought that even if the suspicion were a certainty there would be no justification for the panic he was on the verge of. But he did not become calmer until he remembered that Hollingworth had been a trusted leading member of the Party for a long time and had done very effective work in its service before the war, and that there were no known grounds whatsoever for suspecting him of this kind of treachery. Soon, as Hollingworth sat down at the table, a less improbable explanation of Gatten's presence occurred to Alan : Gatten had been invited to this meeting because Hollingworth intended that no distinction should be made between him and Alan and Elsie and that the three of them should be treated as being equally guilty of conspiring against the Party. But even this explanation, Alan recognized, might be nothing more than a persecutory fantasy of his, and the truth might simply be that what he had reported about Gatten to Mike Tarrant at District Headquarters had never been passed on to Hollingworth. Alan took out from his pocket the piece of notepaper on which he had written a summary of the seaman's letter. At the top of the paper he quickly added in pencil the words: *Has Comrade Tarrant told you that Gatten is a detective?* Before he could get up from his chair to put the paper on the table, Hollingworth said to all the five of them sitting in front of him:

'I don't think I need spend any time telling you why you have been asked to come here this evening.' The acidity which was perceptible in this quietly spoken opening sentence was neutralized as he continued: 'We may as well start at once by hearing from Comrade Mrs Sebrill just what her objections to the Party's policy are.'

He sounded unhostile, not quite as if he thought there was nothing at all disreputable about a rank-and-file Party member's venturing to disagree with the Party's policy but as if he wanted to emphasize his intention of respecting her right as a Party member to explain her conduct fully. Alan hurriedly got up and went to the table to hand him the paper; and was conscious of being watched by Gatten who had chosen a chair at the end of the front row, nearer to Hollingworth than to Alec and Bert.

'Please read this first,' Alan said urgently.

Hollingworth gave no sign of surprise or annoyance at the interruption. He took the paper and put it down on the table, not directly in front of him but to one side as though he meant to look at it later. However he began to read it at once. His head, when turned sideways and inclined downwards, lost the suggestion of sleekness it had had when seen full-face. A tuft of stiff black hair rose from the middle of his forehead, and his prominent nose had an arrogantly curved nostril which exposed the cartilage of the septum near the tip and made Alan think of the beak of a predatory bird. Hollingworth read quickly, and had finished reading very soon after Alan had sat down again. Then, as though he'd found what he'd read quite irrelevant, he looked at Elsie and said:

'Would you begin now.' He added, in a way that indicated he was singling her out as the leader: 'I'll hear the others after I've heard you.'

Alan agitatedly protested:

'I'm not willing to criticize the Party in the presence of a police agent. Gatten admits he has been a detective. I couldn't feel free to say what I want to while he's in the room.'

Hollingworth appeared to be on the point of dismissing Alan's protest, but instead he turned towards Gatten and said in a startlingly loud voice:

'Who sent you?' He leant with his forearms on the table, and he jutted his head forward as he repeated even more vehemently: 'WHO SENT YOU?' Gatten didn't answer, and Hollingworth went on: 'It was the Jugoslav embassy, wasn't it?'

Ridiculous though this accusation seemed to Alan he was inhibited from feeling disapproval of it by his gratification at the vigour of the attack on Gatten – who still wouldn't answer, but perhaps had a very slight smirk on his face. Hollingworth suddenly abandoned the attack and turned to Elsie, asking her again to begin, which she immediately did, regardless of Gatten's presence. Alan didn't renew his protest, because now that she had begun he didn't want to lessen the effect of what she was saying by interrupting her.

'I would like to make clear straight away that I'm not denying there has been an improvement in the Party's line since a year ago. But the wrongness of the policies that were laid down in *Britain's Way Forward* has not been admitted frankly or fully enough yet, and there has been no attempt to "discuss the causes of our errors, to analyse the situation in which they arose, to consider carefully how to remedy them'." Though there was boldness in her words, and though she showed little of the deference which was usual from a rank-and-file Party member when addressing one of the leaders and which she had been so careful to show in her interview with Digby Kelsall two years before, her voice had a modesty in it befitting a communist who expresses criticism of other communists. 'What Lenin said, and Stalin repeated in *Foundations of Leninism*, about the attitude that communists should adopt towards their own mistakes, seems to have been overlooked. Consequently some dangerous mistakes are still being made by our Party.'

It was fortunate that Hollingworth had not mentioned the duplication and circulation by her and Alan of the Australian criticisms. If he had, Alan felt, Elsie would have had to begin more defensively, and less advantageously. Perhaps Hollingworth's motive in not mentioning the Australians might be to avoid drawing attention to the fact that the British Party's policy was being criticized not merely by two insignificant rank-and-filers but also and on exactly the same grounds by the leadership of a brother Party. She went on to say that the most striking change in the Party's policy since a year ago had been the abandonment of the campaign for increased production. Leading comrades were no longer urging the workers 'to have confidence in their own land, to take a pride in building it up' or insisting that 'certainly the politically-conscious working-class will work harder, will bear cuts to solve the crisis' or persisting in the attitude towards strikes which had been expressed by one leading Party member who had referred to the strikers at the Grimethorpe colliery as 'enemy miners'. Her not mentioning the names of the Party leaders from whom she was quoting – McNarney, Hurley and Baxter – no doubt showed a wish to avoid planting an unendurable sting in Hollingworth, but the quotations seemed to Alan to be on the verge of being provocative and he felt some alarm. Hollingworth, however, gave no sign of anger, appeared attentive and calm. She said next:

'Fortunately, after the Nine Parties' statement was issued last October, our Party here came to recognize that Britain is in the camp of reaction, an ally of American imperialism, and that increased production in Britain "would not be used for the benefit of the people".' She couldn't keep triumph altogether out of her voice at this point, but Hollingworth remained impassive. She continued: 'The production drive, which was so dominant a part of our policy, had to be dropped; but it was dropped rather reluctantly, and for a time there were even attempts by some comrades to suggest that though it was now incorrect it had been correct previously. There was never an open admission that it had been quite unMarxist from the start. No discussion of the reasons why such a mistaken policy had been adopted was ever initiated by the leadership.' She paused for Hollingworth to deny this if he could, but he didn't. 'What were the reasons?' she then asked. 'I feel that one of them may have been that the national unity necessary during the war against fascism to some extent blinded us to the realities of the post-war class struggle. But the most important reason of all has been the neglect, by leadership and rank-and-file alike, of theory. If we had remembered Lenin's teachings on the State and on the role of reformist parties such as the Labour Party we could not have fallen into the error of urging the workers to produce to their utmost under a Labour government.'

Next she gave a brief summary of Lenin's theory of the State, in a tone which she obviously tried hard to keep from seeming didactic or arrogant. When she had finished her summary she said:

'Reformists believe — or at least those of them who do sincerely want socialism and are not just political careerists — that the organs of the State in a capitalist country, including its armed forces and police, are impartial and that its parliament and Civil Service can be used to abolish capitalism. What's more, they believe that Socialism can be achieved *only* through the constitutional machinery of the existing State. But the reality is that when a reformist party "comes to power" in a capitalist parliament it finds itself faced with the choice either of adopting a policy helpful to monopoly capitalism or of resigning office and going into parliamentary "opposition" once again. And the same choice would face even a government of left-wing reformists who genuinely wanted socialism, but who rather than call upon the working-class to help them break the resistance of the State would call upon the State to break any unconstitutional action by the working-class.'

Hollingworth had brought a metal-capped pencil out of his pocket, not apparently in order to write anything with it. He was twisting it between his thumb and fingers, metal cap uppermost. But his gaze, which was directed at the pencil and not at Elsie, showed no impatience. She continued, in a voice deliberately modest still, though there was nothing concessive in the sense of what she said:

'The main lessons we ought to have learnt from our mistake of campaigning for increased production are that there is an urgent need at all levels of the Party for an intensified study of Leninist theory, and that the rank-and-file has the duty as well as the right to use its critical faculties when considering statements of policy. But there has as yet been no call from the leadership for intensified study. And as a result we are making further mistakes in policy. The most dangerous of these is our demand for a new Labour government of the Left.'

At this point Hollingworth dropped the metal-capped pencil on to the table and began to speak, even more loudly than when he had spoken to Gatten. Thrusting his face forward in Elsie's direction he accused her of sectarianism and of infantile leftism. But his outburst, in spite of its suddenness and its great vehemence, had something unspontaneous and histrionic in it. As he spoke he moved his fist violently up and down, never quite hitting the surface of the table but seeming about to do so at any moment.

An impulse of disgust caused Alan to make a contrary side-to-side waving movement with his own hand, as if cutting across the vertical movement of Hollingworth's fist, and he said:

'Can't we discuss all this reasonably? We aren't at a public meeting.'

Unexpectedly, Hollingworth at once brought his hand to rest on the table and in a voice no louder than Alan's he preposterously stated:

'It's just my natural manner of expressing myself.' Nevertheless his voice did not become loud again, nor did he resume thumping the air with his fist, as he went on to tell Elsie: 'To refuse to cooperate with the Leftwing of the Labour Party against the right-wing Labour leaders is to reject completely the line laid down in the Report of the Nine Parties' Conference.'

'I'm fully in favour of joint action with left-wing Labour Party members,' Elsie said. 'But shouldn't our aim be to unite them with us in activities which will help the development of a mass struggle against capitalism, not to unite ourselves with them in an attempt at perpetuating the illusion that a reformist government, if only it were composed of left-wingers instead of right-wingers, would introduce socialism ?'

Hollingworth answered her as though she had said something different from this.

'Only anarchists are contemptuous of parliamentary activity.'

His voice remained fairly quiet, and his words were not vituperative, but he unmistakably meant her to understand that the line she was taking had gone beyond the limits permissible to a Party member.

'I'm very well aware of Lenin's teaching that communists should try to use bourgeois parliaments as places from which to make propaganda against capitalism,' she said. 'But he also taught that effective action against capitalism can only come from the working-class and the mass of people, led by the Party.'

Hollingworth again, more completely this time, ignored what she said.

'And what is all this talk about a production drive ?' he asked. 'Your suggestion that the Party's aim has been to urge the workers to produce to their utmost is absolutely false.'

Alan expected him to go on to qualify this astounding statement in some way. But he didn't, and Elsie at last said :

'I have just given several quotations from speeches by leading Party comrades which show conclusively how great an emphasis the Party placed on the need for increased production a year ago.'

'You are playing with words. You are misrepresenting the sense of what these comrades were saying. Anyone can pick out sentences here and there from a speech and make it seem to mean the opposite of what was intended.'

Elsie appeared to be too amazed to retort to this. But now Bert Alldiss intervened:

'There's something here I would like to read out.'

He was holding a copy of *Britain's Way Forward*. He put on his glasses more quickly than he usually managed to. He didn't have to search through the pages for the passage he wanted: the book came open at it immediately, from having been opened in the same place so often before. He began:

'This is what Comrade Jimmy McNarney says here:

The organized workers need to take the initiative now, begin to clear up their own industry and show the Government the way to set about it. It is up to the lads on the job to make the pace. They know where the hold-ups are; they need to smash through them as they did during the Second World War.'

Bert, unlike Elsie, made no attempt to sound modest, was un-inhibitedly indignant at Hollingworth's blatant twisting. He continued reading:

'But I know good trade unionists who argue "That's all very well, Jimmy, but what good is it if we produce more when there isn't a plan? What good is it having a production drive if we have a wrong foreign policy which is going to land us in the soup, no mat-ter how much we produce?" And it is also argued: "If we fight for more efficient production now, won't we be strengthening the Labour leaders in carrying out their reactionary policy abroad and giving in to the capitalists at home? Won't we just be making more profits for the capitalists?"'

It was very evident that Bert was in fullest agreement with these good trade unionists whom McNarney had quoted. His enthusiasm for them seemed to make him forget for a moment that his main purpose in reading this passage had been to give the lie to Hollingworth's assertion that the Party had never urged the workers to increase production under the Labour Gov-ernment. However, he remembered his purpose and read on from McNarney.

'I would like to remind these trade union comrades that just the same arguments were used when the Communist Party launched its great war-time drive for production and the opening of the Second Front.'

Hollingworth interrupted:

'You're taking all that out of context.'

He was unemphatic, almost uninterested, as if to convey that he saw Bert as no more than a minor culprit whose simplicity had enabled the Sebrills to lead him astray. Bert gave Hollingworth a suspicious and puzzled look which Hollingworth conveniently interpreted as indicating that Bert didn't understand the word 'context'.

'By picking on that passage you've just read, and omitting what comes before it and after it, you are giving a wrong impression of Comrade McNarney's meaning,' Hollingworth explained.

He didn't intend this as an invitation to Bert to continue reading, but Bert did continue. Bert read slowly, not just because reading aloud wasn't easy for him but because he was intent on bringing out the sense. He read the whole of the next paragraph, which urged militant trade unionists in the building industry 'to set the example in recruiting labour for the housing jobs and away from luxury work'. When he'd finished the paragraph, Hollingworth said to him briskly:

'That puts rather a different light on the passage you read first, doesn't it?'

For answer, Bert went on reading:

'The miners' production efforts have shown the way. If it was right for this section of workers to do their damndest to get the coal – and nobody thought otherwise when the miners were hacking their way through the snowdrifts to get to work – then it is right for others.'

Bert stopped, and gave Hollingworth a look as if to say 'wriggle out of that one if you can'. But Hollingworth said:

'Go on reading.'

However, Elsie intervened.

'Of course if he goes on reading long enough he'll sooner or later come to a passage which isn't about production, but this won't alter the fact that in the paragraph he read out first McNarney is urging trade unionists to step up production under a reactionary Social-Democratic government in a monopoly capitalist State.'

Hollingworth turned on her, saying venomously though without raising his voice:

'This is sheer quibbling and pedantry. This is the wilful blindness of the doctrinaire leftist intellectual who concentrates on the part and refuses to see the whole.'

He was obviously not sorry to have the renewed opportunity of dealing with her rather than with Bert, whom he couldn't have accused of being an intellectual. Her face showed an undisguised contempt for what he had said, though she declined to retort to him. He didn't turn to Bert again, but spoke next to Gatten instead:

'Comrade Gatten, now perhaps we can hear from you why you have been supporting the Sebrills in their attack on Party policy.'

His calling Gatten 'comrade' though certainly now knowing him to be a detective seemed to prove finally that Hollingworth's intention in having him at this meeting was to present him as someone who however disreputable he might be was less so than Elsie and Alan whose follower he was in a plot against the Party. Gatten began by saying he would admit to having been convinced by the Sebrills that the Party's post-war line conflicted with Lenin's theory of the State. He went on to summarize the theory, or rather to repeat the summary of it that Elsie had just given, but his version was confused – deliberately confused, it must have been, since he had shown previously in conversations with Alan and Elsie that he understood the theory very well. Possibly he was trying to present himself as a muddled political innocent whom the Sebrills had all too easily been able to mislead. He spoke fast and softly, sitting very upright on his chair. His fresh-coloured young-looking face under its close-cut yet still wavy golden hair was the picture of candour. He ended by stressing that everything he had done in connection with distributing the Australian criticisms had been done with the agreement and under the guidance of the Sebrills. Hollingworth quickly, perhaps in order to ensure that Gatten shouldn't suddenly prolong his speech and add details about these criticisms, then asked if any other comrade wanted to say anything.

The only comrade who hadn't yet spoken was Alec Murrayfield. Alan looked at him, hoping that Alec would find a subtler
and more effective way of countering Hollingworth's tactics than
Elsie or Bert or Alan himself had found. But Alec said nothing.
His face appeared almost to have a smile on it, a superior smile.
He gave an impression of tolerant wisdom, of exalted detach-
ment, as though everything that had happened in this room had
been so well observed and so fully understood by him that he was
not prepared to condemn anyone here. His high-arched eyebrows seemed to rise higher up his forehead than ever. Though
Alan himself, because of Gatten's presence, had been unwilling
to argue with Hollingworth, he couldn't help feeling anger at
Alec's lack of fight. Hollingworth didn't even glance towards
Alec. He must have known him to be intellectually and as a
speaker the most formidable potential opponent in the room,
and was no doubt glad that he wouldn't speak. After a very short
pause, Hollingworth firmly told them all:

'Having heard what you have to say, I'm confirmed in what
I thought before – the lot of you are in touch with the Jugoslav
embassy and have been carrying out its instructions.'

No one answered him. To deny the accusation, Alan felt,
might give it a certain status, might promote it from the realm
of the fantastic to the realm of the arguable. The others probably felt as he did. Alec seemed about to say something, but did
not. The corners of Gatten's mouth showed the same slight
smirk – perhaps more distinctly now – as when Hollingworth
had made a similar accusation against him alone. Elsie looked
as contemptuous as when Hollingworth had told her she was
quibbling. Bert's furrowed forehead and his straight gaze at
Hollingworth seemed to state 'I see you now for what you are!'
Hollingworth made no further reference to the Jugoslav embassy
but said in conclusion, almost casually:

'If any of you, after this evening, continue to put about in
the Party the ideas you have been putting to me, you will be expelled from the Party.'

All the combativeness that Alan had been feeling though not
expressing was abruptly quelled by these words. He forgot the

resentment and disgust that Hollingworth's tactics had caused in him. He remembered the intention he had had before the meeting – of making amends for the harm his factionalism had done to the Party and of submitting unreservedly to Party discipline once again. But it was a need for self-justification as well as for submission that made him break the silence which continued after Hollingworth's quiet threat.

'What we have been doing,' he told Hollingworth, 'has at least had the result of exposing these anti-communist agents who have been trying to use us to disrupt the Party.'

Hollingworth gave a histrionically loud, jeeringly ironic laugh, triumphing rather than venomous. Then he stood up, indicating that the meeting was over.

This laugh, which momentarily revived resentment in Alan, made him realize that to submit unreservedly to the Party wasn't going to be easy for him. But the alternative to submission would be unbearable. He felt he could not live outside the Party. And a need came to him to make Hollingworth understand the depth of his love for the Party and the strength of his reluctance to oppose its line. He went up to the table behind which Hollingworth was standing, and said to him:

'I didn't *want* to disagree with the Party. That's the last thing I could ever have wanted.' He found himself at a loss for invulnerable words to tell Hollingworth why this was so. He could not even begin to explain what the Party had meant for him, how it had saved him as a young man from self-centred worthlessness and suicidal despair, how he wanted to live and die for it still. He eventually succeeded in saying:

'I did my best to believe that the Party's post-war policy was correct, but I wasn't able to. Oh if only you could convince me that I and not the policy was wrong.'

The stare that Hollingworth gave him seemed to show at first astonishment and then a condescending pity, as if to say 'You poor simple little fool.' Or was Alan misinterpreting the stare, and might there be in it a sudden brief memory of an earlier period in Hollingworth's political life when he himself had taken Marxist principles seriously? What Hollingworth now said, however, did nothing to confirm either interpretation.

'Have you any industrial contacts?'

Alan didn't at once understand, but then he guessed that the question must be designed to discover whether he had been in a position to spread his anti-reformist ideas among industrial workers and trade unionists, who if they began to criticize the leadership's line might be more difficult to cope with than middle-class intellectuals were.

'No,' Alan not quite truthfully said.

The thought came to him that there was no reason for him to continue to stand here talking to Hollingworth. He regretted having talked to him at all in the way he just had. He had humiliated himself by revealing so ingenuously what he felt to Hollingworth. He turned from the table, and immediately Alec who must have been standing close behind him stepped forward to take his place. Alan didn't wait to hear what Alec had to say to Hollingworth, but went straight towards Elsie who was with Bert Alldiss near the door of the room. He was aware as he went that Gatten, who had not yet got up from the chair at the end of the front row, was watching him – not so much with hostility as with a kind of temperate investigatory curiosity. Elsie and Bert were not talking, but her tenseness suggested that it was only Hollingworth's presence which was restraining her from coming out with everything she felt about him, and when Alan joined her and Bert she at once moved to the door, not waiting for Alec to accompany them though he would be returning by the same bus route as she and Alan would. Alec's lack of fight had evidently disappointed her as sharply as it had Alan. Bert and Alan followed her out of the room and quickly along the passage, and perhaps because of the possibility that the aristo-cratic woman comrade might still be about none of them spoke until they had come down the concrete stairs and across the entrance hall and through the doorway that led to the street. Outside the building they stopped, and Elsie released her fury.

'This is beyond anything I could have imagined that even the most unMarxist among the Party leaders would ever have been capable of,' she said.

Alan asked Bert what impression Hollingworth had made on him.

'He couldn't answer any of our points,' Bert said, 'and he didn't try to.'

Bert began to recapitulate the main points that Elsie and he had made and to recall how Hollingworth had evaded each of these. There was no note of outrage or of rancour in his voice, though he did sound sardonic. He was able to see right through Hollingworth but he regarded Hollingworth's tactics and attitude as a political fact which must be coolly and warily reckoned with. Alan, while listening to Bert with admiration, was increasingly conscious that if they continued standing here outside the entrance of the building Alec Murrayfield or Gatten or worse still Hollingworth himself would soon come out upon them. Unfortunately Bert, to get home, would be taking a different bus route from Alan and Elsie's, and the stop to which he would walk to catch his bus was in the opposite direction from the one where they would catch theirs. However, Alan interrupted him:

'We must meet again soon to talk more about all this. I wish Elsie and I could come back with you now, but Miss Sims is sitting-in for us and will be expecting us.'

'I'll be round tomorrow evening at your house,' Bert said. The glance he gave towards the entrance doors of the building seemed to show that he was no keener than Alan to remain talking here until one or more of the others came out.

As soon as Alan and Elsie had parted from him, and he and they were walking away in opposite directions along the pavement, Elsie said to Alan:

'This evening we have reached a dialectical point of change. Over the past two years we have been recognizing gradually that the Party leaders have become opportunists and reformists, and that they're unwilling to practise self-criticism or to allow the rank-and-file to criticize them, but now during the past hour we've been able to see that they've also become out-and-out political tricksters, as bad as the worst of the bourgeois politicians and much cruder than most of those.'

Her anger was inspiriting to Alan, who said:

'Hollingworth's brazen denial that the Party had ever had a production drive – I can still hardly believe I didn't mishear

159

him. And to think that there all the time on the wall of the room was that slogan "Produce or Perish".'

'Yes, I remembered that at the end of the meeting. But even if I'd been able to include it among my other production-drive quotations it wouldn't have hindered him from accusing me of quibbling. Three little words like those wouldn't have been much of an obstacle to someone who could pretend to be convinced that we have been acting under instructions from the Jugoslav embassy.'

'And the appalling thing is that if there had been Party members at the meeting who hadn't known us they would almost certainly have believed we actually were in touch with the embassy.'

Detestation of Hollingworth made them walk on in silence for a while, till Elsie said:

'The kind of politicians that Hollingworth and McNarney and Dunstable and the others have become are unfit to be in the Party at all, let alone to be its leaders.'

But as soon as she'd said this the objection suggested itself to Alan that if he and she were to regard themselves as no longer bound to feel any loyalty at all towards the elected leadership of the Party they would in effect be renouncing their allegiance to the Party itself. He tried to think of some excuse for the conduct of the leaders, something which would mitigate Elsie's total condemnation of them.

'Perhaps they sincerely believe that their new reformist policy is the only one that can bring about socialism in Britain,' he said, 'and they would like to find Marxist arguments to refute us, but they can't, and this makes them see us as all the more of a menace to the Party, a menace which justifies tactics they would have had scruples against using in other circumstances.'

'I suspect they see us less as a menace to the Party than to themselves and to their power in the Party.'

'If it were just power they were after wouldn't they be in some other organization not quite so small as the present British Communist Party?'

'I don't think the power they have now seems all that negligible to them. Remember, they have "international contacts".

And the portraits of some of them have been carried on banners in processions through the cities of various capitalist as well as communist countries.'

'That is a frightening thought. And also it almost makes me doubt whether we mightn't after all somehow be wrong about them. They are honoured in other countries by communist leaders whom we trust and admire. Can they really have become what we think they are? How *could* it have happened?'

'It could have happened in the war, after Britain became an ally of the Soviet Union against Hitler. They suddenly ceased to be political pariahs and were accepted as useful members of society; they sat on committees with capitalists, were able to make their contribution to the national war effort. And the experience was very sweet to them. Remember that revealing remark of McNarney's just after the war at a Party conference, when he was answering some comrade of the "good trade unionist" type: "We have been *against* for so long, why can't we at last be *for*?"'

'Yes, I know you're right, that's how it must have happened, and they are what we think they are. But however bad they may be, by opposing them we have given help to enemies of communism.'

'Any harm that Gatten and the seaman have done to the Party,' Elsie said decisively, 'is nothing compared with what Hollingworth and his like have done, and will continue doing if they aren't opposed.'

'But if we go on opposing them we shall be expelled from the Party.'

Elsie didn't answer. She and Alan had arrived at their bus stop. Three other people were already waiting there, one of whom – a small man with an evening newspaper sticking out of his duffle-coat pocket – looked up at the sound of the word 'expelled'. Alan and Elsie stood silent till the bus came, knowing that once they were inside it its noise would enable them to talk privately again. But just before the bus appeared they saw Alec Murrayfield approaching along the pavement. He began to run when he heard the bus. He ran like an athlete, with an impressively easy stride – perhaps he had at some time taken up amateur athletics for a while, just as he had taken up acting, archaeology, gliding and even medical studies, each for a while. Elsie, without greeting him at all, got on to the bus before he reached it, and Alan followed her up the steps to the top deck. Alec followed them both. Elsie went to sit on the window side of an empty double-seat half-way along the deck. There was another empty double-seat immediately behind the one she'd chosen; and Alan, in order to avoid the appearance of wanting to exclude Alec rudely from their company, chose to sit behind her. Alec sat down next to her. After giving him a brief glance she looked out of the window, as though intending not to talk with him; but curiosity about why he had behaved as he had at the meeting must have made her change her mind and she turned towards him again and Alan heard her ask his opinion of Hollingworth. With a smile, and in a genially loud voice, Alec said:

'What a charming chap Sammy is.'

'Charming!'

Like Alan, she must for an instant have supposed Alec was being sarcastic – before she astoundedly realized he was being perfectly serious. She turned curtly away from him and stared out of the window. Alan, to whom Alec's remark seemed almost insane in its inappropriateness, tried hard to think of anything about Hollingworth that could justify anyone in feeling that he had charm. Perhaps he had it in private when he was with personal friends or with his wife and children. Also he might have it when he was with other Party leaders, or even – yes, this was quite probable – with rank-and-file Party members who had a properly deferential attitude towards the leadership and didn't question the correctness of Party policies. 'Private faces in public places,' Alan thought, parodying a poet of the nineteen-thirties, 'are slyer and nastier than public faces in private places.'

During the rest of the time that Alan and Elsie were on the bus, Alec made several attempts to talk with her but she wouldn't answer him, not even monosyllabically. The stop at which she and Alan had to get off the bus came before the stop at which Alec had to, and she did just audibly answer his 'good night', as she stood up from her seat to go past him to the gangway. Alan answered it too, more audibly. As soon as he and Elsie had stepped on to the pavement, and even before the bus had moved away from them, she angrily began to express her opinion of Alec; and she continued until after they had turned the corner where their home road met the bus route. At first Alan's feelings were entirely with her in her attack on how Alec had behaved both this evening and also during most of the time since the start of their dispute with the Party. However, it seemed to him as she continued that she was condemning not only the apparently sycophantic way in which Alec had submitted to Hollingworth but even the whole principle of submission to Party discipline – she was condemning, consciously or not, Alan's own attitude at the meeting. And this made him want to try to think of some defence for Alec. As they were walking under the railway bridge he said:

'It's possible he hasn't given up the idea of opposing the leadership's line but means to oppose it by more subtle – and less vulnerable – methods than ours.'

'It's much more likely his motives are what you once said they are: he needs at any price to avoid the risk of a break with the Party because only by working for the Party is he able to justify to himself the kind of "free life" – free from economic compulsion – that his money allows him to live.'

'I know I once said that,' Alan admitted, 'but I think it was very unjust. I'm sure his loyalty to the Party is disinterested.'

'If it is, it's still very different from the loyalty of a working-class comrade like Bert Alldiss. When someone like Bert sees through the leadership he's not prevented from standing up to them by fears that he'll be accused of behaving with the disloyalty typical of a vacillating bourgeois intellectual.'

'We've no grounds at all for thinking that this is how Alec feels.'

'Then what *is* the explanation of his nauseating remark that Hollingworth is a charming chap?'

'Perhaps he doesn't trust us any more. Perhaps he has plans for carrying on the attack we've begun against the leadership's line but doesn't want to take us into his confidence, because of the discredit we've brought upon ourselves by cooperating with Gatten.'

'That's nonsense.'

'It may be. And yet, after you last went to see Alec and Iris at their house you were sure that they already knew we were right and that they themselves would soon be opposing the leadership.'

Elsie did not answer this. Alan wondered whether she might be angry with him also. Neither of them said anything further during the short remainder of their walk from the railway bridge to the gate of their front garden. As soon as they were inside their house Miss Sims came towards them along the hall passage. Elsie did not ask her the usual question 'All quiet?' but Miss Sims said as usual, 'The children have been very good.' Miss Sims smiled, not in the least put out by the distraitness she must have noticed in Elsie and Alan. There was an almost shaming meekness about her, as of an ageing domestic servant in a pre-war bourgeois household. Alan took down her outdoor coat from the coatrack near the front door, and he helped her on with it, pulling it up carefully over her rounded shoulders.

Elsie, after seeing Miss Sims out from the front door and saying good-bye, immediately turned and hurried into the front sitting-room. Alan followed her, not so quickly, and saw her pull open the lid of the bureau in the corner and fetch out her Party card from the pigeonhole where she always kept it (unlike Alan who carried his about with him in his pocket). She held the card out at the full length of both her arms for a moment, and then vigorously tore it across. He recognized that besides anger there was in her a sense of the drama of her action. Nevertheless, having torn the card into two pieces she did not throw them to the ground or into the wastepaper basket, though to have flung them away from her would have been a natural completion to the rhythm of her movement. Perhaps she was inhibited by the beginnings of an awareness of the terror she had caused in Alan. He felt as if he was losing her, as if she was falling into a limitless void which he too was on the brink of. He said desperately:

'But how can you bear to live outside the Party?'

'One thing I shall do now is to go back to teaching.'

'What good will that be if you've abandoned the political fight?'

'I shan't abandon it. I shall carry it on as an individual. I shall try to have some political influence in the staff room. And I could become active in the Union.'

She realized how inadequate this sounded, and she added:

'I would try to start a new and genuinely Marxist-Leninist Party – but for the fact that the Soviet leadership still seems to support the policy of the British Party. We can't go against the Soviet leadership. That would be futile.'

'I can't believe that Stalin approves of the British Party's line, but I think conditions aren't ripe for a new Marxist-Leninist Party here.'

'No, perhaps they aren't,' she had to agree.

'I assume that though Stalin must disapprove of the line he doesn't disapprove sufficiently to think that he ought to interfere. And for as long as he doesn't repudiate the British Party I don't feel that I can.

'But we've seen tonight how utterly rotten it has become.'

'We might still be able to do more good in the Party than out of it. I can't leave it.'

'You know what will happen if you stay in it. The leadership won't just forgive and forget and leave you in peace. They'll send someone down to the Branch to condemn our views and to put the comrades right about us. And you'll have to recant.'

'I think I would be prepared to do that – as a subterfuge.'

'No, you couldn't. Some kinds of subterfuge might be allowable, but to pretend to agree with reformist ideas and policies would be a betrayal of Marxism.'

Alan couldn't avoid recognizing that she was right. And the terror which had come upon him when he had seen her tear up her Party card returned to him more strongly. He felt that he was losing himself, that he was becoming purposeless and helpless. Outside the Party there could be no way for him to continue the political fight. Any hope of continuing it in his poetry seemed to him now to have ended with his discovery earlier this evening that the poem he had recently wanted to write, and had believed to be so much more promising than the other poems he had conceived and rejected during the past two years, was just as impossible as the rest. He was purposeless and he was a deserter from the cause of the exploited and the oppressed. At this thought, a rage against himself arose in him which was stronger than his terror; and he began pacing about the room, oblivious of Elsie, and soon he went striding out into the hall passage and towards the door of the back sitting-room.

As he pushed open this door his rage against himself became rage against the poem whose failure had left him helpless at a time not only when poetry was essential to him if he was to carry on the political fight but when his being forced to leave the Party offered him more freedom to write poetry than he had had for sixteen years. Impossible and repulsive though this poem was, however, it still seemed to him to have been less unpromising than the other poems he had conceived and rejected. It was an advance on those, was perhaps a little nearer to being possible than they had been. Did its failure really prove that any further attempt on his part to write poetry for communism would be futile? What kind of Marxist-Leninist would he be if he allowed himself to make such a despairing assumption?

He went into the back sitting-room without switching on the electric light. The curtains were not drawn across the windows at the far end, and he came to a stop there, staring out through the conservatory into the dark garden. In the distance, beyond the garden fence and beyond the playing-field, street lamps were shining; and where the brightness from these was unintercepted by the leaves of elm trees each of them appeared as a small central dazzle with minutely fine spicules of light radiating from it. They were like insects on fire. Looking at them, he knew that he would go on trying to write poetry. He had no sudden easy hope that he would succeed. He was sure that a far greater effort than he had ever made before would be required of him. If necessary he would take a term off from teaching – this would be financially possible now that Elsie had decided to teach again – and he would work twelve hours a day until he had produced one satisfactory poem, however short. He might even take a whole year off. But the most important thing was that from tomorrow on he must, in his free time, give himself utterly to solving the problem of how to write poetry for communism. This would be his political work. And also in a sense it would be his Party work. 'Even though I shall no longer be in the Party,' he thought, 'as a poet I shall still be able to serve it.'

No fears of failure attacked Alan at the beginning of his year's leave of absence from teaching, even though in the two years since he had left the Party all his attempts to write poetry had come to nothing. During the first three weeks of his freedom, while he was staying in the Sussex village to which he travelled down with Elsie and the children immediately after the end of the summer term at his school, there were mornings when he woke singing – not quite aloud (on each occasion Elsie who was already awake said she had not heard him), but the movements of his lips and throat were as though he was singing and the tune was loud and happy in his head. His not knowing anything clearly yet about the first poem he would try to write now, except that it would be a poem in support of the Party, did not worry him, and he felt no need to be in a hurry to arrive at a definite and detailed conception of it. For five days he gave as little thought as he could to poetry; and when on the sixth day he went with his notebook after breakfast to settle down for three hours by himself, in a room which the elderly woman owner of the house that he and Elsie were temporarily renting had referred to in a letter as the parlour, he spent less time trying to conceive a poem than trying to think why this parlour so insistently and poignantly reminded him of the seaside house where more than twenty years before he had gone to live the poetic life at the invitation of his friend Richard. But the longer he sat gazing around him the less resemblance he found between what he saw here and the room where he had sat with Richard in that other house: here above the mantelpiece there was no big gilt-framed mirror with swans among green reeds painted on its lower corners or with vases of honesty and cape gooseberries reflected in it – there was not even a proper mantelshelf, only a narrow ledge topping the primrose-yellow glazed brickwork and terminating at either side in two descending steps on each of which a small china ornament had been placed; here the furnishings were of the period between the First and Second World War and the armchairs were ponderous and were upholstered not in red plush but in a hard material which, like the carpet, had a jazzy zigzaggy light and dark green pattern on it; and the smell here was not of the sea but of the country, sweet yet musty, as though some small animal – a field mouse it might be, not a rat – had died under the floorboards. During twelve subsequent mornings in this parlour he seemed to make no progress towards discovering definitely what he wanted to write about. However, three days before he and Elsie and the children returned to London a clear and strongly attractive idea for a poem presented itself to him while he was out walking with them in the afternoon.

The children were ahead of Elsie and himself on a chalky path along the side of the downs, Stephen being keen to lead this walk which he had planned out very thoroughly from the Ordnance map on the previous evening. The top of a folded map showed from one of the pockets of his grey flannel jacket now, and he was carrying a butterfly net over his shoulder. As Stephen and Christina, walking quickly up the steepening path, got far enough ahead to be out of earshot, Alan and Elsie talked fondly about them; about Stephen's passion for collecting things, first of all cardboard milkbottle-tops during the war, then used bus tickets no matter how dirty, then stamps and butterflies; about Christina's early interest in the moon, which she had literally cried out for once when she had been in her push-chair, saying 'Christina's moon – 'ave it'; about the poetic imagery that the children had at various times spontaneously come out with, such as Stephen's comparison last year during their holiday in Scotland of sheep on a distant hillside to ant-eggs (just like him to think of something entomological), and Christina's comparison of the foam on the dark water below a waterfall to the pattern on a black and white cow. The children were so lovably present in Alan's mind as he and Elsie talked of them that for a while he ceased looking at them in actuality, and he had a mild shock when he all at once noticed they were no longer visible along the path ahead of him. Then he realized that the path led up through the middle of a small thicket of hazel and hawthorn, and that they must be walking through this. As soon as he and Elsie came up to the thicket he saw them standing out in the open at the far end of it. They were waiting there because they had come upon something they wanted their parents to share the sight of with them – a large abandoned chalk quarry, overgrown with ash trees in the foreground and having so many shrubs and plants rooted on the high cliff-like quarry-face in the background that not very much of the bare chalk could be seen. In front of the ash trees and quite near the path was an impressively tall and stout flower-stem with yellow flowers on it, which Alan – who since leaving the Party had at last started to learn the names of wild flowers as he had long wanted to do – knew to be great mullein. Christina could name it too when he asked her; she said she remembered it from a picture she had seen in his flower book. As they all began to move on along the path, he happened to look up at the steep face of the quarry again and was startled to see, on a broad grass-covered ledge not far from the top, a man and a woman sitting. Both of them were rather plump, and they were playing cards. The woman was dealing the cards on to the grass while the man watched her. The ledge was recessed into the quarry-face and behind it a ten-foot wall of chalk was topped by the sky. Alan was reminded of a lawn he had once seen high up within the secluding walls of a castle. The two card-players were quite unaware of being stared at. How had they got there? Presumably the grass-covered ledge must be much longer than Alan had noticed and either it must slope up gradually to reach the top of the quarry or else the top of the quarry must slope downwards to meet the ledge; but he never discovered how the man and woman could have got where they were, because ash trees as he continued walking intercepted his view of them and the ledge. He felt an intense pleasure, which seemed to arise from the contrast that they and their card-playing made with their surroundings. At a whist drive in a parish hall they wouldn't have been marvellous at all. For an instant he came near to wondering whether they might have been some kind of an hallucination, and he stopped walking and turned round to try to glimpse them through the foliage of the ash trees. He thought he could see them, dark against the high chalk, but he was not sure. What he did vividly see, before walking on again, was the thicket through which he had come up to reach the quarry. Or, rather, he saw the path through the thicket. It made a tunnel, not straight though only slightly sinuous, under the hawthorn and hazel leaves – a culvert for the upflowing of light from the plain below the down. Why did the plain, viewed through the framing leaves, seem more extraordinary even than the card-players had seemed? Perhaps its marvellousness arose from the contrast between it and them, just as theirs had arisen from the contrast between them and the quarry. The whole plain, with a small bright river crossing it, appeared to be very close to him, although in reality it stretched at least ten miles before terminating in another line of hills. He felt suddenly that what he was seeing was something much more than a luminous landscape: it was the poetic life. There was no nostalgia or Utopianism in his vision of it. He was seeing the poetic life not as it had been when he had tried to live it years ago, nor as it might be lived by others in the distant future, but as he could begin to live it in the present, from this moment onwards. It was a life which though it would be given above all else to poetic creation, just as the earlier poetic life had been, instead of to political activity as the Party life had been, would at last enable him to write the poems for the Party that his life in the Party had inhibited him from writing. And the first poem he would write would glorify this new poetic life and would describe the incidents that had led up to his discovery of it during this afternoon's walk.

In the remaining three days before his return home with Elsie and the children to London he was able to plan this poem out in detail. By the end of the last morning of their Sussex holiday he felt he was fully ready to begin the actual writing of the poem. But on his first day back home, when he came upstairs with his notebook after breakfast to sit alone in his and Elsie's bedroom, he was soon aware that his feeling of readiness had left him. Though the plan he had worked out for the poem still seemed feasible it no longer excited him as it had done in that musty parlour which had been so strangely reminiscent of the earlier poetic life. Staring now at the limed-oak dressing-table with its rectangular vertical mirror, and through the windows behind it at the gables and chimney cowls of the houses across the road, he had the thought that he might stand a better chance of writing this poem really well if he were to go out of London for at least a few more weeks and to stay somewhere in the country again or by the sea. But he immediately reminded himself that the new poetic life must be a life he would be able to live after as well as during his present free year, and that he ought not to begin it in surroundings he could not remain in later when he had to go back to work as a teacher. His supreme and final fight to become a poet again must be fought out here in London and in this room. He must set himself a time limit for starting this poem: he must write the opening lines of it not later than the day when he would have been due, if he hadn't obtained this year off teaching, to return to school for the autumn term.

His hope was that before this day arrived the poem would regain its attractiveness for him sufficiently to enable him to start it without his having to force himself to do so; but during the next three weeks, though he was able to improve his plan for it in a number of details, it became less rather than more attractive to him. On the first morning of term, after he'd watched from the bedroom window while several of his pupils riding bicycles with drop handlebars had passed along the road on their way to school, he sat down and by an act of will he began against strong disinclination to write the poem. By the end of the morning he had completed five lines of it, and he found them tolerable, and he was conscious that the zest without which he had been so reluctant to start writing was reviving in him now that he had compelled himself to start. On the second day of term he wrote six lines; and, though on the third day these seemed unsatisfactory to him and he had to re-write them, by the end of the first week he had got twelve tolerable lines down on paper in his notebook. He reckoned that the length of the poem as a whole would be between ninety and a hundred lines, which meant that within eight weeks at the present rate he would have finished it and then there would still be plenty of time left for him to write other poems before the end of his free year. However, at the beginning of the second week he realized that the last seven of the twelve lines he had so far got down were much less satisfactory than he had thought, and he spent the rest of this week and the beginning of the next in a difficult attempt to improve them. One night during the third week he knew that the whole of the existing opening was wrong and would have to be reconceived. For the first time since the beginning of his free year a fear came to him that by the end of the year he might not have succeeded in writing a poem at all. He asked himself what he would do if that were to happen, and he found that he did not know. The only acceptable answer he could think of, after several hours of sleeplessness, was a quotation from Shakespeare – 'But screw your courage to the sticking-place/And we'll not fail', though he couldn't wholly convince himself that this wasn't an evasion of his question. He decided that in order to rewrite the opening successfully what was required from him above all was more determination and a stronger effort, and that in future he would work in the evenings as well as the mornings. (In the afternoons he must go out walking for exercise as hitherto: his struggle to write would become still more difficult if he didn't keep himself in good physical health.) But during the fourth week he had to recognize that the whole conception of the poem, and not just its opening, was at fault. Its central theme, that he could serve the Party by living the poetic life, was a nostalgic lie. This poem, which was to have been his first during his free year, had totally collapsed. He had reached a dead end. 'I am on trial for my life,' he thought. He must not panic. There were still nearly eleven months to go before he would have to return to teaching. The only thing to do now was to conceive a new poem with a new theme.

Towards the end of October his problem of finding a convincing theme was complicated increasingly by the problem of how to keep up his morale. There were mornings when after coming upstairs to the bedroom with his notebook he spent less of his time till lunch in thinking about poetry than in attempting to overcome his apprehensiveness and despondency. Nevertheless he did overcome them sufficiently to be able, at the beginning of November, to discover a theme in which he could have some confidence. After the total collapse of his first poem he had for several mornings considered the possibility of once more trying, as he had tried five years ago, to write one that would directly praise the Party life. However he was soon forced to admit to himself that there was no real feeling in him on which such a poem could be based. The only emotion, even now, that seemed strong and persistent enough for poetry to be made out of it was his shameful yearning to return to the poetic life. Why shouldn't he use this emotion to create a poem most of which would describe the poetic life of more than twenty years ago in all its apparent desirableness and which would end by showing how it had led him into a near-suicidal misery that nothing except his turning to the Party had been able to rescue him from? This theme, though it came to him in the middle of a night of restlessness and bad dreams, and though it wasn't altogether new, still seemed valid to him next day, and he began work at once on planning a new poem that would embody it. Half-way through November he decided that his plan for this poem had reached a stage where it was as satisfactory as he would be able to make it, and that the time had come for him to get the opening lines down on paper; but fear of a false start delayed him day after day until the greater fear of never starting at all drove him during the last week of November to begin the actual writing. He soon knew that the lines he was getting down were poetically lifeless; nevertheless he persuaded himself that the only possible course for him was to continue writing and not to attempt to revise anything until he had completed a first draft of the poem as a whole. But the more lines he added the more frighteningly flat the poem seemed. The revulsion and dread which he had to conquer when he sat down to work grew stronger every day. And besides having difficulty in getting to sleep at nights he began to wake very early in the mornings, and instantly when he woke he felt – even before he had time to remember consciously how bad his poem was – an anxiety like a stab of ice or fire in the centre of his body, a concentrated physical pain which took some while to diminish. It resembled what he had felt when his attempt to live the poetic life years ago had been nearing total failure, though now it was worse because it was followed by such a quivering of his whole body that even his jaw trembled and his teeth chattered audibly enough for Elsie to have heard if she had been awake. He found he could stop his trembling by thinking of Stalin and by speaking the name of Stalin, repeatedly but not quite aloud, much as a religious believer might have called on the name of God. Yet though this was an effective method of suppressing the physical symptoms of his anxiety it did not help him in the least with his writing. During the first week of December he realized that nothing – and least of all the illusion that by producing such lifeless trash he would in some way be serving the Party – could justify his struggling on with this poem. He must completely rewrite it from the start, must begin a new version of it without a day's delay. Half-way through the second week of December he did begin. The new opening lines were better than anything he had written previously during his free year; but his morale hardly improved at all, and he made slower and slower progress, like someone pushing a snowball which accumulates weight as it is rolled over the snow. There were hours during his afternoon walks when he had a sensation even in the sunlight that he was moving in the shadows, as though the sun had been partially eclipsed. He began to have fears of mental derangement. During the mornings an image which had nothing to do with the poem he was working on came often into his mind: it was of a man running up a downward-moving escalator at the bottom of which was a sump filled with sulphuric acid. There were hours, however, when by telling himself that his struggle was in support of the Party and of communism, he was still able to surmount his depression and even to feel hope. He found relief too by taking an occasional day completely off from writing, but when he began work on the poem again his gloom and dread seemed to be all the greater because of the pause. Soon after Christmas he was in a misery so deep that he did not know how he would ever be able to clamber out of it again. And then, on New Year's Day, he was suddenly sure that this present poem also, though technically less unsatisfactory than his previous attempts had been, was based on a theme he could not believe in. To write a poem condemning the poetic life would be just as impossible for him as to write one glorifying it. That night he did not sleep at all. Next day there was a qualitative change in his anxiety: it seemed to have become rooted in him physically, causing a persistent tremor of his hands and an acceleration of his pulse rate, and neither by self-exhortation nor by calling on the name of Stalin was he able to alleviate it. He recognized that he was ill, and that until he was better he would have to give up all thought of trying to write.

He went to see a doctor, who gave him a prescription for barbiturates, and these helped him to sleep for at least an hour or two each night. And in the mornings he occupied himself by reading Wordsworth's *The Excursion* – a poem he had long been meaning to read in order to find what similarities there were between Wordsworth's disillusionment with the French Revolution and the disillusionment of twentieth-century intellectuals with the Russian Revolution – though the intensity of his wretchedness often made concentration on the poem very difficult for him. The prospect of having to live through the remaining eight and a half months of his free year without trying to write poetry was often terrifying to him. But he did not doubt that if he were to force himself to go on trying now he would soon become mentally as well as nervously ill, whereas if he could resign himself to not writing there was just a chance that even before he had to return to school next autumn he might recover sufficiently to try again without danger. And in fact, towards the end of January, he began slowly to get better. The progress of his recovery was not steady – he had moments of morbid exaltation, usually and inexplicably when during his afternoon walks he was passing along some particularly ugly London street, and he had moments of melancholia almost as deep as any he had had previously – but by the second week in February he felt well enough again to risk going up to the bedroom with his notebook one morning after breakfast. His

intention was not to try to conceive a new poem but to beg
investigation into why for so many years all his attemp
write poetry had failed, though behind this intention there was
a half-hope that if he could discover the true causes of his failure he might even now succeed in writing a poem before the
end of his free year. During eight mornings he covered thirty-
five pages of his notebook with a discussion of the causes; and
then, as this occupation seemed to bring no deterioration in his
nervous condition, at the end of the third week of February he
allowed himself to try once more to conceive a poem. Within
three days his illness returned and it was far more severe than
it had yet been. He was afraid to go out of doors, and he was
afraid to be alone in the house. Elsie got leave of absence from
her school so that she could be with him. For more than a
week he spent several hours each day talking with her about how
he felt. He knew what a strain this was imposing on her, but he
could not keep his misery to himself. He began to have fears that
he was developing cancer and that two of his colleagues at school
were intelligence agents who were scheming to prevent him from
ever returning to his job there; and, though he was always able
to recognize that these fears were groundless and were nothing
more than disguises put on by his real terror about what was
going to happen to him now after the total collapse of his
struggle to write, he could not ignore them, and she helped him
to defeat them. And then the news came, at the beginning of
March, that Stalin had died. Alan was able to ask himself why
this, instead of driving him into a wretchedness still deeper than
he was already in, caused him hardly any additional grief at all.
He thought the reason for his near-indifference might be that
recently he had begun to wonder whether Stalin's never having
come out in support of the Australian criticism of the British
Party had been due not, as he had hitherto supposed, to an intention on Stalin's part of refraining from interference in the
affairs of Communist Parties outside the Soviet Union but to
Stalin's being perhaps in agreement with the line taken by the
British Party. Another reason might be that Alan was too mor-
bidly and self-centredly miserable for any external event to make
him feel either worse or better. However, he was soon to find

that he could feel worse. At the end of the first week of March the realization came to him, in the outer scullery of his house after dark, that the only way for him to become and remain well again would be to renounce all thought of trying to write poetry not just during the rest of his free year but during the rest of his life. He had been on his way through the outer scullery towards the side passage in order to go out for a walk. When he decided that he must give up hope of ever being a poet again he came to a stop in his movement towards the passage. A terrible dread rose in him that he might not be able to bear continuing to live after abandoning the struggle to write. He felt strengthless: it seemed that only the rigidity of his bones kept him standing there and that if he were to try to move at all his joints would fold up and he would fall vertically to the concrete floor. And he recognized that compared with this anguish his remorse at having left the Party had been nothing. The loss he must learn to endure now was of an occupation which had long ago become part of his own nature, in a way that Party political activities never had and never could have become. He wasn't able to lessen the anguish, or to move from where he stood, until he told himself that he had a duty to Elsie and the children, and that he must live for them, and that his having driven himself into a nervous breakdown for the sake of poetry had been a disgraceful folly. After this moment his cure really began.

By the end of April his worst symptoms – his hypochondriacal fears, persecutory imaginings about his colleagues, bodily shudderings as if he were a ship which was being struck by storm waves – had disappeared, though a slight tremor of his hands remained. He had succeeded in resigning himself to the prospect of living neither the poetic life nor the Party life but the ordinary life, the schoolmaster's life. This didn't mean he had decided he would be unable to do anything at all in future to help the political struggle against capitalism, but he saw himself as being able to help only as a layman and never again as a Party member, only in a small unorganized way and as a more or less isolated individual. And he would continue to be faithful to poetry at least to the extent that he would not cease being a reader of it, especially during the four and a half months that were still to go before his free year ended. Nevertheless his acceptance of the ordinary life was not complete enough to free him from a persistent sadness, a feeling as of bereavement, which did not lessen as time went on. One evening early in May he had the thought that he might be able to overcome this feeling if he were to write something about it, provided he wrote for himself only and not with the idea of publication. Soon after finishing tea with Elsie and the children he took his notebook upstairs and went to sit alone in Stephen's room, having first asked Stephen's permission. He preferred not to sit in his and Elsie's bedroom because of the noise there at this time from the evening rush-hour traffic passing in front of the house; and because, instead of being able to see the apple blossom at the end of the garden as he could from here whenever he chose to look out of the window, he would have been faced there with the gables and chimney cowls of the houses across the road that he had stared at for all too many hours during the months of mornings he had recently spent trying to write poetry. Opening his notebook he was conscious of the danger that in proposing to rid himself of melancholic feelings by writing about them he might really be aiming to re-enter poetic creativity by the back door, and that the consequences might be as disastrous for him as if he were to try to write poetry again. For ten minutes he sat with his notebook open on his knees, afraid to begin writing; and when he did he wrote very slowly, alert for any warning nervous signs, but there were none, and at the end of three quarters of an hour he was sure he had done himself no harm and he believed he was better than before he had begun. However, he thought he might be wiser not to go on writing for any longer than three quarters of an hour this first time. He decided he would stop and go out for a walk. The traffic would be past its worst by now.

He found Elsie in the kitchen when he came down from Stephen's room. The look she gave him was a little anxious: she evidently hoped his reappearing downstairs with his notebook so soon didn't indicate that he'd been forced to stop writing in it by a temporary recurrence of the neurotic despair which he had lately seemed to have almost completely recovered from.

She was reassured by his relaxed tone when he said to her, 'I thought it might be a good idea for me to go out for a bit.' She smiled to show she trusted his judgement of what would be good for him. Smiling back at her he remembered with love how much she had helped him and how much she had endured from him during the worst period of his illness when the only relief he had found had been in expressing to her again and again the misery he had felt. Now he put his arms round her and kissed her. As they released each other they both became aware that while they had been embracing he had still been holding his notebook clutched in his right hand. They laughed, and he said, 'After that revelation of my absentmindedness I'd better go out at once.'

He went into the front sitting-room to put his notebook away inside the bureau where he ordinarily kept it, and then he left the house by the front door. As soon as he was outside he felt a heightening of the sense of well-being which writing in his notebook had already brought to him. The traffic was no longer continuous, and in the springtime evening he did not find it offensive. Though most of the cars were closed saloons, one or two open tourers with their hoods down passed him during the time he took to walk his first hundred yards along the pavement; these open cars seemed to bring a gaiety with them, as from the early days of motoring. And the prunus trees which stood at intervals along the outer side of the pavement between him and the road had small whitish flowers among their coppery leaves. He had never previously, this year or any other year, noticed these flowers properly. Coming to a stop to look more closely at them on one of the trees he felt how much more exciting they were than the larger and profuser blossoms on the apple trees at the end of the garden. At the same instant, so powerfully that he had no chance to put up any resistance, the longing to write poetry revived in him; and he knew, with the keenest happiness and without the least fear, that very soon he would try once again to write it, and he was extraordinarily sure that this time at last he would succeed.

He did not immediately, as he walked on, know what any of the poems he would write would be about, but a vivid and precise idea came to him of the poetic form they would have. It would be similar to the form he had used for one or two of the poems he had written soon after joining the Party but which he had not used again because he had come to believe that it didn't accord with the requirements of socialist realism. It was a form which his increasing uneasiness about writing in verse had for a long time been unheededly indicating that he should return to. It would not be verse but prose-poetry, and it would go much further than those earlier poems in employing rhythmical devices that would bring it to the verge of verse without ever disrupting it as prose. There might even be occasional rhymes in it, vowel or consonantal rhymes or a combination of both, though he'd have to avoid letting them establish any kind of regular pattern, just as he'd have to avoid letting the rhythms become regular enough to give an impression of concealed metrical verse. And he mustn't make the mistake of supposing that prose-poetry could be as concentrated in its effect as good verse could be: his prose-poems must have the length of short stories rather than of sonnets. Yet whatever disadvantages prose-poetry might have in comparison with verse, he was enthusiastically confident now that this form would enable him to break out from the poetic sterility of his last fifteen years. An objection did momentarily trouble him: in choosing the form for his poems before knowing what they would be about wasn't he guilty of the same bourgeois aestheticism as when, walking along this same pavement one autumn afternoon three years ago, he had decided that his aim must no longer be to use poetry to make political statements but to use his political experiences and feelings to make poetry? He quickly answered this objection: his having thought of the form before the content needn't prevent him from choosing whatever content he wanted for it. But what exactly would the first poem he would write in the new poetic form be about? He knew there was one subject he must at all costs avoid, a subject which the springtime evening and the prunus trees and the cars with their hoods down were already beginning to tempt him with. The poem must absolutely not make any reference to the poetic life.

Instantly after he had given himself this warning, and when

he was still not much farther than three hundred yards from his house, a subject for a poem came into his mind which there seemed no reason for him to reject. He would write about his recent illness. That would certainly have no less emotional force as a subject than the poetic life would have had. The poem would start by describing the alarmed waker in the dark bedroom to whom the rumbling of the railway bridge at the end of the road betrays the time of night, even though he forbids himself to look at the luminous dial of his watch; because if the trains are passing over the bridge at long intervals he knows that he has woken very early and that he must lie in bed for hours with his heart thumping and with fear flowing through him, whereas if the trains are more frequent he knows that the morning is near and that he will be able to face a day of anxiety unweakened by a night of sleeplessness – though there is a possibility that the greater frequency of the trains may mean that he has woken very early indeed, perhaps only half an hour after falling asleep, when the traffic of the previous day is still on the move, and then he knows he has before him a whole night of frightened wakefulness and that during the next day his fear will be beyond his control and he will not dare to go out of the house or be alone. Alan, continuing to develop this poem in his mind, ceased to notice the prunus trees and the decreasing traffic, but arriving at the T-junction where his home road joined a major road he stopped for a moment before deciding not to turn back yet, and when after this brief interruption he thought of the poem again he had a misgiving about it. It would not be, in any sense, a poem for the Party.

But how could he expect, and how could he ever have expected, to write poetry for a Party that he had increasingly been losing faith in year by year at least since the end of the war? The only thing which had enabled him to retain any faith in it at all after what had happened at the meeting with Hollingworth had been that the Soviet leadership didn't oppose it; however, since Stalin's death news had come from the Soviet Union which undermined for Alan the authority of the Soviet Party. The recent official Soviet statement that the group of Kremlin doctors who before Stalin's death had confessed to a plot to murder various Soviet leaders were in fact completely innocent, and that their confessions had been obtained from them by illegal methods, suggested to Alan the question whether (unless the doctors really were guilty and had now been exonerated because the present Soviet leaders didn't regard a plot to murder Stalin as a crime) some of the confessions made at Soviet trials before the war might have been extorted from the accused by similar methods; and if the Soviet leadership had been capable of such utterly unsocialist practices in the past what certainty was there that its past tolerance – which it still continued in the present – of the British Party's line was based on socialist principles? Alan need not be afraid that the poem he was now planning was at fault for not being in support of the Party. On the contrary, the time had come when he must recognize that what above everything else had prevented him for so long from writing poetry had been the duty he had felt to write for such a Party. The truth was, he thought with joy, that his break with this revisionist organization was the essential pre-condition for his being able to write again. However, his joy was soon qualified by the realization that his proposed poem besides giving no support to the Party would give none to the political struggle against capitalism either. Nevertheless it wouldn't oppose the political struggle, he assured himself with reviving confidence, wouldn't be reactionary. And it would be a victory after years of poetic sterility. And it would be followed by other poems which would be for the struggle – but the essential thing was to get down to writing this poem as soon as possible, not to risk setting up an anxiety in himself by searching for a new subject now.

He stopped abruptly on the pavement, and turned, and began to walk back home. His walking was not faster, was perhaps a little slower, than before. He became wholly concerned with planning his poem. By the time he had arrived home, and had fetched his notebook from the bureau in the front sitting-room, and had gone upstairs to Stephen's room once more, the plan had become sufficiently detailed for him to feel he could begin to think about the wording of the opening sentence of the poem.

Ten days later, on a Sunday morning an hour and a quarter

after breakfast, he finished the poem. He was in Stephen's room again, and after finishing the poem he sat looking for a minute or two out of the window at the small high cumulus clouds against a strongly blue sky, postponing the necessity of reading through as a whole what he had written and of judging its value. When he did bring himself to read it through he was much happier about it than he had expected: it was verbally and rhythmically alive, which his unfinished poems during the past fifteen years had mostly not been (had perhaps been afraid to be – as though he'd felt that any vitality of style in them would have been a departure from socialist realism). Admittedly the content of this present poem was politically neutral, not only in the sense that it gave no direct political message but also in the sense that, by ignoring the causes of the pathological misery and fear which it faithfully described, it failed even to be indirectly political. However, now that he'd found a poetic form that was exciting to him in itself he would be able to go on to write other poems which besides being stylistically alive would be political in content, some of them directly so, though perhaps many of them indirectly. There was no danger that in future his occupying his free time with writing would bring on a neurosis. His recent recovery, which had begun from the moment when he'd finally stopped trying to write for the Party, had been furthered by his writing this poem about his illness and would be completed when he went on to write poems that were indirectly or directly in support of the struggle against capitalism. The sooner he wrote a political poem the better. He could begin to try to conceive one this morning. He still had an hour and a half before lunch.

There was a knock on the front door. He heard Elsie go to open the door and then he heard a man's voice – slow, deep and amiable – which he soon recognized as Pete Naylor's. Pete, who was Literature Secretary for the Branch, still called now and again at Alan and Elsie's house, usually on a Sunday morning, bringing with him pamphlets and other items of Party literature some of which they sometimes bought from him. Of late he had been coming less often – his last visit must have been more than a month ago. Alan told himself not to give way to a wish to go downstairs and talk with Pete: an interruption, even if for no more than five or ten minutes, might put an end to the possibility of conceiving a new poem this morning. Nevertheless, as the sound of conversation between Pete and Elsie continued steadily from downstairs, Alan thought of Pete and not of poetry. Among all the Branch members with whom they had once been so closely friendly, Pete was the only one who still came to see them. The others, though none had become hostile to them — except possibly the Whiddetts — were genuinely too busy with Party activities to be able to spare the time for a non-political friendly visit. Pete himself, it was true, was ostensibly doing Party work when he brought literature to Alan and Elsie, but he knew quite well that they were interested in reading it only for the purpose of finding further fault with the Party's policies, and there could be no doubt that his main motive for continuing to visit them was the unpolitical liking he felt for them. Alan realized, as he sat looking at the sky without even trying to think of poetry, how much he reciprocally liked Pete. He knew that this feeling was partly due to their common interest in poetry and also perhaps to the similarity of their attitudes towards the work they did for a living — Pete while aiming to be efficient at his job as a quantity surveyor practised a technique of disassociating himself from it inwardly — but what most of all attracted Alan to him was that Alan saw in their relationship a survival of the unique kind of friendship which existed among Party members and which he had been more unwilling to lose than almost anything else when he had left the Party. Now, at the thought of how many friends he and Elsie no longer had, he decided that in spite of the risk of losing a poem which he might otherwise have conceived before the end of the morning, he must go downstairs and see Pete immediately.

Pete was standing near the front door and sideways to it, talking with Elsie, and in the hall passage the children — who also liked Pete — were interestedly listening to him. From the top of the stairs Alan noticed that as usual he was wearing quite different clothes from those he had appeared in when he had last come here. At one time the interest he took in clothes — not only his own but other people's too, as he'd shown once again a few weeks ago when he'd remarked that he admired the new shoes he saw Elsie was wearing – had seemed to Alan to be not quite proper for a Party member, but at present Alan's attitude to clothes, like his attitude to poetic form, was less puritanical than it had been. From half-way down the stairs Alan called out to Pete in a tone of greeting:

'And what have you brought for us today?'

'Just one or two of the usual,' Pete answered, smiling warmly; and from a brown canvas shopping bag that he had with him he fetched out first several copies of *World News and Views* – small and printed on thin paper – and next, almost with a flourish, one copy of the large, handsome, and remarkably low-priced magazine *Soviet Literature*. Alan took them and paid for them, saying, 'Come in and sit down.' Pete seemed very willing, though to judge by the amount of literature remaining in his shopping bag he still had to call at a number of other houses this morning. Elsie said, 'I hope you'll forgive my retiring into the kitchen. I'm in the middle of making a cake. Now that I've gone back to teaching I have to put my weekends to good domestic use.'

The children went off into the back sitting-room, while Alan led Pete into the front sitting-room and asked as they both sat down, 'How are all the Branch comrades getting on?' He always asked this when Pete came, but today a wistfulness may have made itself heard in the question. Pete looked at him, then said with quiet enthusiasm:

'Oh, they're all flourishing.'

'Bert Alldiss – what's he doing now?'

'There's a strike on at his factory. I expect you've read about it. He's taking a very active part in that.'

Though Pete's tone entirely avoided reproaching Alan for inactivity, Alan did not ask him anything more about Bert.

'And the Murrayfields?'

'Iris is still Branch treasurer and Alec is going ahead with the special political work he's been doing among university graduates,' Pete said. Alan detected that he was embarrassed about the Murrayfields, particularly about Alec. This might indicate that Alec had been withdrawing more and more from ordinary Party activities, out of disillusionment with the leadership, and that his political work among graduates had been the excuse he had given for non-attendance at the Branch. Alan was very much tempted to question Pete further about Alec, but he refrained for fear of being unable to disguise the satisfaction he would feel if Pete had to admit that Alec was no longer coming to Party meetings. Alan asked instead:

'Have you heard anything new about Maldwyn Pryce?'

'No. He's still very busy in the evenings with this Youth club job he's got in South London.' Pete, though seeming to imply that Maldwyn was no longer very active politically, showed no embarrassment, possibly because he felt that Maldwyn's having to do a paid job in the evenings was a more defensible reason than Alec's for giving up ordinary Party activities. Pete added: 'I must go along and see him again soon, when I get a free evening.'

Alan had the wish to ask if anything had been heard of what Gatten was doing now in Birmingham; but distaste at the thought of Gatten quickly overcame his curiosity and he didn't mention him. Instead, remembering something he wanted to talk to Pete about even more than about any of the Branch comrades, Alan abruptly said:

'Since you were last here I've started writing poetry again.'

'That's wonderful news.' Pete was really glad, was not just being amiable. And he was glad not only for Alan but – as he made evident by what he said next – for the socialist movement too. 'I always believed you would do it. "One doesn't help socialism by neglecting to use one's best talents." Can you remember saying that?'

'I'm not sure.'

'It was in an article of yours I read during the war when I was on board ship going to India.'

In spite of Pete's gladness, and of the admiration which his memorizing of that sentence from the article seemed to show, Alan was for a moment hurt by the phrase 'neglecting to use one's best talents' with its reminder of the years he had wasted, and he could not hold himself back from saying now:

'The fact is that after I joined the Party in the thirties I found poetry more difficult to write each year.'

He immediately regretted he'd said it. The last thing he wanted this morning was to begin a combative political argument of the kind he had got into during more than one of Pete's previous visits. Pete, as though equally eager to avoid an argument, appeared at first to be going to make no comment on what Alan had said, but then he very mildly objected:

'I think you once told me that before you joined the Party you hadn't been able to write for some time, and that joining was what made you able to start again.'

'It helped me to start, but not to go on,' Alan had to explain. 'It gave me something to write about, but it increasingly hindered me from writing.'

Pete put the best construction he could on this. 'You mean that your political work allowed you too little leisure?' he asked sympathetically.

'Partly that, though to be fair I must admit that the District Committee raised no objections in the thirties when I let them know I would like to have three evenings in each week off for writing.' Alan wished he could change the subject, but unless he finished this sentence he was in the middle of he would be inviting Pete to ask him to explain himself further, so he added: 'And partly also, as fascism advanced and war seemed more and more inevitable, I was hindered by becoming less and less able to believe that poetry mattered.' At this point Alan realized that his desire to avoid being provocative had led him into doing himself an injustice, and he went on: 'But even the war itself mightn't have stopped me if the Party's own attitude to poetry had been different.'

Pete was surprised:

'Surely the Party has always recognized the importance of poets – much more than other parties have.' With a smile he added: 'And what other political leader quotes poetry as often as our Jimmy McNarney does?' Pete's use of the word 'our' suggested he had forgotten for a moment that Alan had left the Party.

'Yes,' Alan said, smiling also, 'even though McNarney always quotes the same poets and the same passages – Shelley, Byron, Morris, "Rise like lions after slumber", "Yet, Freedom, yet thy banner torn but flying / Streams like a thunder-storm *against* the wind," and "What is this, the sound and rumour? . . . 'Tis the people marching on." '

'But those are good poems,' Pete protested unindignantly, though he was no longer smiling.

'Yes, of course they are,' Alan willingly agreed. Nevertheless he couldn't refrain from going on to say, 'But I suspect that McNarney, and many other Party members too, would be inclined to regard any poem as good if it expressed sentiments which they could fully approve of, and any poem as bad if it didn't.'

'I don't think you're being quite fair there, Alan.' Pete spoke with friendly reasonableness. 'You must admit that during the Popular Front period in the thirties the Party gave encouragement to a number of writers whose work was by no means wholly socialist in tendency.'

Alan resisted a temptation to say, 'And sometimes the Party proclaimed a writer to be great not because it admired his actual writings but simply because he had made a politically progressive speech at a public meeting.'

Pete continued: 'I think the Party has the same literary principles as Marx and Engels – who for instance valued Balzac very highly because of his realistic descriptions of bourgeois society, even though he was politically a royalist.'

'All right, I'll admit that the Party does recognize merit in writings which aren't communist, provided they can be regarded as progressive in some way, but the point I really meant to make was that their literary quality matters much less to the Party than their political quality.'

Alan was beginning to feel he didn't care if he did get into a discussion with Pete, so long as it was mainly about literature and so long as it remained friendly.

'I wouldn't agree that the Party isn't interested in literary quality, if that's what you're suggesting,' Pete said with gentle decisiveness. 'Writers in the Soviet Union are constantly being urged to improve their craftsmanship.'

Alan, repressing an impulse to exclaim 'It certainly needs improving,' said with a careful avoidance of any direct reference to the Soviet Union:

'The question is whether real poetry can ever be produced when the poet's first aim is to make a political statement rather than to create a poem.'

'A poet whose first aim is to create a poem could soon arrive at something very like art for art's sake, don't you think?' Pete had no difficulty in keeping his tone mild.

'He could, if the poem were his *only* aim,' Alan said. 'However, I'm assuming he's a communist for whom the political struggle is the most important thing in the world, and who wants his poems to serve it, but who realizes that the political message in them – unless they are to be tripe and of no help to the struggle – must serve and be secondary to the poetry.'

Pete looked unconvinced, had a slight smile which suggested he thought Alan was being over subtle. Alan became a little more assertive:

'And of course I believe that a Marxist-Leninist Party must aim at influencing poets to write poems in support of the struggle for socialism – provided the Party never forgets that good poetry cannot be obtained by compulsion.' Pete, perhaps suspecting an implied accusation here against the Soviet Party, seemed about to make an objection, but Alan quickly continued: 'I believe that poetry is necessary to the struggle, and also that supporting the struggle is necessary to the poet if he is to produce the best poetry he is capable of.'

Pete, obviously quite sure that what Alan was saying at this point was wrong, objected now:

'I don't see how a poet's being politically progressive can improve the poetic quality of his writing.'

Pete's tone was wholly unaggressive, but Alan was sharply irritated by this comment which seemed a stupid echo of the bourgeois notion, increasingly in vogue since the naughty nineties, that art can have nothing to do with morality. Alan said, 'The great poems of the world are great not solely because of the technical skill with which they have been written – even though skill is the first essential in poetry – but also because of the depth and subtlety and scope of the emotional truths they tell us about the world.'

'When I said "poetic quality" I meant what you're calling "technical skill". Of course I would agree that a poem must be judged on ethical and political grounds as well as on aesthetic grounds.' But Pete's face clearly showed there was something he still did not agree with in what Alan had said. Before he could word his disagreement, however, Alan continued:

'What you seem to be saying is that the emotional content of a poem can be condemned or praised on moral grounds but that it in no way affects the quality of the poem as a poem.' Alan gave Pete no time to deny or admit this. 'Whereas I think that the content of a poem is just as much a part of the poem as the form is.' Alan knew his voice was beginning to sound vigorous and he tried to make it gentler. 'I think that a poem praising Hitler's treatment of the Jews, for instance, would not only be morally and politically evil but – no matter how skilfully it might be written – it would be poetically bad also. And' – here the vigour got the better of Alan's effort to control it – 'the more skilfully such a poem was written the worse, the more meretricious, it would be poetically.'

Agreement alternated with disagreement in Pete's look as he listened, but he seemed unsure which to come out with first, and Alan was able to go on:

'Poetry is not just something the poet adds as a sort of decoration to a political or moral statement that he wants to make. Poetry deals with life directly and in its own specific way; it has its own language and laws and its own kind of truth which is not the same as political or moral truth.'

'I should have thought there was only one kind of truth,' Pete said, unsardonically.

'Oh, what kind?'

Alan couldn't prevent the tone of his question from being a little truculent.

'Well, if you want me to qualify it,' Pete said, 'I'll call it scientific truth – using "scientific" in the broadest sense.'

'Don't you think that our emotional attitudes to the world, as well as our scientific theorizings, can be true or false?'

'Yes, but only in the sense that they can be either genuinely felt or deceitfully simulated.'

Pete came out with this so readily that Alan was taken aback for a moment, before saying:

'They can also be true or false in the sense of corresponding or not corresponding to external reality.' All at once Pete, sitting calmly in the armchair opposite to Alan, appeared to him to be wholly different, even physically, from the amiable and good-looking person he really was, and to be the ugly embodiment of all those ideas in the Party which were harmful to artistic creativity. Alan hardly tried to keep an angry impatience out of his voice as he added: 'Why is it that so many Party members adopt the fashionable habit of using the word "scientific" to mean "true" and the word "emotional" to mean "false"? I don't know where the idea originates from that emotions can't correspond to anything in the objective world, but it certainly isn't to be found in Lenin, who said that they reflect reality.'

'Where did he say that?' Pete seemed to try to avoid sounding as if he doubted Alan's word.

'In his *Materialism and Empirio-Criticism.*'

'Did he mention "emotional truth"?'

'Not that I remember,' Alan had to admit. 'But if emotions reflect reality they can surely reflect it with a greater or less degree of truth – or of distortion.' Awareness that Pete remained as calmly unconvinced as ever made Alan even less calm than before. He could not suppress a note of fanaticism in his voice as he went on: 'The concept of emotional truth seems to me of the utmost importance. If we reject it we've got no answer to those modern bourgeois critics who say that poetry – and art in general – ought not ever to be regarded as being *about* anything at all.'

'I see what you mèan.' It was evident that Pete would have liked not to disagree with Alan, would have liked to avoid provoking him. Yet in spite of himself he had to add: 'But I can't help thinking that this "emotional truth" of yours savours just a little of mysticism or metaphysics. Doesn't it suggest an affinity with what religious believers speak of as "spiritual truth"?'

'Not in the least,' Alan said sharply. 'Spiritual truth so-called does not correspond to objective reality, but emotional truth is just as much about the real world as scientific truth is, only in a different way.'

'Just as much?' Pete's slight smile seemed to say that though he found Alan's claim preposterous he did not want to press the argument any further. However, he couldn't quite bring himself to leave the last word with Alan, who after all had been criticizing the Party even if only for its attitude to poetry. 'Can you give an example from an actual poem' – something rather like slyness came into his voice – 'of what you would regard as an emotionally true statement?'

For more than an instant Alan could not think of an example, and the one that did at last randomly enter his mind seemed a little ridiculous to him.

'"Cowards die many times before their deaths,"' he said. 'Scientifically that's false.'

'It certainly is,' Pete firmly agreed. Then he may have suspected Alan of laying a trap for him. 'Or at least, it's false if you take it literally. Of course, it could be paraphrased as "Cowards experience in imagination many times before their actual deaths all the horrors of dying." That would be a perfectly rational statement.'

'Yes but it would have lost its point,' Alan said eagerly; 'it would have lost the emotional force that Shakespeare's use of the word "die" gives it. It would no longer be *poetically* true.'

'"Poetically true".,' Pete said with a not quite genuinely innocent puzzlement, 'do you mean the same thing by that as by "emotionally true"?'

'Poetic truth – and artistic truth in general – is emotional truth communicated in a specially skilled way.' Alan's right arm made a movement of exasperation and he brought his hand down almost with a slap on the copy of *Soviet Literature* which he'd bought from Pete this morning and which he'd laid on the arm of the chair when he'd sat down here. He wasn't able to stop himself from adding: 'And artistic truth is just what has been missing from most of the stories and poems and reproductions of paintings I've come across in past numbers of this magazine.'

Alan soon realized that for the first time this morning he had said something now which came near to making Pete feel seriously antagonistic towards him.

'The aim of Soviet writers is to depict life,' Pete said gravely; 'and depicting life is the proper function of all art that deserves the name.'

Alan, much as he would have liked to try to placate Pete, couldn't let this last assertion go unquestioned.

'If that's so, how does art differ from — for instance — sociology?'

'Art doesn't necessarily describe actually existing individuals or places. It creates types which are generalizations based on actuality, and which at the same time are unique in themselves.'

'Sociology also can generalize about actualities,' Alan said temperately.

Pete stared at him, then asked:

'Are you opposed to realism in art?'

Pete's tone was almost as if he was asking 'Are you opposed to communism?'

'No, I'm in favour of it,' Alan said. 'But the point is that no matter how realistic a work of art may be its main purpose is to evoke feelings, and its depicting of life is only a means to this end.' In spite of the risk of deepening Pete's antagonism Alan went on with excitement: 'The communication of emotional truth is the one essential thing which all good imaginative literature, from Homer to Lewis Carroll, has in common; and the weakness of so much of the writing that is published in this' — Alan briefly lifted up the copy of *Soviet Literature* from the chair-arm beside him — 'is that its prime aim seems to be to put over a political message. It may communicate political truth, but artistically it is too often false.'

'Do you think,' Pete asked in a controlled voice, 'that recent writing in the non-socialist countries is on the whole more true artistically?'

'No I don't,' Alan was quick to say. 'And I far prefer the sort of artistic untruth one finds in even the most artistically lifeless socialist-realist attempt at depicting life to the sort one finds in even the most artistically skilful work of some bourgeois writers

' — I mean those whose secondary aim is to persuade us that the vileness of capitalist society is part of an unchangeable "human condition", as they call it.'

Pete was evidently not appeased. He said, 'I think that most of the work published in *Soviet Literture* is of a very high standard indeed.'

'I ought to make clear,' Alan said, in a further attempt to be conciliatory, 'that I'm criticizing Soviet writing only as it is in the immediate present. Some first-rate work was done in the years soon after the Revolution, and I don't doubt there will eventually be Soviet poems and novels which will be greater than any the bourgeois world has been capable of.'

'I think they're already greater,' Pete said with a quiet firmness which did not conceal that he was deeply aroused. But Alan couldn't bring himself to retreat any further:

'Perhaps the word "great" shouldn't be used of bourgeois or Soviet writing at present. Compared with the bourgeois classics they both, in their opposite ways, seem unimpressive.'

'There's a very real sense in which Soviet literature today can be said to be greater than classical bourgeois literature,' Pete asserted tenaciously.

'What! You think that in the Soviet Union now there are better writers than Tolstoy?'

'I mean Soviet writing as a whole is on a higher level than bourgeois writing was in the time of Tolstoy – or at any other time.'

The fantastic opinion was given unexcitably, with the stubbornest certainty. Alan was amazed temporarily into dumbness. Pete went on:

'Soviet writing is superior to bourgeois writing because it is the product of a more advanced stage of social and economic development.'

'You might as well say that the literature of modern Greece is for the same reason superior to the Greek classics.'

Pete either didn't take in this objection or he found it too frivolous to refute.

'Soviet writing expresses the experiences and aspirations of a higher type of human being than has existed in the world before. And since it deals in a straightforward style with things which interest ordinary working people it is read and loved by millions, as bourgeois writing never was.'

Alan did not try to stop himself from saying, with a crude grin, 'So you think the quality of a book is to be judged by the number of its readers? That seems rather a quantity-surveyor's way of looking at literature.'

Then he converted the grin into an innocuous-sounding laugh, less in order to take away the sting of his remark than to prevent Pete from resenting it. But Pete was too sure of being in the right to be offended. He grinned back at Alan, not as if admitting that Alan had scored a point but as if acknowledging that a joke had been made – a joke which brought serious discussion to an end for the present.

'It's time I set out on my rounds again,' Pete said, taking his canvas bag by its handles and getting up from the armchair. 'But I'd just like to say good-bye to Elsie first.'

Alan's feeling of having had the better of their argument was suddenly removed as he watched Pete go out of the room and turn the corner into the passage towards the kitchen. Could such an unshakeable confidence as Pete's be totally mistaken? Perhaps after all he was right in thinking Soviet literature superior to bourgeois literature. Artistically it might be inferior, but at this period of history when imperialism was threatening the world with genocide surely the sort of writing which expressed belief in social and scientific progress was preferable not only to the recent bourgeois sort which showed man as a helpless worm but even to the greatest tragic masterpieces of the past? And wasn't Soviet writing, with all its faults, infinitely superior artistically as well as politically to those poems of Alan's whose quality he'd cared so excessively about that they'd never come into existence on paper? The incipient self-disgust that this thought caused in Alan was prevented from developing by the re-appearance from the kitchen of Pete, who paused to call out good-bye to the children in the back sitting-room and then came on towards the front door. Alan told him:

'I've realized you were right about Soviet literature. I was just being captious.'

Alan said this because for the moment he genuinely felt it and also because he was afraid that, by having allowed himself once again to draw Pete into discussing an issue they were likely to disagree fundamentally about, he'd taken a step nearer to estranging the one Party member with whom he had up to now been able to remain on terms of something like Party comradeship.

'Oh, I wouldn't say that. At the 19th Party Congress Soviet writers themselves were very critical of some aspects of Soviet writing.'

The smile on Pete's large face seemed to show there had been no risk at all of his being estranged by anything Alan had said to him this morning. He would come here again on other Sunday mornings with Party literature, Alan was sure, and the friendship he felt for Alan could survive greater ideological strains than it had been subjected to yet.

As Alan shut the front door after watching Pete walk down the path to the front gate, the persuasive effect on him of Pete's total certainty about the greatness of Soviet writing was already beginning to wear off. And by the time he came back into the sitting-room he felt wholly disinclined even to glance cursorily through the copy of *Soviet Literature* which he saw again on the arm of the chair. He knew he had not been wrong when he had said to Pete that the writing published in this magazine was too often artistically false. And now he realized that he would not have been wrong either if he had said also that often it did not even depict life truly, that it was false sociologically and politically as well as artistically. And next time that Pete came here Alan would not be able to refrain from telling him so. Pete perhaps would not be irreconcilably antagonized by this, but Alan's own feelings towards Pete would be changed by the obstinately confident assertions which Pete would certainly once again come out with in defence of Soviet writing. Alan's hope that with Pete he would be able to keep alive the kind of comradeship which was possible between Party members had been a delusion. Alan together with Elsie must become resigned to being without comrades now.

What would be the worth, Alan thought as he was on his way

upstairs again to Stephen's room, of a comradeship which required him constantly to suppress his real feelings about the Party? If he were to be silent when Pete, following the leadership's line, said things to him that were contrary to Marxism-Leninism, he would be an accomplice of the leadership and would be helping them to betray the struggle against capitalism. Comradeship between him and Pete could be restored only when a broad new political movement of the Left eventually arose in which they could work together. Meanwhile, for so long as Pete continued coming to the house Alan should not give up trying to win him over by argument, though Alan would have to argue more patiently than he'd managed to yet. He must do what he could to defend Marxism against the Party leaders – and he would defend it not only in talking with Pete but also in the poems he would write. This thought exhilarated him as he came into Stephen's room again.

He picked up his notebook from where he had left it on the floor beside the armchair here, and sitting down low in the chair – a habit of his – he stared out of the broad high window at the altocumulus cloudlets which covered more than a third of the visible expanse of the sky. Then he looked at his wrist-watch and saw that he had less than three quarters of an hour left before lunch. Perhaps, in so short a time, instead of making a concentrated effort to conceive a poem, he would do better to let his thoughts have free play : he might be less likely to succeed in conceiving a poem by this method, but also he mightn't feel so disappointed if he didn't. The sound of the voices of Stephen and Christina came up to him from the garden. Below the alto-cumulus cloudlets and to the left of them was an elliptical blue clearness with marginal islets of whiteness in it, and to the right the cloudlets were progressively closer together and slightly larger, at first like silkworms' cocoons and then like a limestone pavement cracked in varying directions. Other likenesses were quickly suggested to him : roches moutonnées, megaliths as at Avebury or Carnac, a dinosaur's spinal column with vertebrae dwindling in size towards the tail tip, cowrie shells, the spotted breast of a thrush, white maggots infesting a blue wound, a semicircle of massed cherub heads as in a baroque painting, a

Venus' flower-basket sponge, the reticulations on the cap of a stinkhorn fungus after its mucus has been sucked away by flies. He began to remember clouds he had noticed at other times than now: small bright curls of highest cirrus which had once suddenly brought a theme on the oboe into his mind from Gluck's music for the arrival of Orpheus in the Elysian fields; multiple parallel sequences of separated cumulus shapes varying in size from hedgehog to hippopotamus and chasing one another across the sky on a windy summer's day; lenticular clouds remaining stationary in the airflow over a hill summit and making him think of how a permanent water-ripple can form over a stone in a brook, and of how the horizontal undulations of an adder's body in movement maintain their positions unchanged until its whole length has been drawn through them, and of how when the leader of a single-file of flying flamingoes dips in his flight the others successively imitate him only when they reach just the same point relative to the ground as he has reached before dipping. Next Alan remembered shapes that had appeared among large congested-looking cumulus clouds whose edges (except where the cloud-tops had reached a height at which they expanded into anvils and became fuzzy with ice crystals) had been very sharply defined: heads of cockatoo and basilisk and of Dr Syntax with his wig; turbulent monks in heavy hoods; stout-limbed arquebusiers and round-cheeked Flemish peasant women and sidewhiskered early nineteenth-century aristocrats; faces of politicians which remained recognizable sometimes for more than a minute until their slowly altering outlines transformed them into faces of other politicians or of animals; ruined buildings, torpedoed ships, crashed aircraft, smashed motor vehicles; a cockheaded laugher and a bearded weeper; a thin-nosed face on its death pillow; the beak of a vulture; the beak of a dolphin; a vast plain covered with complicated statuary representing innumerable past disasters; a towering armless giant, his head viewed from behind in foreshortened semi-profile, looking away into immense distances, grimly though not hopelessly, as if he could see not only the disasters yet to come but also an eventual world-wide peace And Alan was confident that most of the resemblances he was remembering had not been merely subjective inventions of his: on several occasions various people to whom he had pointed out one or other of them had been able to see just what he had seen. But he realized that, however objective these resemblances might usually have been, the times when he had noticed them had been times when his imagination had been poetically alive – as it was now.

His eyes once again focused the present sky beyond the broad high window, and at the same moment he remembered how eight months ago during his walk with Elsie and the children on the downs the conviction had come to him as he had looked back towards the plain that a new poetic life was an immediate possibility for him. The conviction returned to him now, even more strongly. But this time he did not see the new poetic life as a life which would at last enable him to write poems for the Party. He recognized that his seeing it like that had been the sole reason for his failure to begin to live it then. He saw it as freeing him wholly from the Party. He saw it still as a life in which his chief voluntary activity would be poetic creation, but the poems he would create – and they would be primarily poems and only secondarily political statements – would be against capitalism and not for a Party that no longer seriously opposed capitalism. He knew that being without a Party, and having to rely solely on his own judgement and on Elsie's, he would run the risk of sometimes writing poems which might not serve the anti-capitalist struggle as well as they ought to. The poet needed the help of a Party, just as the struggle needed the help of poetry. But when a Party ceased to be Marxist-Leninist and abandoned the struggle and deserted the cause of the oppressed and exploited peoples of the world and betrayed the children of the world, then the poet must repudiate it, no matter how isolated he might as a result become for a while. There would eventually be a change: either the Party would cleanse itself, or else a new and genuinely Marxist-Leninist Party would be formed. And the poems that Alan was going to write would be the best contribution he could make towards expediting this change. He knew what the first of these poems would be about. It would reproduce his thoughts and feelings during the past few minutes since he had sat down in the armchair here. It would begin with his seeing the clouds. It would glorify the new poetic life.

He got up quickly from the armchair and went striding over to the window. Below on the lawn in front of the apple trees the children were playing French cricket with a tennis racquet and a blue plastic ball. They too would be in the poem. But he wasn't for the moment able to develop its details any further. The sense of being a creator, of having found himself again, displaced the poem itself temporarily from his consciousness. He had not felt anything at all like this ten days ago when he had conceived the poem he had just finished about his recent illness. He had not felt like this since his earliest days in the Party, and perhaps not since he had tried to live the poetic life before then. For a long while he had strayed from poetry, but he had not betrayed it in the end. 'I have come home again,' he thought.

As he continued standing at the window, Elsie came out into the garden from the kitchen and went up to the children, probably to tell them to get themselves ready for lunch. Soon, although he made no movement, all three of them caught sight of him almost simultaneously. They waved to him; and he saw that they were glad to be reminded of him in the room up there working once more at his writing.

More about Penguins

Penguinews, which appears every month, contains details of all the new books issued by Penguins as they are published. From time to time it is supplemented by *Penguins in Print,* which is a complete list of all available books published by Penguins. (There are well over three thousand of these.)

A specimen copy of *Penguinews* will be sent to you free on request, and you can become a subscriber for the price of the postage. For a year's issues (including the complete lists) please send 30p if you live in the United Kingdom, or 60p if you live elsewhere. Just write to Dept EP, Penguin Books Ltd, Harmondsworth, Middlesex, enclosing a cheque or postal order, and your name will be added to the mailing list.

Note: *Penguinews* and *Penguins in Print* are not available in the U.S.A. or Canada

Christopher Isherwood

Mr Norris Changes Trains and its sequel
Goodbye to Berlin

Walter Allen, writing of these two books in *Tradition
and Dream,* concludes: 'Isherwood's originality is to
show us the collapse of German civilization obliquely,
through characters eccentric or bizarre, characters who
for one reason or another – sexual, racial, economic – are
lost. These books . . . capture the disintegration of
Germany, the years of crisis and chaos, of mass
unemployment, internecine warfare between Nazis and
Communists, the whole horror of a nation's degeneracy,
as no other work of fiction has done.'

Both these works are Penguin Modern Classics.

A Meeting by the River

This novel is organized around letters – from Patrick to
Tom in California, and to his wife and mother in
England – interpolated by extracts from Oliver's diary.
Isherwood utilizes with great realism the intimacy of the
epistolary style.

Not for sale in the U.S.A.

Christopher Isherwood

Prater Violet

Although it is autobiographical in form and recounts
the author's experiences while working on the script
of a musical film in the thirties, *Prater Violet* is a
consummate and living portrait of one man – Friedrich
Bergmann, the film director.

A Penguin Modern Classic.

A Single Man

Christopher Isherwood writes in a style that is a complete
breakaway from the objective reportage of *Mr Norris
Changes Trains*. With devastating candour he strips away
the protective skins of the lonely, frightened, homosexual,
single man.

Exhumations

A collection of Isherwood's stories, book reviews, articles,
and verses written over a period of almost forty years:
'fragments', as the author himself calls them, 'of an
autobiography which tells itself indirectly, by means of
exhibits'.

Not for sale in the U.S.A. or Canada

George Orwell

Animal Farm

In this searing satire upon dictatorship George Orwell
tells the story of a revolution that went wrong. The
animals on a farm, led by the pigs, drive out their
master and take over the farm. But the purity of their
original doctrine is soon perverted.

Nineteen Eighty-four

1984. Throughout Oceania 'The Party' rules through the
agency of all-powerful ministries. The authorities use
every device to keep a check on the people's thoughts,
words and deeds. Against this nightmare background
is played out the drama of Winston Smith, who rebels.

Down and Out in Paris and London

Orwell's lively and factual record of his experiences
among the poor of two capital cities.

Homage to Catalonia

Told with all the honesty and bitterness of a fighting
man only a few months after the events, this book not
unnaturally offended the Left.

Decline of the English Murder and Other Essays

A collection of some of the less accessible essays by
George Orwell, including his lament for the inferior
quality of modern murders and his comments on the
changing face of fictional crime.

Also available

*The Collected Essays, Journalism and Letters
of George Orwell, 1920–1950*
Edited by Sonia Orwell and Ian Angus.
In four volumes.

Not for sale in the U.S.A.

George Orwell

A Clergyman's Daughter

Scandal rocks the East Anglian parish when, after an incident with an elderly freethinker, the clergyman's daughter disappears.

The Road to Wigan Pier

These factual and shocking reports, shot with a wary mistrust of the political cant of the intelligentsia of all hues, make Orwell's contemporary comment on the miner's life, on class, on slums, unemployment, and malnutrition 'as fresh and stimulating as when he first wrote' – *Daily Telegraph*

Coming up for Air

The First World War, eighteen years in insurance, and marriage to the joyless Hilda have been no more than death in life to George Bowling. This and fear of another war take his mind back to the peace of his childhood in a small country town.

Keep the Aspidistra Flying

George Orwell was well aware that political creeds are often rationalizations of emotional problems. Here, with insight and humour, he shows us a man in process of maturing.

Burmese Days

One of George Orwell's earliest novels, *Burmese Days* is a passionately felt indictment of imperialism as he experienced it as a Burmese Police Officer.

Inside the Whale and Other Essays

This volume contains such masterpieces as *Down the Mine, Shooting an Elephant, Boys' Weeklies,* and *England Your England*.

Not for sale in the U.S.A.

EDWARD UPWARD

The Rotten Elements is the second part of a trilogy
that began with

In The Thirties

This novel introduces the character Alan Sebrill, a
conscientious, sensitive, middle-class poet, who chooses
the Communist Party as offering the only possibility of
hope. His conflicts of conscience and imagination, his
web-fine involvements with the other Party members,
especially Elise, are described with Chekhovian simplicity
and subtlety, with the gentlest irony and warmest
compassion.

In his unassuming, direct way, Upward has done the
impossible; he has united poetry and prose.

Not for sale in the U.S.A.